# Damaged

*It is our scars that make us human.*

Shayne McClendon

**Print Edition Copyright © 2013 Shayne McClendon**
**Digital Edition Copyright © 2012 Shayne McClendon**
**Published by Always the Good Girl LLC**
www.alwaysthegoodgirl.com

**All rights reserved.**

No part of this book may be reproduced or transmitted in any form or by any means, electronic or mechanical, including photocopying, recording, or by any information storage and retrieval system without written permission from the author and publisher. This is a work of fiction. Names, characters, places, and incidents either are the product of the author's imagination or are used fictitiously, and any resemblance to actual persons, living or dead, business establishments, events, or locales is entirely coincidental.

ISBN: 978-0-9896755-1-2

## **Also by Shayne McClendon**

The Barter System

Yes to Everything

In the Service of Women

The Hermit

Being Delightful

A Little Bit Country Collection

The Endurance Collection

The Great Outdoors Collection

Love of the Game Collection

Ready to Rumble

Revenge is Best Served Hot

Woman's Best Friend

*Shayne McClendon*

## **DEDICATION**

In the midst of tragedy and personal loss, we sometimes believe the pain will never ease, the hurt will never heal.

It does. Not overnight…and you'll always carry the scars…but it does get better. All of us are a little bit damaged. All of us have our scars. It is part of the human condition.

Instead of focusing on the pain that caused the scar…recognize that you survived it.

To each of my followers who have shared their stories and their personal struggles with me:

**You are still here. Keep fighting. You can do this.**

### **My Daily Mantra**
*I will not quit.*
*I will not go down without a fight.*
*Life will not break me.*
*Circumstances will not make me bitter.*
*I'm a survivor.*
*Nothing is ever going to change that.*

Much love,
*Shayne*

# CONTENTS

## DIRTY LITTLE SECRET – NOVELLA ONE

| | |
|---|---:|
| CHAPTER ONE | 1 |
| CHAPTER TWO | 15 |
| CHAPTER THREE | 23 |
| CHAPTER FOUR | 26 |
| CHAPTER FIVE | 30 |
| CHAPTER SIX | 35 |
| CHAPTER SEVEN | 39 |
| CHAPTER EIGHT | 44 |
| CHAPTER NINE | 53 |

## LET YOUR HEART LEAD - NOVELLA TWO

| | |
|---|---:|
| CHAPTER ONE | 55 |
| CHAPTER TWO | 62 |
| CHAPTER THREE | 75 |
| CHAPTER FOUR | 82 |
| CHAPTER FIVE | 87 |
| CHAPTER SIX | 91 |
| CHAPTER SEVEN | 97 |
| CHAPTER EIGHT | 105 |
| CHAPTER NINE | 110 |
| CHAPTER TEN | 121 |

## COMING HOME - NOVELLA THREE

CHAPTER ONE ................................................................. 135
CHAPTER TWO ................................................................ 141
CHAPTER THREE .............................................................. 148
CHAPTER FOUR ................................................................ 154
CHAPTER FIVE ................................................................. 163
CHAPTER SIX .................................................................. 167
CHAPTER SEVEN .............................................................. 175
CHAPTER EIGHT ............................................................... 180
CHAPTER NINE ................................................................ 186
CHAPTER TEN ................................................................. 195
CHAPTER ELEVEN ............................................................. 204
CHAPTER TWELVE ............................................................ 215

## EXTRAS

SCARS BY SHAYNE MCCLENDON ............................................ 230
OBSESSION BY SHAYNE MCCLENDON ...................................... 239
ABOUT SHAYNE MCCLENDON ............................................... 246

*Damaged*

*Shayne McClendon*

*We're all just a little bit…*

# DAMAGED

*…and that's alright.*

*Shayne McClendon*

# Dirty Little Secret
## *Novella One*

### Chapter One

*Seven years ago...*

Jared Stalzer parked his pickup truck at the shopping center and walked three blocks to the quiet residential street in the poorer section of town.

He wore a heavy coat and a baseball cap pulled low over his eyes. It wasn't his high school senior letterman jacket which was easily recognizable in their small town. Nothing making it obvious that Number 3, Tomina High's best quarterback in twenty years, was in their presence. The team was tracking to go to State this year. He was going to take the whole thing...get recruited to a great school and play in the NFL. One day, he'd mention his sleepy little hometown on the Pacific to reporters, but he'd never come back. His parents could visit for the holidays in whatever tropical location he chose.

It was late fall and the wind had developed a definite chill. Jared pulled his coat more snugly around his body and approached the third house in, entering the gate and walking around the back of the small cottage style house. Kneeling to knock against the basement window just above the ground, he waited for the sound of locks turning and walked down three steps to enter the dark space beyond.

Kendall Torres closed the door behind him and he fell on her; pushing her against the wall and claiming her mouth with the same hunger she always made him feel.

She was not his girlfriend. Wasn't even publicly a friend or someone he spoke to in the halls at their high school. More times than he could count, he'd passed her without acknowledging her existence. She did the same…it had been her idea, after all.

His friends often mocked her funky clothes and hair styles. He made sure it wasn't when she might hear them; he didn't want to lose the perfect arrangement they had going so he kept them under tight control.

Three months ago, they'd gotten internal suspension together. Kendall for protesting the installation of vending machines offering Red Bull and Monster to still-developing teenagers. Jared for getting caught fucking one of the cheerleaders in the girl's locker room.

They'd been seated alphabetically side-by-side and the first day, she hadn't even looked at him. The second morning, he sketched a cartoon of the substitute teacher forced to supervise them. He'd captured the essence of the very tall, very skinny, incredibly angry man perfectly.

She glanced over and had been unable to hide her snicker.

Surprised, he turned it to her for a better look and she gave him a real smile. Something about that smile had tugged at him. At a part of him he didn't even know existed. Kendall's smile was stunning. Full lips and sparkling white teeth set in naturally tanned skin.

It was the first time Jared had really *looked* at her. The first time he'd noticed her pale green eyes surrounded by long lashes. She had adorable dimples. Her hair was thick and black, done in crazy braids and little knots all over her head and he wondered absently how long it was. She wore her clothing in layers; tank top, t-shirt, button down shirt, baggy jeans, and thick-soled Doc Martens.

He wanted to know what she was hiding under all those clothes.

Jared had really *seen* her and immediately accepted with a sense of shock how much he wanted to fuck her. Not date her. Not introduce her into his clique or his life. All he wanted…all he *needed*…was to fuck her.

For the rest of that day and the next he'd drawn cartoons for her. Drawn *for* her and drawn her *in* with the natural charisma he'd been born with. When they walked out together at the end of the third day, he turned to her in the deserted halls and kissed her.

She didn't pull away or slap him, so he deepened the kiss, showed some of his hunger for her. He resisted grinding his erection against her stomach, somehow knowing she wouldn't be convinced just by the size of his cock. She wasn't like the other girls he dated. Nothing like them at all.

So when Kendall opened for him like the sweetest flower, he plucked her easily.

He asked her quietly if she needed a ride and she told him that would be nice. When he stopped in front of her home, he leaned over and said he wanted her. Told her he'd never wanted anyone physically more than he wanted her.

She was silent for so long, simply staring at him, that Jared wondered if he'd gone too far. Scared her off. Then she told him her parents worked constantly, that her bedroom was the converted basement and it had an entrance from the outside.

Her next words shook the hell out of him, "I know you're just looking to fuck me. I find I'm strangely okay with that. I expect the use of protection whether we're together once or a dozen times. No exception or we're done."

The smile she gave him sent a small flutter of actual nervousness along his spine. "I hear my name mentioned in relation to our time together from anyone and we're done. I will tell the entire school you couldn't get it up because you're secretly gay but don't want to fuck up your football career. That you confessed this to me in tears when you'd tried several times without success. Some people will know it's bullshit but a bigger percentage of the student body look for a reason to hate people like you so it'll spread like wildfire anyway. You get me caught by my parents and we're done because my father will likely kill you. Are these conditions suitable to you?"

Jared nodded in a daze.

"Fine. Park your truck at the shopping center on Phillips. Walk back to my house and knock on the back window to the basement. I'll let you in." With that, she got out of his truck and walked across her lawn, her funky messenger bag swinging at her side. He watched until she unlocked the side gate of the house and disappeared.

Driving to the shopping center, Jared sat thinking for several minutes. He was the person who pursued, got what he wanted, and got the fuck out. Kendall had turned the tables on him. The first girl to ever manage it; that fact made him wary.

It also made him want her more. He got out of the truck and slipped a baseball cap over his head, walked back to her house. When he knocked, the door opened immediately and she stepped aside to let him in.

He took in the space that seemed so different from her with a touch of surprise.

Pale purple walls, small porcelain lamps, a quilt on her platform bed featuring delicate vines and violets, a corner desk with a laptop beneath shelves filled with books, a small seating area with two covered recliners and a small table between, deep purple throw rugs over the painted concrete floor. Groupings of photos on every wall comprised of landscapes, people, and objects.

One door led to a bathroom. Another to her closet. A third to what appeared to be a darkroom.

There were two windows; four feet long and one foot high. They were covered in gathered sheer material in purple and white. The dim light in the room was provided by one corner lamp currently on, glowing off the walls and creating the most intimate and strangely adult space he'd ever seen.

Kendall had already removed her boots and socks as well as the two over-shirts she'd been wearing earlier. In bare feet, she was about five-seven. She stood before him now in a tank top and baggy jeans and Jared saw she'd been hiding a *lot* under her clothing.

Lifting her arms, she began taking down her hair. As the first knot was unraveled, it fell in a curling wave down over her breast. He watched her, fascinated. One by one, she removed all the small arrangements until half her hair was wavy, the other half crimped from the braids. It was heavy and glossy. The effect on her face made him even harder than he had been.

"I'm not a virgin, but I'm not a slut either. I've had one boyfriend I was with twice before I dumped him. That was...just after we moved here from Columbia."

"You're from Columbia?"

"Thought I was Mexican, didn't you? White people think most of us with permanent tans are Mexican. Guess we all look alike, huh? Yes, I'm Columbian, Jared." He could tell he'd annoyed her and had no idea what to say in response.

When she moved to continue undressing, he released the breath he hadn't known he was holding. Her hands worked at her jeans and she pushed them from her hips. His balls drew up painfully as she kicked them away and stood in white bikini panties and a white tank top. Her legs were long and curvy. Her feet were pretty; her toenails tipped with delicate bronze polish.

She lifted the tank top over her head and he felt his body tighten from neck to calves. A white demi-cup bra seemed to offer up her full breasts specifically for his appreciation. Reaching around, she unclasped the bra and dropped it to the floor, then skimmed her panties off.

Standing before him nude, her hands on her hips, she was like something from every teenage boy's imagination. Full breasts, flat belly, flared hips, and long legs. For the first time in his life, he saw a real-life pussy bare of all hair. His dick twitched eagerly in his pants and his mouth dropped open.

Jared managed to raise his eyes. She was staring at him, waiting. He pulled his t-shirt over his head and removed his wallet, walking to place it on the table beside the bed. As he unbuckled his belt, she watched the movements of his hands, never taking her eyes away from them as he stripped.

When he stood naked in front of her, he knew exactly what she was looking at. A body every teenage girl, and some grown-ass women, lusted after. Six-two, tall and rangy, his entire body cut from thirty hours of football and gym a week, shaggy blonde hair, brown eyes, bright smile, and a *'you know you want to fuck me'* attitude. His cock stood at full attention, ready for action.

Jared closed the distance between them and wrapped his arms around her, his mouth dropping over hers possessively. As long as he was with her, she belonged to him. He'd be sure she didn't *want* anyone else to fuck her.

He devoured her, working her with his lips, teeth, and tongue until she gave him the moan he'd been waiting for. Already an experienced lover, there were things he wanted from each of the women he was with. The more vocal they were, the more he liked it. He turned her, backing them both to the bed. He reached down and yanked back her quilt. Pushing gently, she sat and scooted backward.

When he bent to follow her, she said, "Protection, Jared."

His smile was predatory, "We have a while before we'll need it. I don't plan to just fuck you, Kendall. I have the reputation I do for a reason. Lie back and relax." He liked to play a game with himself, seeing how long he could go before he *had* to come. Her smooth pussy called to him. No hair was a novelty he'd never experienced and he was going to take his time to truly enjoy it.

He settled between her thighs, paying attention first to her beautiful breasts. Licking and sucking them until her hands went into his hair, her nails scraping his scalp. Raising his head to look at her, he asked, "How long before someone comes home?"

"No earlier than seven but I doubt you're going to need four *hours*, Jared," her voice was breathless, already husky with need.

He laughed, "It'll be close, baby, but I wanted to check." Her eyes went wide, her lips slightly parted. "Enjoy." He went back to sucking nipples that were the same light coffee color as her lips, tugging them lightly with his teeth until they were hard and distended.

Moving down her belly, he kneaded the soft skin there. She was flat and toned but not hard. He found he really liked that. Stroking his hands over her full hips, he found the same there. Full but not flabby, toned but not hard. Feminine in a way he wasn't used to.

He kissed and licked her everywhere, fighting the lure of her pussy and its slight musky scent that begged for his attention. Jared touched her, kissed her, licked her until she was clenching and unclenching her fingers in his hair, writhing beneath him, moaning softly.

As he traced his fingers over her mound, down one outer lip, up the other, a light caress down the cleft of her, she jerked under him. He positioned one of her thighs under his armpit, his forearm over her pelvis, using the fingers of that hand to hold her folds open for him, baring her pretty dusky pink clit. She was held down now, forced to endure what he did to her pussy with no ability to grind her hips. It would build the sensation for her.

He slipped one finger of his other hand inside her, finding her slick. "You're already wet, Kendall. So hot and ready." He stroked in and out of her a few times, gathering her moisture on his finger before smoothing it over her clit and labia. When he reentered her, he used two fingers. She was so tight; he wanted to be sure she was prepared for him.

As his tongue slid through the folds already slick with her juices, tasting her for the first time, her upper body arched off the bed. "Touch your breasts for me, Kendall. Play with your nipples," he murmured against the wet silk of her flesh.

She hesitated but when her slender hands finally cupped her own breasts and she took her nipples between thumbs and forefingers, he had to grind his cock into the bed to keep from coming.

Jared went back to eating her pussy, dividing his attention between watching her and learning every inch of her. When he removed his fingers and replaced them with his tongue, the other hand rubbing little circles over her clit, she came harder than any woman had with him before. It was stunning to watch, to *feel*, as her snug pussy spasmed around his tongue.

He lapped up the warm nectar her body produced, smoothing more over her clit and focusing there. Jared licked her down from her first orgasm and took her back up to another. The second time she came, she pinched her nipples to the point of pain and he groaned against her.

As her breathing became normal again, she stared at him down the length of her body. "You need to either fuck me, or turn around and give me your cock to play with. Your choice, Jared."

He sat up and removed a condom from his wallet, tearing it open and rolling it along his throbbing shaft with hands that weren't completely steady. Settling between her thighs, he pressed forward, sliding his dick through the natural lubrication glazing her mound.

All Jared could think about was being inside her. Fucking her deep. He managed to mumble, "No blowjob...I'd never last now." He slid his hands under her back, clutching her shoulders from behind to anchor her, supporting his weight on his forearms. Kendall tasted her own flavor on his lips and found it oddly exciting, ramping up her already oversensitive nerves.

After he coated his cock, knew the head was slick enough, he slid just the crest inside her pussy. She was tight and Jared was not small. He took his time, small thrusts in and out while he kissed her thoroughly. When he was fully seated, he went still and kissed over her jaw line and down her neck. Her hair smelled like lime and coconut. He kissed along the back of her ear for a long time, enjoying the scent.

Kendall's hands roamed over his shoulders, down his back, over his firm ass where she dug her fingers into the muscle there and pulled him into her. He raised his head to look at her, surprised at how involved she was. Most girls expected him to just do the work while they soaked up the benefits.

"Jared, I'm dying...*move*." He smiled and started rocking with shallow thrusts. When her smooth legs lifted and wrapped around his low back, he slipped deeper; gaining another inch until the head of his cock was being cupped by her cervix. Kendall's upper body arched into him, her pebbled nipples pressing against his chest. "Yes...oh, *yes*, Jared."

He gritted his teeth against the eroticism of her slight accent, her voice pitched low and affecting him like a physical touch. "I want to go hard, Kendall. Tell me if I'm being too rough."

She nodded and he pulled almost all the way out of her before plunging home. She gripped him tighter and he smiled in surprise. Jared turned himself loose on her, giving a female the full power of his body for the first time in his sexual experience. Holding tight to her shoulders, he drove again and again into Kendall's welcoming pussy.

After a handful of minutes, he felt her body tighten until he could barely move past the grip her vaginal walls had on him. Her breath started to race, the pulse at her throat beating so fast, and he watched as a flush spread from her chest to her neck.

She came hard, screaming his name and digging her nails into his back. He didn't stop; he wanted to draw her climax out as far as he could. When she began to settle back to the bed, she met his eyes and said, "Again...I need more, Jared."

His eyes held an animal heat as he smiled and nodded. He brought her to the brink again, at the last second circling his hips into her, and pushed Kendall over so thoroughly she spoke to him in Spanish. He had never been so hard, so desperate to come that he was almost in pain. He had to hold back; he wanted to see her come one more time.

"Drop your legs, Kendall." She did and he pulled out, sitting back on his heels. "Roll over."

Kendall smiled and rolled to her stomach. He pulled her up on her knees and slid smoothly into her again from behind. One hand grabbed her shoulder, the other went into her hair, fisting around the soft length. Bracing her, he slammed his body into hers with everything he could put behind it.

"Yes, Jared, *hard*. Fuck me *hard*."

"Reach under your body; play with your clit while I fuck you, Kendall. *Do it*." She slid one hand over her breasts and stomach, going tentatively between her legs. He knew when she felt what he'd wanted her to feel because she tightened around him like a vice. "That's it, baby. Play with that pretty clit while I fuck you. God, you feel good."

Within moments, she went hurtling over the edge, throwing her head back and milking him with the silken walls of her pussy. His name on her lips, the full-body way she came, the sight of his cock stroking into her wet heat, all combined to bring him to the limit of his endurance.

"I'm coming, Kendall...fuck yes, that feels so good...so fucking good." He gave her everything he had, continuing to stroke until her body began to loosen, and he'd pumped himself dry.

Her body was trembling and Jared lowered her carefully to the bed, moving her hair away from her face. He kissed her back and pulled out, going to the bathroom to strip away the condom and rinse his cock, slick from his own come.

When he walked back into the bedroom, Kendall was still on her stomach but up on her elbows watching him. He knew for a fact he'd never seen a woman so naturally sensual. He sat on the edge of the bed and reached to brush her thick hair back, tracing his fingertip over the shoulder he bared, down the line of her back, over her ass. He returned using the flat of his palm and she smiled.

"I'd say that was a success," her voice was just naturally sexy. "I wasn't sure if your reputation was inflated. Glad to see every sordid detail is true."

He laughed and lay down beside her on his back. "I appreciate that, Kendall...at least I think it's a compliment."

"Yes, it is. I rarely pay compliments, Jared." She crossed her arms and put her head down looking at him. "I'm kind of surprised you're still here though. I've heard you fuck and run before your breathing even returns to normal."

He turned his face to her with wide eyes. "*Nice*. Where the hell did you hear that?"

Kendall gave a throaty chuckle, "I'm totally invisible, Jared. Most people don't know I exist. Those that do tend to forget. It's exactly the way I prefer it for my own reasons. The side effect is people say the most amazing things around me. Luckily, I'm just the photographer for the paper, not the reporter. The tidbits are tantalizing. Anyway, your groupies, the cheer and dance squads, have study hall at the same time I tutor in the library. I've heard things that would curl a lesser woman's hair. Mine, already being curly, wasn't affected."

Jared turned his face back to the ceiling, absently noting she'd painted it the same color as the walls. "Hmm. I suppose I *do* typically fuck and run. I never really thought about it. I know I came harder with you than I ever have before. Maybe I'm too tired to run."

She rolled to her back, "Or maybe, you know you don't have to pretend shit with me because no one will ever know about the time we spend together. There are no illusions about who you are, what you want, or the impression you're trying to give. Honesty is liberating. I'm sure you don't get a lot of it in your life, with your usual friends and girlfriends. Enjoy it. Stay or leave, come back or don't. I won't judge you because I don't want anyone judging me."

They simply existed together in silence for a long time, something Jared had never done with a female before. He found he liked the stillness of being here with Kendall. She didn't need to fill the empty space, had no need to constantly draw attention to herself. She wasn't like anyone he'd ever dated or had sex with before.

Kendall remained there, naked and comfortable with her nudity, her hands crossed behind her head. Her eyes were open but she looked truly relaxed with him lying naked beside her.

The thought crossed his mind that it was the first time before, during, or after sex that he'd felt like a grown man. Not a boy, not a football player, not a student. Kendall was an eighteen-year-old girl who carried herself like a grown woman; she'd somehow shared that same sensation of maturity with him.

Glancing at her, he asked, "Kendall, are you tired?" She smiled and asked if he had more condoms which made him laugh and reach for his wallet. "Yeah, I have more." She rose above him, taking the condom from his hand, and rolling it over his dick.

When it was in place, she straddled him, lowering her body, and taking him deep. He gripped her hips and watched as she began to ride him. It was intense watching her move over him. It was unique. More than a little frightening. He slid his hand over her belly and placed his thumb over her clit, circling gently. When she came the first time, she leaned forward and kissed him, running her hands over his chest and shoulders.

He felt a strange tremor of vulnerability. Taking control back was necessary.

Jared flipped her over, still inside her, and moved with her to the edge of the mattress. Lifting one leg to his shoulder, he draped the other over the bend of his elbow while his feet remained on the floor. Grasping the tops of her thighs, and turning to kiss her knee, he fucked her without mercy. Told her to play with her tits and her clit so he could watch. He had her ass suspended off the bed, the force of his thrusts driving her down into the mattress. He broke into a sweat from the cardio of the position.

She climaxed less than a dozen strokes later and as she came down she said, "Talk dirty to me, Jared."

Stumbling in his strokes, he regained his rhythm and complied, shocked that she wanted it. "You like it dirty, huh, baby?" He groaned and fucked into her faster and harder. "You have got to have the sweetest pussy on the planet, Kendall. Smooth and golden, silky and wet, so fucking tight." He rotated his hips a couple of times and she took her lower lip between her teeth, her head rolling side to side on the mattress. "Tug on those nipples for me, honey. Get 'em all ready for me to suck on. Oh yeah, just like that…all swollen and hard."

Jared continued a steady stream of dirty talk until he felt her clench around him and climax, her entire body lifting from the bed, supported by her shoulders. "Oh yes, Kendall, that is exactly what I like to feel, you coming hard around my cock. Makes my balls draw up so tight. I'm desperate to come. I have to shoot my load right now. Yes, yes…all for you, baby, and it feels so damn good."

He stroked a few more times and lowered her legs gently, lifting her and edging her up the bed, still buried inside her. Her pussy spasmed around him, milking him even though he had nothing left to give. He still throbbed, his heart raced, his breathing hard enough to move her hair with every exhale at her shoulder. "Kendall…*damn*."

"I hear you. You are very, *very* good, Jared. *Fuck*." Her eyes were closed and she was casually playing with the hair at the base of his neck. "I have no idea, nor do I want to know, how much you've practiced but it certainly made perfect."

He chuckled, "Thank you. I don't think I can see. I can guaran-damn-tee I can't stand up."

"I'm okay; you're not as heavy as you look." She had one hand on his back, tracing circles over his muscle definition.

"Hey…I look *heavy*, Kendall?"

"You look *big*, Jared. Much bigger than me. But you're very lean.

Gorgeous, but I don't need to tell you that."

He lifted his head to look at her, loving the several shades of green in her eyes. They were mostly light green, but there were tiny striations of darker green and amber. Her lashes were so thick it looked like she was wearing makeup but he would have sworn she wasn't.

"I feel like you *do* need to hear how gorgeous you are, Kendall. I can't believe the body you have under all those clothes." Her eyes drifted closed and he swore it was so he couldn't read them.

When she opened them again, her voice was soft, intimate in the silence of the room. "Thank you, Jared. But no, I don't need to hear it. Your eyes are brown from a distance but there is the prettiest gold ring around them up close. You seem shy for me to talk about your eyes. Why is that?"

"No one ever talks about my eyes. No one else has ever noticed the ring. Weird, huh?"

"Nah, probably their eyes were all crossed from mind-numbing orgasms so they couldn't focus." He laughed loudly and kissed her thoroughly. He didn't want to pull away from her, but he didn't want the condom to slip off inside her either.

Kendall seemed to sense his dilemma. "Go ahead, Jared. We lose it and I have to go in after it. Takes the fun right out of everything." He gave her another smacking kiss, laughing against her lips, and went up on his arms to slowly pulling out of her. They both lowered their gazes to watch and it turned them both on, their eyes meeting hotly. "Really. We can't continue to fuck like bunnies. No matter how badly I want to."

He groaned as he pulled the rest of the way out and gave her a half smile, heading to the bathroom to get rid of the condom. He poked his head out the door. "Shower with me?" Kendall climbed off the bed and Jared watched her cross the room; her movements reminded him of an exotic cat.

They stepped into the small shower together and took turns under the spray. When Kendall stepped under to wash her hair and body, he said, "You are so hot, Kendall. Jesus." She laughed and shook her head.

They got out and dried off with fluffy violet bath towels. Kendall wrapped one around her and walked to the other room. She pulled white panties, pale blue sleep shorts, and a white ribbed tank top on before gathering her thick black hair in a haphazard bun at the top of her head.

"Oh, Kendall. Damn."

She smiled but said nothing as she took the damp towel back in the bathroom. He pulled on his boxer briefs then his jeans. As he raked his fingers through his wet hair, he realized she was holding a serious camera in her hands and taking photos of him.

"You are *not* taking pictures of me half dressed."

"Oh, I really am. I'll develop these later and make you copies. Trust me, I won't show them to anyone. They're all for me and my extensive collection of beautiful photos. When you're forty with a little pot belly, you'll like having these. You will." He kissed her as a distraction and wrestled the camera from her, chasing her around and taking a few of her. "If I could conceal our faces, I'd love to get photos of us together. Naked, of course. We'll see if we can make it happen."

Jared put her camera down and gathered her in his arms, backing her into the wall and pulling the clip from her hair. As it fell in thick waves over her shoulders, he slipped his hand into it and kissed her until he felt her knees weaken. Resting his forehead against Kendall's he asked, "What time is it?"

"Almost six-thirty," her voice was barely a whisper.

Jared sighed and kissed Kendall again lightly before letting her go. "Gotta go or your parents are going to flip the hell out." He pulled his t-shirt over his head and quickly put on socks and sneakers. When he was fully dressed, he grabbed her for one final kiss and was out the door.

# **Chapter Two**

Since that day, he'd seen her at least three days a week. No one suspected anything. No one was ever home when he was there. His friends had no idea where he spent his time when he wasn't playing football or in school. There was a huge parking party this weekend and he'd been told in no uncertain terms to be there.

His center on the team, a huge fucker they called Big Country, said he was tired of their team captain and primary hell-raiser being MIA. Thanksgiving was in a couple of weeks and he was expected to play the holiday game and entertain hordes of visiting relatives.

He still dated other senior girls and he fucked them. Amy Stonehouse was his current 'girlfriend'. The stereotypical bubbly, blonde cheerleader who put out. Jared could barely tolerate her and had to close his eyes during sex to pretend she was the woman he really wanted to be having sex with. He made sure he was rarely available to Amy and slept with her as few times as possible…but it didn't get any easier and he felt like shit after.

The worst part was that Kendall knew but didn't want to talk about it.

A month after they'd started sleeping together, he'd tried to justify it by telling her if he appeared celibate, everyone would wonder what the fuck was going on but even as he'd said it, he'd felt ashamed. He'd felt like a coward.

Jared knew she dated no one else, wanted no one else. Kendall had stopped him from talking by putting her nipple to his mouth and he'd latched on to it like a life preserver; wanting to please her even more than usual to wash away his unfamiliar guilt.

They weren't a formal couple but the sense of cheating on her again and again didn't go away.

Right now, there were no expectations. There was only Kendall. He'd finished practice, hung with his friends for a few minutes, stopped by his house. Now it was her time. Time to worship her body, allow her to worship his, and forget the world, the pressure, and his reputation.

She'd barely gotten the door closed when he had her topless, the tank top hardly settled on the floor before her sweat pants and panties joined it. He unbuckled his belt and slid his clothes away enough to free his cock, pulling a condom from his back pocket. When it was rolled on, he took her hard against the wall, her legs wrapped around his waist.

Neither of them needed foreplay today. Some days were like that. There were days when they worked one another over orally until they were too wrung out for regular sex. Then there were the straight fucking days. It was what Jared needed today and Kendall always seemed to understand. She pulled his shirt over his head as he slammed into her, taking her hard while he ate at her mouth.

Whatever he wanted, she did for him. Whatever he needed, she gave him.

They'd tried every position on every surface in her basement room. They went through two boxes of condoms each week and there were times they almost ran out. Kendall was also on birth control from Planned Parenthood. In almost four months of non-stop fucking, they hadn't had so much as a scare. She always smelled good, looked good, tasted good and he was thoroughly addicted to her sexually. The rest of her was taking root inside him and he had no idea what to do about that.

Being with other women not only felt wrong, it was flat and uninteresting. The captain of the cheer squad thought she gave great blowjobs but Kendall could turn pro. She'd practiced on him again and again, had even made him jack off for her, until she had the perfect combination of pressure, suction, and teeth. Kendall could make him come within thirty seconds or torment him for thirty minutes, not allowing him to climax.

He loved how well she knew his body, how well he knew hers.

Today, his need for her was insatiable. He couldn't kiss her enough, touch her enough, fuck her deep enough. Jared made her come once explosively then carried her to the bed. Undressing, he flipped her to her stomach and took her hard – too hard, he sometimes worried – from behind.

The tension riding him, the need to make her coast the boundary of pleasure and pain, seemed to evaporate when he felt and heard her climax a second time. Frustration, guilt, and an unexplained fear left him in a rush. There was only Kendall. His Kendall. His woman.

Settling on his heels, he brought her back to his chest and held her gently. One hand across her ribcage cupped the breast on the opposite side, his other hand drifted over the soft skin of her stomach and smoothed over her mound, his long finger stroking along her cleft.

Kendall's arm was above her head, her hand in his hair, raking softly at the base of skull. Her other hand was on his hip, kneading the muscles there, her knees spread wide on either side of his. Her head rested on his shoulder, his mouth caressed her neck as she started to ride him, lifting and lowering herself in a lazy rhythm. Kendall's hair fell like silk thread around them, adding yet another layer of erotic sensation.

It was this intimate position, making love rather than fucking, that a few of his teammates and his girlfriend witnessed as they busted through the unlocked basement door.

Kendall went rigid. Jared went insane. "Get the fuck *out*!"

"Oh hell no, you are not cheating on me with fucking *Kendall Torres*," Amy's voice was less cheer happy and more bitter harpy as she put her hands on her hips and stuck her ass to the side, needing to strike a pose even in this situation.

Big Country and the other guys took a different tack, "She is fucking hot; can totally see why you're nailing her, buddy. Does she travel with the team?" This was code for girls they passed among them.

Jared whipped the quilt completely over Kendall up to her neck two seconds after he saw them in the doorway. Sunlight now streamed into their personal space, making it too bright and shattering their illusion of being the only two people in the world.

Her face was turned away and he didn't think she was breathing. "Out…right now…I swear to God. *Get the fuck out.*" Jared's voice had gone low and deadly. Each of the guys he played with recognized the danger and sensed there might be more going on than they'd figured.

Amy started screeching and throwing out threats. Big Country threw her over his shoulder and hauled her back outside. The rest of the team followed, suddenly realizing they might have made a huge mistake. The last young man out pulled the door closed behind him.

Utter silence descended on Jared and Kendall. Neither said anything or moved for almost a minute. When she braced to lift herself from him, he held her in place. "Wait, Kendall, wait. I can fix this." That was when he felt her tears hitting his forearm, still across her torso. "No, baby, please don't cry. I can fix it, I swear it. Don't cry, Kendall." She shook her head, sending her beautiful black hair sliding over his chest. "Yes, I can. It's going to be alright."

Still holding on to her, he pulled out and turned her in his arms. The sight of Kendall crying hit him like a fist in the heart. She wouldn't look at him, but tears slipped silently from under her eyelids.

Stroking from her temple to her jaw, he whispered and tried to soothe her. "I know it seems really awful right now, worse for you, but I'll make it right." He kissed her lips and hugged her to him, "I can, Kendall. Please don't cry, baby, I'm so sorry. So, so sorry. Let me fix it. Please let me fix it, baby."

He got off the bed and pulled her with him. Walking into the bathroom, he disposed of the condom and stepped with her into the shower. He washed her hair then her body. Scrubbing himself quickly and wetting his hair, he took her out and dried her off. Kendall still hadn't spoken.

"Get clothes on, honey. Just throw something on." He dressed fast and pulled the quilt over the bed. When he turned back, Kendall wore jeans and a soft t-shirt. She pulled her hair up in a bun on top of her head. Curling up in one of the chairs, she stared off in the distance.

He'd never seen her sad before and everything inside him was screaming to make it right, to bring back her smiles. The laughter Kendall always gave him; that he hadn't realized he had come to depend on until now.

Jared crouched in front of her and guided her chin around, forcing her to look at him. "I'm calling them in. Do *not* freak out. I will handle this."

He opened the basement door to the outside and his three teammates and fuming girlfriend were huddled together ten feet away. "Get your asses in here." Pointing a finger at Amy, he said, "Say one more fucking thing to Kendall and I will *ruin* you, Amy. You know I can. Do not fuck with me." Looking at the other guys he added, "You three better watch yourselves."

They nodded uncertainly and filed past him through the door. Standing together just inside, Jared closed the door and walked to stand beside Kendall, dropping his hand possessively to her shoulder.

"Tommy, Slade, Big...what the *fuck* are you doing here? And why the hell is *she* with you?"

Big Country looked incredibly uncomfortable. "Dude, we thought you were like, into drugs or something. You've been weird for months. Not really hanging, not drinking, not whor...I mean, not really dating. Amy wanted to know where you were and none of us knew. She got crazy on us, said she was going to figure out what was going on and we didn't want her happening on anything without us. We just never expected...*this*." He gestured at Kendall helplessly.

Slade stepped slightly forward. As their best wide receiver, he was built more like Jared, tall and lean. "We followed you from your house to the parking lot. Tommy trailed you here, saw you go into the backyard. When he looked around the corner, you were going into the basement. Had no idea, man. I swear to God, man...we had no idea."

"I mean, given the neighborhood and all, we figured you were here to buy drugs." Tommy's eyes jerked to Kendall, "I mean...that is...*fuck*. Sorry." Tommy was one of their offensive backs; huge and not real bright.

Slade continued, "We just didn't know, man. Thought you might need help. Thought maybe you'd gotten into something that would ruin your playing chances. Why didn't you...you know, tell us?"

Jared gave an irritated laugh. "Because Kendall didn't want to deal with the bullshit associated with me. I've been with her for almost four months." Amy gasped. "Yeah, Amy...I was cheating on *Kendall* with *you*...not the other way around. I did it to keep our cover and I'm feeling even *shittier* about it now actually."

Amy flipped her hair, "So cannot believe you'd choose *that* over *this*!" She ran her hands down the slender body she obsessed over every minute of every day. She needed constant reassurance that she wasn't "fat" or "ugly". Why hadn't he listened to his conscience? At least to common sense?

"Oh, yes, Amy. *Absolutely* I choose Kendall over you." He pulled Kendall to her feet and stood her in front of him against his chest, his hands cupping her shoulders protectively. "Guys?"

All three of them looked at Kendall as if seeing her for the first time. Tommy's mouth was hanging open. Big Country looked at Jared, "She is stunning, dude. I had no idea she was so…just…hot."

"I'd pick her over you, Amy," Tommy said quietly before adding a mumbled, "Sorry."

Slade was half black and gorgeous. He said quietly, "Kendall, without the heavy glasses, funky hair, and baggie clothes…you're probably the hottest chick in school. I don't get it."

"Yeah, well, I also took gymnastics and dance for ten years before we moved here, but I didn't sign up for cheer squad either. Those things…being pretty, being popular…they just don't matter to me." Amy's sharp intake of breath made her smile for the first time, "Not that being pretty and popular shouldn't be someone *else's* only goal in life. I don't judge."

Amy narrowed her eyes and Kendall propped a hand on her hip. "Girl, please don't give me that catty look. I'm not stealing your man. I'm *fucking* your man. There is definitely a difference. You can all go back to your happy and totally oblivious lives. I'd appreciate it if you left me out of it." With that, she walked to the basement door and held it open. "Everybody out. I'm tired."

Glancing at Amy she added sweetly, "School all day and fucking all afternoon just wears a girl *out*." She pointed at the door; Amy tossed her hair and put her nose in the air, stomping past Kendall. "Bye guys. You too, Jared."

The other three filed out quickly and Jared walked to her. He stood in front of her for a long moment, staring down into the face he knew he couldn't live without. "Don't do this, Kendall. Be with me officially.

Publicly. I want you, I need you so much. I don't want to hide you like something I'm ashamed of anymore."

She put her palm on his cheek. "I can't, Jared. Maybe one day I can explain it to you. I *cannot* draw attention to myself. Not in any way. You can't help the attention you get." Her thumb stroked the corner of his mouth and she attempted a small smile. "I'll always look back on this time and say it was the best time in my life. I've loved having you in this little cocoon; this little world away from reality for both of us. I will miss you *desperately*, Jared. I promise you."

Kendall stretched up and pulled him down for a deep kiss, wanting him to know what she was feeling. When she broke it, she didn't meet his eyes as she gently nudged him toward the door.

Jared was almost over the threshold when he turned back. "I'm giving you the weekend. Then we're going to talk, baby. I can't be without you." He reached out and pulled her to him hard, staking claim to her mouth. He clutched her to him, one hand in her hair and the other gripping her ass. Then he gentled the kiss and stroked his tongue over hers until she was limp in his arms. "Monday. We talk Monday. I need you, baby. I…I love you, Kendall."

She rested her head on his chest, a hitching sob broke from her before she whispered, "Oh, Jared, I love you, too. You don't understand. I really hope one day I can explain so you don't hate me."

She pushed at his stomach and he felt her watching him as he turned to go. Everything inside him was screaming silently not to leave her, not to let Kendall out of his sight. To lock himself in the quiet solitude he'd come to cherish with her and let the world get fucked. He kept thinking she'd call him back, tell him to wait, tell him Monday was too far away.

But she didn't.

Instead, Jared heard a low sob an instant before the door closed and the lock clicked into place.

He managed to walk up the steps and join his shell-shocked friends in the backyard. He glared at Amy, "You say *one thing* against her, and I tell everyone I caught you and Brianna eating each other out. It won't be a lie. I'll just add that you call people Brianna when they go down on you. I will fuck up your life, honey, if you say one word about my Kendall."

With that, he turned and stalked out of the yard, the others following behind him.

## **Chapter Three**

Kendall listened until she heard the gate on the side of the house slam shut. Burying her face in her hands, she gave herself a moment to feel the loss of the man she'd fallen stupidly and irrevocably in love with. Washing her face in the little bathroom, she took a deep breath and kicked her own ass into gear.

Moving to the back of her closet, she pushed a curtain aside to reveal a door. Unlocking the multiple deadbolts, she walked up the stairs into the house above. It was completely empty, abandoned. No one had ever lived in this house but her.

And she was about to leave it for the last time.

At the front window, she watched as the man she loved led his friends back to the shopping center three blocks away. Placing her hand on the door frame, she allowed the futility of their situation to wash over her. Too soon, he was out of sight. Kendall sobbed brokenly and clutched her arms tightly around her middle, forcing herself to keep it together. When she finally got herself under control, she got to work.

Walking into the garage off the kitchen, she opened the door of the brand new SUV her father had purchased in cash before he was killed. She took out the new tags and traded them out. She pulled the fake title and registration from her file under the seat and replaced the other set in the visor.

Back in the house, she pulled her duffle bags from the secret compartment in the pantry her father had always warned her to create somewhere in any house she lived in. One held more than a million dollars in cash. The other held several new identities and not much else.

Carrying them down to the basement, she gathered up her personal things. The quilt her mother had made years before she was shot execution style and left to die in the dirt. The camera equipment her father had given her before they'd run the first time…two years before he'd been tortured to death a few feet from her. The few things she carried from place to place.

She removed every photo from every surface. Emptied her darkroom.

The photos she'd taken last week of Jared and her making love. Their faces weren't visible, just their profiles, but their bodies were beautiful, their passion obvious. There were at least a hundred photos of him and a few of her.

Choosing one that didn't show her face clearly, her favorite of him from their first day, and the most beautiful of them together, she put them in an envelope to include in the letter she planned to write him.

Other than the quilt, everything had to fit inside the second duffle bag. Choosing her favorite clothes, her few mementos, and photos, she was fully packed and ready to move out within twenty minutes of Jared walking out the door. Everything else had to stay behind. Nothing could be traced to her. It was just one more room of stuff she'd never see again.

After she loaded the SUV with the duffle bags she did one more sweep over the place, checking under the furniture she had to leave behind. Pulling on boots and a thick jacket, she took stationary from her desk. Writing quickly, she folded the letter and addressed it to Jared. She gave no return address; simply stamped it and took it with her.

With one final glance at the sanctuary she'd had for almost nine months, the longest she'd stayed in one place since she was twelve, she headed back upstairs and into the garage. She checked the hidden compartment beneath the backseat and made sure the two 9mm's were loaded and waiting.

Taking her wallet from her backpack, she pulled out her old driver's license and replaced it with one that bore a different name. She was now twenty years old with a new social security number, high school diploma, and job history.

In a small metal bowl, she burned all the old identification. She'd never be Kendall Torres again. Her father's brother provided her new documents every six months. Her given name was Gabriella Garcia-Moreno but she hadn't used that name in almost six years.

She got behind the wheel and took a deep breath. In her mind, she'd always be Kendall. That was the name Jared had called her, the name he had used when he told her he loved her. She raised the garage door and backed the SUV out to the street. As she drove away, she cried, wishing things could be different. Knowing they never would. Not for her.

She mailed the letter, got on the highway, and drove east. She didn't know where she was going or how long she would drive. She knew it would be hundreds of miles. Too far away from the man she loved and would miss with everything inside herself.

# **Chapter Four**

By Saturday morning, Jared knew he couldn't wait to see her another day. He *needed* Kendall, missed the feel of her in his arms. He'd been hard since he woke up. Leaving the bathroom freshly showered and dressed, his mom called him into the kitchen.

Debbie Stalzer was the All American Soccer Mom. Small and brunette, she headed the PTA, organized bake sales for church, volunteered at every charity she could fit in her schedule, and was proud to say her family came first.

She handed her oldest child, her favorite – though she'd never admit that out loud – a tall glass of orange juice and a letter that had come in the morning mail. He opened it with a smile, recognizing Kendall's handwriting and briefly thinking it was odd there was no return address. His mother rambled on happily as he began to read.

When Jared collapsed into a chair, the glass of orange juice slipping from his hand and shattering on the floor, his mother almost had a heart attack. Kneeling in front of him, she begged him to tell her what was wrong, what had happened. He couldn't talk. Then he did something he hadn't done since he was six years old.

He burst into tears and held on to his mother.

*My darling Jared,*

*I'm sorry I can't say goodbye to you in person. You don't know…can't know…how it hurts me. I have to leave now…today. By the time you get this, I'll have already been driving for almost twenty hours and have a totally new identity. Please don't try to find me. It isn't safe. I'll tell you what I can and no more. It's better for you, and for me, that you know as little as possible.*

*<u>I am eighteen and from Columbia</u>. Nothing else about me is true. Not even my name, though to tell you my true name would sign your death warrant. I will look different six months from now. Change again six months after that. I pray my face changes as I age.*

*I've been living alone since I arrived here nine months ago. My mother was murdered when I was twelve. My father when I was fourteen and I've continued running on my own. I took the basement as my personal space because it was more easily defended. Imagine my surprise when I realized I'd forgotten to lock the door for the first time in six years. If your friends noticed you acting differently, other people likely would have, too. I wanted you so badly, selfishly wanted one thing for me. One thing just for me.*

*My mother witnessed something she shouldn't have when we were on holiday. My father and I witnessed her murder two days later. We went home to Columbia and he cashed out our life. We ran and kept running.*

*Once we were together that first day, I knew I'd risk everything to stay with you. It was only today when I realized I was risking not just my safety, but yours. I had no right to do that. No matter how lonely I was. How scared I've been for so long now. I love you, Jared. When I said our time together would always be my best memory, I meant it. Your potential to become the most amazing man is unparalleled. Don't waste your life, baby. Take the gifts you've been given and do good things. My greatest wish is for you to be happy.*

*I miss you desperately already. Your smile, your laugh, the way you hold me, the sound of your voice. I can never see you, never contact you again. I carry my favorite photos of you with me. Reminders of the man who loved me so well, so beautifully...no one else will ever compare.*

*Forgive me. Forget me.*

*Love,*

*Kendall*

After a long time, Jared handed his mother the letter and asked, "Where's Dad? I need to talk to him *now*." She texted her husband then read the letter. Gary was the county Sheriff. "Mom, I need your keys, you're behind my truck." When Debbie picked up the photos of her son and the young woman who'd written the letter, she felt herself blush. "No judgment, Mom. We were ridiculously safe. And I love her."

She nodded and handed him the keys to her Volvo. He drove them to Kendall's home, unable to speak. This time he pulled into the driveway and walked up to the front door. He even knocked, knowing she hadn't lied in her letter. His Kendall was long gone and it had been his fault.

When his father's Sheriff's department truck pulled in behind them, his mother rushed to him. Slightly shorter than Jared with a barrel chest, Gary Stalzer approached his son and put his hand on his shoulder. Jared handed him Kendall's letter and he read it with a professional eye.

"Let's check out the house." He led his wife and son to the basement entrance, picking the lock and opening the door. Jared rushed in and the weight of the truth hit him like a truck. He collapsed beside the bed and gasped for breath into the sheets that still smelled like Kendall.

He stood and went up the stairs to the main part of the house. It was obvious to all three of them no one had lived in this part of the house for a long time. The wood floors were covered in a sheet of dust, small booted footprints tracking through the house. There was a bare wall in the pantry that ended up being a small hidden storage space.

The garage that was empty but tracks through the dust showed a large vehicle had backed out recently. A small metal bowl of ashes where a tiny corner of her driver's license still remained.

"I didn't question it. She said they worked all the time. I never saw the empty upstairs, the vehicle. She's lived alone since she was fourteen. No wonder she tried to be invisible. *Oh my god*." His mother rubbed his back as he pinched the bridge of his nose before rubbing his eyes hard.

He went back downstairs and walked into her bathroom. She'd left all her shampoo and soaps. He pocketed a small bottle of perfume she used sparingly. Everything looked almost the same. Her closet still held clothing as well as a mini fridge and microwave, something else he'd never questioned since he had a mini fridge in his own room.

The darkroom where they'd made love once as she developed pictures of him. Feeling along the walls, he found a forgotten picture of her laughing in bed against the pillows. He took it with him to keep anyone from finding it, and because it was the only full facial shot he had of her.

His father said he'd see what he could find out, but more than likely, all the paper trails would end up being false. Taking a deep breath, Jared told him, "Nothing official, Dad. I won't endanger her. I want every single item in that basement. I'll carry it out myself."

The three of them left the house, returning to their own. Jared went to bed and slept more than twenty hours. When he woke late on Sunday night, he knew he would see her again. Someday, he'd find her. In the meantime, he would make himself a man she would be proud of.

# **Chapter Five**

The rest of his senior year went quickly, though Jared applied himself as never before in classes. He stopped drinking and partying completely.

It was his father who took him aside to talk about how lonely he obviously was. "Son, you're too young to be alone all the time. You're going to throw yourself into a full damn depression at this rate." His gruff voice was softer when he added, "Your mother worries about you all the time, Jared. Just…try, okay? Try to get out of the house and have some fun."

He started dating again six months after Kendall disappeared into thin air but only dated women with dark hair who weren't fake.

Over his years in college, some of the women he dated fell in love with him but he didn't - *couldn't* – return their feelings. There was always too much he held back because it wasn't his to give. He was more respectful to women after Kendall. He never dated more than one at a time and was always more careful about protection than any of the women would have been. If things ended, he tried to keep things civil.

Jared found he went out of his way to talk to loners, people no one else seemed to talk to. Kendall had taught him that the surface of a person's supposed life didn't mean shit. You had to dig deep.

In the summer after high school, Amy had gotten pregnant by the son of the town banker who also owned the country club. She hadn't gone to college but lived the shallow life she had always planned for herself.

Not one whisper of his relationship with Kendall had ever spread. Everyone wondered and wild rumors flew but Jared didn't confirm or deny them.

His high school buddies still hung with him. The four of them were split between UCLA and USC on football scholarships. He and Slade had been snapped up as a team completer in passing and receiving with UCLA. Big Country and Tommy rounded out a lagging offensive line for USC.

They met up every couple of weeks. He had finally told them about Kendall when they'd been in college for over a year and the three men were speechless. Big wanted to know how the hell he still managed to talk to them after the situation they'd caused.

He told them she wouldn't have been able to stay forever anyway. Kendall would have had to leave eventually; she probably should have left months before she had. There, in front of the friends he'd had since first grade, Jared had shed tears for what he and Kendall had shared...and what they'd lost. That simple show of emotion had matured them all, had brought them closer. Jared was grateful not to bear the secret alone anymore.

He graduated and was drafted to the Broncos where he played three stellar years before a hit took out his shoulder and ended his throwing days. He took the money he'd made being a first-round draft pick and started several businesses in his home town.

One of them was a private investigation firm with some of the best investigators on the west coast. He bent all his resources to finding the love of his life; determined that one day he'd have her with him again.

Jared gave time and money to community sports and charities, using his notoriety to encourage the wealthy to write fatter checks. He tried to live his life as a better man than he would have been without those four beautiful months with Kendall.

He had never planned to return to this small town in Oregon, but losing her had ensured he'd have to. It was the last place he'd seen her. It was where his memories of her were strongest.

After leaving the NFL, he'd purchased the little house she'd lived in. He put her furniture, the possessions she'd left behind, back in it just as he remembered. His parents had stored everything for him since high school.

He remodeled the upstairs and bought the vacant lot next door. Little by little, Jared made it into what he needed and eventually moved into it to the shock of the surrounding neighborhood. Leading a community revitalization effort, he worked with local government and residents to make it an area they could be proud of and that was safe for their children.

He was the local boy who made good and he found he felt better spending holidays here with his family and friends than he would renting some sterile place on a tropical island to cook turkey in.

So it happened that seven years after Kendall had disappeared without a trace – at a moment when he hadn't really been looking – he found her.

Big Country still played for the NFL, currently with the Seahawks. His girlfriend often roped him into local art exhibits and museum openings despite his agony. The night before he called Jared, he had attended a gallery opening for Ken Jacobs, a reclusive photographer whose work was world-renowned. The man had not attended his own exhibit but every piece on sale had been purchased.

One of the displays had caught his old friend's eye. It was a couple obviously having sex. Though no faces were revealed in the photograph, Big thought he recognized some features of the models as well as the hazy background of the room they were in.

Jared listened with white knuckles as Big explained the attention it had received from the patrons. Other artists asked if the couple in the photo were available for further modeling.

*How beautiful. How passionate. Almost as if they are truly in love...really making love.*

His oldest friend bought the picture, outbidding everyone else by thousands of dollars to the shock of his girlfriend. She was even more shocked when he told her it was a gift for his best friend. He gave Jared the courier information and said it would arrive within hours.

After hanging up, Jared walked his house all day, waiting for the package to arrive. When he saw the delivery truck pull to the curb, he was almost rude to the driver; grabbing the oversized box and slamming the door after a rushed *thank you, goodbye.*

He took his time opening the crate, worried about damaging what was inside; stalling in case it wasn't what he'd hoped for at all. When the last of the packing material fell away, Jared dropped to his knees in front of it.

It was one of the many Kendall had taken of them in her basement room. This was one he hadn't seen. Her breast nearest the camera was covered by his large hand and her head was thrown back, only her cheek and edge of her mouth visible. His own head was bent, his mouth at her neck, his brow and cheek the only part of his features exposed.

It was a photograph he hadn't seen but he remembered every moment that was captured and it made him instantly hard to the point of pain. He carried it to the bedroom and leaned it against his dresser mirror. He remembered that day so clearly. How she'd set up the tripod, how nervous he'd been. Then they'd gotten so caught up that neither of them paid attention to the camera that went off every twenty seconds for a long time.

Jared sat down at the computer for a long time, searching for every scrap of information he could find about Ken Jacobs. Everyone believed him to be an older man though there was no detail on his exact age or even when his birthday was. There were no photos of him, no way to contact him. All correspondence went through the gallery that handled his work and they were fiercely loyal.

Jared packed a bag, tucking his laptop inside. With his phone, he took a picture of the framed photo and saved it.

Stripping to shower, he couldn't bear the tension in his dick another moment. Sitting on the edge of his huge bed, he stared at the photo and took his cock in his fist. He stroked slowly at first, remembering how they'd played that day, how she'd sucked him for a long time, making him wait so long to come. When she'd allowed him to at last, he had retaliated by pulling her over his face and eating her while she moaned and worked against his mouth.

After she could move again, she'd set up the camera and come back to bed, positioning them to the side. At first self conscious, she'd lowered herself on him, her legs around his back while he knelt on his knees, sitting back on his heels. He remembered sucking her nipples while she raked her fingers through his hair and whispered to him about how good he made her feel, how he played her body like an instrument.

Like so many other days, their goal had been mutual pleasure. Never in a rush, never selfish, they had loved one another almost from the beginning, Jared thought now. Kendall had come so hard in his arms when she couldn't bear another moment. She had collapsed against his shoulder while he thrust hard and deep inside her; he'd climaxed moaning incoherently against her neck.

By the time he replayed the entire experience through his mind, Jared was fisting himself hard and fast, his balls drawn up painfully tight. His come felt like it was boiling in his body, the need for release urgent now. The orgasm clawed its' way from his low back and the tops of his thighs, his semen exploding from his body and splattering in wave after wave on the hardwood floor in front of him, Kendall's name a heartbroken whisper in the silence of her old home.

When he'd pumped himself dry and the shaking began to ease, he collapsed back on the bed, breathing hard and knowing now more than ever that he had to find her. Jared pulled himself up wearily and used his discarded clothes to clean his spilled seed from the floor.

One final look at the photo made his spent cock twitch.

He showered and dressed as quickly as possible. When he found himself somewhat presentable in jeans and a button-down with boots, he grabbed his bag and headed downstairs to the garage.

Taking the folded picture of Kendall laughing in bed from his wallet – creased and worn at the edges – he put it in the visor and reversed to the street, heading for Seattle.

# **Chapter Six**

Kendall Torres, known for the last couple of years as Ken Jacobs, was anonymous at last. The only price for her anonymity had been her soul, her heart…her peace of mind.

So many pieces had finally come together to allow her a small semblance of normalcy. To give her a life of her own. *Too late*, she often thought to herself in the dark of the night.

Three years ago, her father's brother had heard from a source in the DC police department that a young woman fitting Kendall's description had been found dead of a drug overdose. No one had claimed the body of the woman thought to be a lifelong street person.

Knowing he was still watched by the drug cartel searching for his niece, Uncle Francisco contacted the local funeral home and arranged for the young woman to be shipped back to Columbia so 'his little Gabby' could be laid to rest in their family plot.

An open-casket service was held after the unknown woman was made to resemble the young Gabriella Garcia-Moreno even further. Her head had been shaved to the scalp and Kendall had cut almost a foot of her hair to be used to make a wig. The body was dressed carefully and placed in the casket. She even wore a locket that contained pictures of Kendall's parents.

Kendall's extended family – people she had been unable to see in more than a decade – attended the funeral and sobbed over her lost youth as well as the loss of her much-loved mother and father. The tears shed had not been pretense.

Two unknown men had arrived during the memorial where large family photos were displayed of the Garcia-Moreno family in happier times. One had discreetly photographed the dead woman lying peacefully in the casket.

The woman who had given Kendall back her life was cremated that same day and her ashes placed in an urn that was buried on the estate. A party was held immediately after the urn's interment and more than a hundred people paid their respects to Rodrigo, Amelia, and

Gabriella's family.

Her Uncle Frank was a furniture maker and spoke to dozens of people every day. He passed messages to her disposable phone through those he trusted. Anyone watching would have had difficulty determining who to watch.

For three years since the funeral, Kendall had stayed in the Seattle area, moving every few months to a new hotel or apartment. Last month, her uncle told her he believed it was truly safe. There had been no inquiries about her in more than a year and a shift of power in the cartel had seen many of those previously in power killed or replaced.

After so many years, she could stop running. She kept Ken Jacob's anonymity. She tried to live a somewhat normal life. She dated a few times, taken the occasional lover when she'd gotten so lonely she couldn't stand another day without physical contact. It helped but didn't satisfy her.

Today she walked the produce market, her shorter black curls catching the breeze and cupping her face. When she'd cut so much to make the wig she'd decided it suited her and left it shoulder length now. Two tiny clips held it away from her face. There were blue contact lenses in her eyes. Her sense of fashion was classic these days; the ultra feminine sundress and heeled sandals very different from styles she'd adopted in the past.

Choosing various fruits and cheeses, Kendall wandered with no real destination in mind. She paid the vendor and placed her items in a leather net bag over her shoulder. As she stepped into the uncovered center of the market, she soaked up the rare sunshine Seattle was blessed with and lowered stylish sunglasses over her eyes.

At one of the numerous coffee bars she laughed and talked with the young woman behind the counter, wondering if she shouldn't get her number. She found female lovers offered her a physical connection without having to compete with Jared's memory.

The woman handed her a receipt and she saw a cell phone number jotted on the front. She smiled and nodded, walking through the floral stalls as she sipped the delicate brew. An hour later, her coffee finished, she stepped into a small open-air bistro for crusty bread and olive oil, selecting a Mediterranean salad as well.

Nearby, a group of athletic college students played with one another, laughing as they played an older version of leap-frog. The joy and simplicity of the scene called to her and she removed her camera from her bag, taking several photos before lowering it with a soft smile. It turned melancholy as she remembered watching Jared play with his friends the same way in high school.

Back then, she'd often watched him, been captivated by something she didn't fully understand. From the beginning, she'd seen the potential Jared was wasting. Internal suspension, sitting beside him for three days, had been more temptation than she could ultimately deny.

She hadn't intended to fall in love with him and she was certain loving her had been the furthest thing from his mind. There were no regrets. Not for one moment she'd had with him. Those memories had helped her keep going.

Pulled into the past, she ate slowly, ordering white wine when she was done. Sitting back in the plush chair of the patio restaurant, she enjoyed the sun and idly wondered how Jared was getting along. Sometimes she searched his name on Google; more than she felt comfortable admitting actually. She liked to see updates about all the good things he was doing in his hometown.

He was still so beautiful, even more since becoming the man she'd always hoped he would be. Her heart clenched and she wiped sudden tears from under her sunglasses. The glass clinked as she set it on the table with trembling hands.

After blotting her eyes with the linen napkin, she picked up her bag to pay the check. It was time to head home. To the home that was beautiful but empty of the things she'd dreamed about as a young girl. She doubted she would ever have a husband and children of her own now.

Standing and turning to the counter, she froze at the male voice that said quietly, "Kendall."

She shook herself from a moment of shock and put double the amount due on the table, signaling the approaching server. She could not respond to a name she hadn't used in seven years. Terror almost brought her to her knees.

Placing her bag over her shoulder, she sped through the tables to the sidewalk beyond, intending to get lost in the crowds of the market. She was afraid as she hadn't been in so long. The thought of losing her life, as barren as it often felt, had her shaking and panting for breath.

A gentle hand on her shoulder had her turning too quickly, her heels throwing her off balance. Kendall gasped at the sight of Jared behind her, looking down at her with the same intense expression he'd had the last time he kissed her.

It was impossible. It had to be her imagination. Perhaps the stress and trauma had finally caught up to her. She couldn't get enough air, couldn't slow her heart, and felt him catch her as her knees gave way and everything faded to inky black as if someone had turned off a light.

## **Chapter Seven**

Sunlight through trees overhead caused her to blink rapidly in confusion. She was disoriented, remembered fear thrumming through her.

Turning her face, she found Jared's above her. "Hi, baby." He held her across his lap on a bench in the quiet park across from the market. He was supporting her with his forearm, his other arm over her waist. Her bag, sunglasses, and shoes sat beside him.

Three rapid beats of her heart and she threw herself at him, her arms going around his shoulders as she sobbed brokenly against his chest. She breathed in the warm mixture of sandalwood and male, soaked up the hardness of his body, and let the sound of his voice soothe her aching soul.

Jared had his face in her hair, his body surrounding her as he whispered, "Pretty baby, it's alright. Everything's going to be alright. I promise. It's okay, Kendall." His arms were locked around her as if he was afraid of her disappearing on him.

Minutes ticked by but his hold didn't loosen and she didn't want him to let her go. One hand stroked from the fall of her hair down her back. So long since she'd held this man, since she'd felt safe and cared for. Finally pulling her face back to look at him, she waited while he wiped her tears and laid his big palm along her cheek.

"How? How are you here, Jared? How did you find me?" she asked him quietly.

His brilliant smile stole her ability to think. "Your exhibit last month. Big Country plays here in Seattle and happened to go. He shipped our photograph to me. It's sitting in my bedroom." A small frown appeared between his eyes, "I've been here almost a month trying to find you. I staked out the gallery." Kendall had gone there the day before to drop off more work and pick up a substantial check from the showing. "I followed you home. It took everything in me not to bang on your door."

"Jared. Oh my god, Jared."

"I can't let you go again, Kendall...I can't." She saw desperation in his eyes and recognized it from her own reflection. He lifted her until she was fully on his lap, their faces level. "Every day I've thought of you. I've searched for you."

"Jared. You don't know what you're saying. You know we can't be together. I explained," she reminded him with her heart breaking all over again.

He gripped her shoulders and gave her a tiny shake. "I know exactly what I'm saying. I can't go through this anymore, Kendall. I can't be apart from you. I've had a hole inside me since the last time I held you and *you* are the only one who can fill it."

"It's too dangerous, Jared. Don't you understand?" She wanted what he offered too much. She *needed* this man as she'd never needed anything in her life. It was temptation unlike anything she'd ever felt before, reaching inside her and twisting her best intentions.

Warm, strong fingers cupped the nape of her neck, stroked into her hair. His touch was electric. "There is *no way* I can bear letting you go a second time. I barely survived it the first time. I can protect you, I can protect myself." She opened her mouth to protest and he kissed her. Hot, wet, deep he took her lips, imprinting on her again. It was as if a missing puzzle piece fell into place for both of them. The kiss went on and on, saturating every corner of her that had been dying for him.

When he lifted his mouth from hers, he stared deep into her eyes and said roughly, "I want you, I need you, I love you...so much, Kendall. I am *begging* you – as the man who gave you half his heart – please don't leave me again." He slipped her shoes on her feet and stood her up. "Your home or my hotel...it's your choice, but wherever it is, we're going together."

She nodded and grabbed her bag in one hand, linked his fingers through hers, and started running for a row of taxis parked near the market. They slid in the back, their sides sealed from shoulder to knees. She gave the cabby the address of her house.

He pulled her closer and inhaled the scent of lime and coconut that still suffused her hair. Kendall's skin was so soft and warm. His fingers stroked up and down her arm, letting his fingers remember the feel of her. She turned her cheek and laid it on his chest, listening to his strong heartbeat. Neither of them trusted themselves to speak.

When they pulled into a quiet neighborhood and stopped in front of her little bungalow, she handed bills to the driver while he was pulling out his wallet. "Go, Jared." He climbed out of the cab and she followed, moving around him and tugging a key ring from her bag.

She flung the door wide and disengaged the alarm system. Kicking off her shoes, she reached behind him to lock the door and reset security before jumping into his arms.

Her legs wrapped tightly around him and he was kissing and touching her everywhere. Sliding his hand under the hem of her dress, he tore her panties away. She unbuckled his belt, pushing his slacks and underwear just past his hips. Wrapping her fist around his cock, she savored the hard silkiness of him. She'd forgotten how big he was. He was hot and throbbing against her palm.

Jared turned, slamming her against the wall, one hand dipping between her legs. Assuring himself she was wet and ready, he felt Kendall position him an instant before he stroked into her fast and hard. Kendall screamed his name and kissed him, devoured him, her fingers fisted in his hair. "Yes, baby, please. I need you so badly. I've missed you so much. Hard, Jared, go hard and remind me. Make me remember everything."

Bracing his feet against the tile floor, he powered into her with the force he had never shared with any lover but her. "It's like home. Your sweet pussy remembers me. How I missed you, baby. Fucking into your beautiful body, making you come. You're so tight, so wet for my cock."

Again and again he drove deep, their bodies growing slick with sweat. His eyes locked to hers. "*Feel me*, Kendall. Feel me fucking you and know that no one else will ever love you like I will. You feel so good, so damn good. Come for me, Kendall. I have to feel it."

"Don't stop. Jared, I'm coming so hard. Come with me, baby." Her body tightened around him as they shouted their mutual release into the quiet house. He didn't want to stop stroking, didn't want to let her go for a single moment. They had so much to make up for. So many lost years.

Both of them were shaking and there were tears on Kendall's cheeks. Jared sank to his knees on the foyer floor and rocked her, still inside her, holding her tight enough to probably hurt. Her arms and legs gripped him just as desperately.

Her face was pressed to his neck, her voice breaking with her tears. "I was so alone, Jared. I slept with other people. I missed you, I needed you. I was too afraid for you. Please forgive me. Say you forgive me…for everything. Forgive me."

"Sweet Kendall. I can't imagine how alone you've been. I understand. I missed you so much. I dated rarely but I did do it. I'm sorry. I was tense, stressed all the time. Sexual frustration made it worse. I could pretend if they had dark hair and didn't talk. I wanted them to be you. I needed them to be you, Kendall."

Jared felt himself getting hard inside her again and pulled her dress over her head. She pulled his shirt over his. He stood and toed off his shoes, kissing her while he stepped out of his pants and boxer briefs. He moved deeper into the house and she directed him to her bedroom.

Her work table in the corner proved to be the right height to lay her down and watch all of her as he started thrusting deep and slow into her pussy again.

"Baby, take out the contacts." Kendall sat up and her fingers shook as she removed the colored lenses and dropped them on the floor. Jared held her chin between his fingers and smiled. "Oh, yes, baby." He drove into her and she laughed. He placed his palm flat on her chest and pushed her gently down to her back.

Her nipples were so hard and she held his gaze as her palms moved up her torso and took the pebbled tips between her fingers. Squeezing, tugging them out from her body caused Jared's eyes to darken with unconcealed lust.

"You know how much I always loved that. God, I'm so hard again." He draped her knees over his elbows and gripped the tops of her thighs. Her ass was suspended above the table as he fucked her without mercy. Keeping her off balance, speeding up and slowing down, shallow thrusts amid deeper ones, he held off her climax.

She was begging in English and Spanish, her hands leaving her breasts to grip the edge of the table. Curling one hand around her leg, he stroked over her clit and watched as she came so hard her scream was silent. Her body arching, tightening, while his name became a chant through her clenched teeth.

"More, I need to make you mine again, baby. To mark you as my woman. To make you come until our bodies aren't able to survive without each other ever again."

# **Chapter Eight**

Jared lifted her and padded to the bed covered in the same quilt he remembered. He pulled it back and sat on the edge of the bed with Kendall straddling him. She began lifting and lowering on him, "I have missed you very, very much, Jared. To have you here, holding me, inside me when I never thought I'd see you again is like magic. It scares me to have you here. I don't know what to do."

Warm, strong palms lifted to cup her face. "Kendall, we *will* work this out, but we'll do it together. You've been alone too long, and I've ached for you every day for seven years, needing to feel your pussy around me, to have your nipples in my mouth, to kiss you, lick you, taste you, *love* you."

He lowered his mouth and took a hard nipple in his mouth, cupping her breast in his palm and kneading it while he licked her, sucking just the tip first, then pulling her deeper and sealing her to the roof of his mouth. Then she was coming again, bracing her hands on his broad shoulders while her body gripped him inside.

Jared let her settle from the orgasm before laying her gently on her belly and slipping into her from behind; their bodies pressed fully against one another. Gliding over her hip and around to her stomach, he went to her mound, stroking over her clit while he moved into her slow and easy.

"Your body feels so good, Kendall. You were made for me. I could go all day like this. A nice steady rhythm, making you come again and again until you can't stand up. You're so wet, pretty baby. My fingers slip over you so smoothly. I want to lick you slow later, suck your clit into my mouth, and play my tongue over it. Stroke my fingers in and out of you until you give me more of your juices to lap up."

She was moaning and grinding against his hand in the same tempo that he fucked her, "You still love me to talk dirty to you, Kendall. Talking about fucking you with my cock, my fingers, and my tongue. Taking you in every position." She reached back and stroked his muscled thigh.

"Jared, you are so hard all over, around me, inside me. I watched every one of your games in college. I even saw one live. I watched the draft for hours…" Her voice trailed off with a laugh. "That gets really boring, by the way. I was afraid I was going to miss you so I watched all the pre-draft stuff."

He nuzzled the nape of her neck, licked, and kissed her as his heart hammered with the knowledge that she'd followed him all these years. "Then there you were holding a Bronco's jersey. I thought I'd die you looked so gorgeous. I recorded every game you played, I saw when you were hurt, and fought myself for *three days*. I was a raving lunatic, screaming and crying. I followed the Internet constantly, waiting for news on your surgery. I knew you'd be devastated…I sent you a card."

Jared stilled, closing his eyes and remembering. *"You played beautifully but don't forget there are bigger things for you than football…*that was you?" Kendall nodded below him. "I kept that card because it made me think of you, of the letter you left me. Oh, baby."

He pressed more firmly into her and Kendall moaned. "It made me take that letter out of the safe and re-read it. I spent the weeks I was recovering walking the town. Really *seeing* some parts of it for the first time. I'd lived there my entire life but hadn't noticed the youth center had been closed for years. The municipal pool was broken. The parks were a mess. I started making a list. I called it my KT list. Ways I could make a difference; to make you proud of me, wherever you were."

His strokes increased in pressure, fingers circling, circling over her clit. "I've been proud of you since the day I had to leave, Jared. The way you handled things made it so hard for me to go. I raged at myself all the way to Chicago." She sighed. "I don't think I have the hydration to come again, baby."

Jared chuckled and rose to his knees, bringing her with him, settling back on his heels with her over his lap. It was the same position they'd been in when they'd been interrupted years before.

"We never finished what we started that afternoon. The next day, I was so hard for you. I needed you so bad. Then I got your letter and it felt like someone pulled the rug out from under me." Kendall's head rested on his shoulder while she used gentle movements of her hips to deepen his thrusts. Jared kissed and licked down her neck. "There were nights I dreamed you'd been killed. I'd panic, not even knowing where to look. I knew you were out there, waiting for me to find you."

Her movements increased in strength and speed as he worked her over, talked to her. "I want you with me every day, Kendall. To know you're safe because I wake up beside you. To hold you and stroke you like this." His fingers slid more quickly over her clit.

"To be able to touch and suck your beautiful breasts…" He went from one to the other, cupping and testing their weight, pinching her sensitive nipples. "To feel you around me, hot and wet, my cock ramming into you again and again. Feeling you come so hard, milking me with the walls of your pussy. To shower with you, eat meals with you, and argue over stupid crap. I want us to take care of each other. To not be alone anymore."

Lifting her, he took control of the thrusts and felt her beginning to tighten, her body ready to come. "Come for me once more, baby. Let's finish what we started seven years ago." Jared powered into her, working her clit and nipple as she imploded, her body constricting in, squeezing him like a vice. Kendall whispered his name and he roared hers, grasping her to him, come shooting from the head of his cock and coating her pussy.

It felt so good, so hot.

Both of them went still at the same time. *"Jared…"*

His heart was slamming against his ribs. "Kendall, I forgot. I…I was so caught up. I'm sorry, baby. You're the only one ever. I swear you don't have anything to worry about as far as STD's. I know how careful you are. We're fine."

Her voice was barely a whisper but he heard the terror inside it. "Uh…pregnancy?"

Jared lifted her from him, laying her on her back as he stretched out beside her. "I would *love* for you to be pregnant, Kendall." The look of complete and utter shock on her face made him smile, "Marry me, baby." This time she actually jumped.

"Jared, you do not know what you're *saying*. A marriage between us would never be binding. I couldn't marry you under my real name so it wouldn't even be legal. All my documents are forged. I used to have a real birth certificate and a passport. Now, I have nothing real. I honestly couldn't prove my true identity if I had to."

"What is your given name?"

Her voice was barely audible. "Gabriella Garcia-Moreno. My parents called me Brie." Then she burst into tears and he gathered her to him, stroking her back, and whispering to her. She cried quietly for a long time with her arms around his back.

He encouraged her to get it all out, to grieve her parents, and acknowledge the hell she'd gone through. He wanted her to admit her fear and loneliness and then let it all go. It was time for her to let someone else worry for a while.

It was time for her to trust him to take care of things, to take care of *her*, and to love her. When she went totally limp, Jared realized she'd drifted to sleep. He pulled the quilt over them and watched her for a long time before following her.


The room was in almost total darkness when Jared opened his eyes. Kendall wasn't with him. He shot up in a panic yelling her name, knowing he'd lost her. She appeared at the bathroom door, rushing over to climb up beside him, touching his face, and whispering soothingly. "I'm here, Jared. I had to use the bathroom. Shower with me."

He grabbed her hard. "I thought you'd run again. I thought you were gone. Please don't ever do that again, Kendall. Swear it to me." She nodded and held him, feeling his heart race against her chest.

After a while he began to relax and scooted to the edge of the bed, pulling her with him. He lifted her and she wrapped around him, her head on his shoulder. They showered, taking their time washing one another's hair and body. When they were rinsed, he lifted her and took her against the cool tile wall. Their cries echoed in the small room.

Jared kissed her with a smile as he tugged her from the shower and dried her. After he'd dried himself, they collected their clothes from the foyer. Kendall dropped her sundress over her head and he slipped on his slacks before they padded barefoot into the kitchen. She sliced fruit and cheese while Jared made thick ham sandwiches.

When Kendall went to sit, he tugged her onto his lap and her arms went around his neck. "Tell me yes, Kendall. Marry me." She started to launch into all the reasons she couldn't and shouldn't, marry him. He put his finger over her mouth.

"Kendall…baby, I won't have you go off alone again. I have resources and an amazing team of people who work for me. I don't know what you looked like as a child, but you look much different than you did seven years ago. You're leaner, your hair is shorter, and you dress differently." Long fingers raked through her silky curls.

"It's time to hide in plain sight, honey. What good is running? You never get to put down roots, have a family, or live your life. If you can't live it in happiness, what good is it anyway? You deserve to be happy. I can make you happy. We do what we can to protect ourselves and never take one moment together for granted. Say yes, Kendall. Marry me."

She sat staring at him for a long time, chewing her lower lip. Jared waited for her, determined to let her see reason on her own. Either way, he wasn't going to let her go. He was not going to have her wandering the world in fear for her life. He wanted her with him. He wanted babies together. To be able to hold her and love her every day. He wouldn't settle for less.

"Are you sure you're willing to risk your safety just to be with me, Jared?" He nodded and hugged her tight. "I'm scared…but…*yes*."

The grin that broke over his face was priceless. "You won't regret it. I will make sure you never regret it." They hugged and kissed; kissing more while they ate their food.

After they cleaned up, she took him into her studio. He was amazed at how many photos there were of him…of the two of them together. "This is one of my favorites. You'd accidentally fallen asleep. You never fell asleep like that." He was stretched out on his stomach, his head on his arms, the sheet barely covering his lower body; one leg was exposed, the curve of his hip, and the slope of his ass. "You have always been such a beautiful subject, Jared."

He took out his wallet and showed her the ratty picture he'd carried with him since the day she left. The one he'd found in her darkroom. "This is my favorite. You're laughing and so beautiful. The others I had copied, blew them up, and had them framed. They're on my office wall. You have no idea how many people comment on them." He turned to her and took her in his arms, "We will make this work. This time, we'll tell everyone we're together. No more keeping you a secret. No more sneaking around. No more hiding. I love you."

They spent two glorious days in bed, talking about everything that had happened over the time they'd been apart. When Jared brought up their future, she still worried. He didn't let it deter him.

On their third day, he helped her pack her studio and load it into her SUV. She shocked the hell out of him when she showed him the duffle bag with almost a million in cash inside. "There's more stashed in safe deposit boxes across the country in totally different names. You have to access them in order. Open one safety deposit box; get the cash and ID out of it to access the next one. There are a total of eight, each holding a million in either diamonds or cash. Dad sold everything we had except the estate. He put that in his brother's name when we left Columbia."

She rubbed her upper arms, warding off the chill her past caused. "I have the ninth case. My father had the tenth case, down to about half a million, when he was murdered and his killers took it."

"What the hell did your father do for a living?" Jared asked as he stared at the cash with a small frown. He had millions himself, but he'd never actually just seen it in stacks like this.

Kendall laughed bitterly, "Before I was born, my father was a drug lord. He'd been a famous soccer player in his youth but his knee was destroyed. He took his soccer earnings and invested in drugs. A lucrative business apparently." Her eyes were flat, dull with sadness.

"He met my mother when she was eighteen, a sweet Catholic girl who could not be more opposite to the man he was. He wanted to court her but she refused, saying a man who dealt drugs was not meant for someone like her. The man *she* would marry would have a legitimate job, a life of growth and building things; not a life of destruction and death."

Turning, she met his eyes. "For two years he slowly pulled out of the drug trade. Liquidated his assets and brought it to the US to hide. He bought a plantation, devoted his life to ranching. She married him in her childhood church and introduced him proudly to her family. They were very much in love and I was born within the year."

She cleared her throat, swallowing past the tears that threatened to clog it. "When I was twelve, we went to the coast on holiday. My mother hadn't come down to the beach with us. She was feeling ill. It turned out that she was pregnant but didn't know yet. After we left, she went to a corner store for crackers to settle her stomach. She walked into a shakedown by the local drug runners and watched as they shot the owner and his wife. She ran and they chased her. They lost her in the hotel traffic."

Staring at Jared bleakly, she whispered, "She didn't tell my father what had happened. She was afraid. That he would be pulled back into the life he'd worked so hard to escape."

Closing her eyes, her voice was hoarse as she continued, "Two days later, they shot her in the back of the head as she was coming out of a gas station restroom. My father was pumping gas, heard the shot, saw her fall. The shooter jumped into a waiting vehicle and the driver of the getaway car recognized my father from his drug days."

"He took us home and we buried my mother. They tracked us to the estate and we hid in a root cellar out in the orchard for three days." Jared held her tight, so tight, wanting to keep the horrible memories at bay. Knowing he was powerless to take the pain from her.

"We came to America, running, always moving. When I was fourteen, we were living in Dallas. My father hid me in a crawl space behind the refrigerator. He killed two of them before the last three brought him down. They tortured him for over an hour before they killed him, wanting to know where I was. He tried to bribe them for my safety but they laughed." Uncontrolled tremors shook her body as sightless eyes stared into her brutal past.

Kendall took a deep breath, staring out the kitchen window to the yard beyond. "He began to mock them. Told them they had small dicks. Told them he'd fucked their mothers. He said he knew they were fucking each other up the ass while they traveled together. He knew I was listening, you see. He knew it was only a matter of time before I came out to beg them to stop torturing him. They wouldn't have killed me quickly…"

The thought of what could have happened had Jared's blood roaring in his veins. He crushed her against his chest, wanting her to stop but knowing she had to finish. "He taunted them until he saw their rage grow. The last thing he said was *my daughter will survive*. Then there was the small sound of the silenced bullet before the killers walked away. I stayed where I was for a full day. Enough time to know if anyone had stayed behind. Then I crawled out and kissed my father goodbye. It was the first time I loaded the SUV alone. I scanned it and drove away. Two counties over, I called my father's murder in from a payphone. I moved constantly with ID that said I was eighteen. Five states before ending up in Oregon."

Kendall turned to him, taking his hand in hers. "I stayed in Oregon longer than anywhere. When I left, I never stopped moving." She told him about the unidentified girl who'd been buried with Kendall's birth name in Columbia.

Then she explained how she'd taken one of her father's ID's when she'd arrived in Seattle. "I thought changing gender and aging drastically would throw them off since they knew my father was dead. I told people I was his adopted daughter. I've been here three years, using Ken Jacobs and Katie Jacobs alternately. When I left Oregon, I destroyed my ID under the name Kendall Torres. It was Dad's protocol."

He hugged her hard. He was more thankful than he could ever show that she'd survived more than a decade of running from the drug cartel intent on ensuring her silence by whatever means necessary.

"You're going to stop running now, Kendall. We'll figure out what to do about your name. If you have ID that will stand up to background checks, we'll just have Kendall legally added to the front. That way, I don't mess up."

Jared stroked her hair back from her face. "I say we get married here, have the name change done here, then we'll head home. We'll ship all your stuff and my truck. My mom will go by the house. She'll take care of putting your stuff in the garage until you get there and decide where you want it." Jared kissed and hugged her for a long time. "You've been through so much. I'm going to make up for all the things you didn't get to do, didn't get to experience. I love you. I love you and I'll keep you safe, baby."

"I want this. I want this so much, Jared. I'm scared to hope."

"Walking out your front door in the morning is a risk, Kendall. For all of us. You can't live your life in fear anymore. We do everything we can to protect ourselves and we *live*." He took her back to bed and made love to her all afternoon. Jared took her over and over again until she finally slipped into an exhausted sleep.

For the first time since the death of her mother, Kendall dreamed of a future.

# **Chapter Nine**

Six weeks later, they pulled into the driveway of the home where they'd fallen in love. Kendall couldn't believe the changes, how different and yet, still the same it was. He gave her a tour, not allowing her to see the basement yet.

The framed photograph in what was now *their* bedroom brought her to tears. After Kendall stored her duffle bags in the crawl space, Jared told her to take a nice soak in the Whirlpool tub upstairs in the master bath. He'd already showered and changed into sleep pants. She soaked for a long time. When she came out, she walked around the house barefoot looking for Jared. She found him in her old bedroom in the basement.

Her new husband had his back turned to her, lighting candles. She couldn't help but gasp at the beauty of the space. It was set up almost exactly as she'd originally had it. He'd placed her quilt over her old platform bed, hung several of her photos of them around the room, and scattered candles on every surface.

He turned to her with a hungry smile. "I think we should always keep this space like this. Our own little getaway right downstairs. We'll be sixty and still feeling young, remembering ourselves at eighteen in this room."

She nodded and ran to him, allowing him to catch her up as he always did; to hold her hard to the point of almost not being able to breathe. He laid her on the bed and knelt above her, running his fingers through her soft hair.

"You are so beautiful, Kendall. I've never been as happy in my entire life as I am now, having you home, having you as my wife. Thank you for taking the chance on us."

Her breath whooshed from between her lips and she blurted, "I'm pregnant."

His eyes widened and his mouth dropped open. "You are? How do you know?"

"I bought a test earlier today when we ran to get supplies. I just did it upstairs. When I was unpacking my bathroom stuff this morning I realized I hadn't had to replenish *products* in a really long time. It got me wondering." She took a deep breath to steady her nerves. "The stakes are higher now, Jared. Are you still sure?"

His mouth was all over her, kissing and nibbling and sucking until he felt the tightness ease from her body. "I love you so much, Kendall. I'm so excited. Please be happy and don't worry. We're going to have a little baby, a little symbol of our love for one another. Just like you're a symbol of your parent's love. They made sure you survived, that you knew how to protect yourself, and that you knew how to love when it was your turn." He kissed her face all over.

"We're going to love one another for another sixty years, baby. Watch our children and grandchildren grow. You'll see." He slid deep into her body, moaning with her as the familiar sensations washed over him.

For a long moment Kendall just stared at him. Then a slow smile broke over her face. "I love kids, Jared. I never thought I'd have any of my own. I wonder how far along I am? If it's a boy or a girl? You're going to be such a wonderful father."

He laughed and began to move. "That's my girl. Time for me to love you all over, Kendall."

Then he worshipped her body from head to toe and showed her how much he loved her. Hours later, they drifted to sleep together in the same bed where they'd first made love.

And there were no more secrets.

# Let Your Heart Lead
## *Novella Two*

### Chapter One

*Junior High...*

Mrs. Augusta Whitehall stormed into the office and demanded she be given a tutor for her daughter as if it were a privilege not every student had access to.

The school administrator took in the woman's bleached hair and expensive rings on every finger that attested to a woman unused to money, who'd apparently fallen into it fairly recently and felt the need to flaunt it gaudily. She was a pretty woman who'd become a caricature of herself but she obviously didn't see it.

Beside her stood her daughter, Amelia who was the complete opposite of her mother in every way. The belle of the school district and easy favorite of every teacher, not to mention the scores of male admirers she had from every grade level.

The receptionist stood behind the desk and started to ask a question, when Mrs. Whitehall set eyes on the young man just entering from a side door. Leonardo Stefan De La Cruz had been running errands for the principal.

The vulgar woman took one look at him and said far too loudly, "You there, you look ethnic. Usually the ethnic kids are pretty smart. Are you smart?"

Amelia Whitehall moaned, turning beet red before grinding out,

"Mom, please stop. That's Leo and he's the smartest kid in the school district. He works really hard so please don't disrespect him or embarrass me."

Leo rose to his full height, still nowhere near as tall as he prayed he'd be one day, and faced the woman proudly. He offered his full name with a slight bow and held out his hand. Amy's mother shook it briefly and muttered, "Yeah, you *look* like a Mexican Leonardo Dicaprio."

Noting Amy's utter humiliation over her tactless mother soothed Leo's normal irritation over the stereotype. "Actually, my family is from Spain and Scotland. Not Mexico. And I was named for Leonardo Da Vinci…not Dicaprio." Flicking his eyes over the woman's shoulder, he met Amy's too bright gaze and realized she was about to cry. It moved him. "How can I help?"

"I got a letter. She's failing core classes and I need her grades up quick or her father won't let me take her to anymore pageants or auditions. How fast can you work?"

Amy had the tips of her fingers pressing hard into her temples and Leo had never seen a person more in need of a kind word than this young woman with her awful mother. He sent up a silent prayer of thanks for his own mother.

Before he gave himself a chance to think about it, Leo nodded, "I am happy to assist. Amelia, if you'll meet me at the library, we can establish a plan to pull your grades back up. How's that?" She looked up, surprised, and smiled with a small nod.

Leo felt as if someone had punched him in the chest. Her blush of embarrassment was still evident on her fair skin but it did nothing to detract from the way she lit up with her happiness. He smiled back. "Mrs. Whitehall, it was nice to meet you," he lied smoothly.

He turned to go and the woman called after him, "Young man, I'm happy to *pay*. I know you probably have a bunch of brothers and sisters at home. I'm sure you could use the money."

Amy gasped and turned away, this time she truly was crying in complete shame, her small shoulders trembling with her hands clasped over her mouth in horror. Even the office staff was struck silent.

Pivoting to her with slow grace, he clasped his hands behind his back to keep from strangling the ignorant cow. When he responded to the plethora of insults she had delivered with ten seconds of speech, his words were laced with steel. "*Madame*, I assure you, I am an only child, and I do not need the money. My family's wealth has been passed down through generations of Spanish and Scottish nobility. I help because my help is needed. There is no ulterior motive."

With a slight bow, he turned to go. At the door, he called quietly to Amy and she glanced up with tears on her cheeks. "It will be alright," he said softly and then he was gone.

Hours later, Leo realized sitting across from Amy at this little library table was going to kill him. Fourteen-year-old males were not created to withstand this kind of torment. She smelled fantastic, her dark hair was shiny and long, and her perky breasts were pressing against her cheer uniform.

Then her eyes lifted and he was lost in the depths of the clearest green eyes he'd ever encountered and stumbled over what he'd been saying. She smiled when he faltered, but she didn't laugh. Amelia never laughed at him or anyone else he knew of.

Amelia was queen of the popular kids. She had her pick of friends, parties, and dates but she wasn't stuck up. She didn't act entitled. So beautiful; when most girls her age were going through awkward growth spurts and body changes, Amelia seemed to breeze through puberty with a beautiful figure honed from hours of gymnastics, dance, and ballet. Her clothes were always perfect; assembled by her mother's personal shopper so she always looked just right. She was also skilled in piano and acoustic guitar, due to more lessons her mother subjected her to.

"Leo? You okay?" The smooth sound of her voice flowed over him and he knew he was in danger of embarrassing himself.

Taking a deep breath and squaring his narrow shoulders, he replied in the strongest voice he could, "Yes, of course. Just trying to decide which subject we should focus on first." From a long line of proud Spaniards on his father's side and a long line of Scottish highlanders on his mother's, he willed his body to obey him, to not disgrace him. "I believe you have the most missing work from Earth Science…"

She was nodding. "It's the last class of the day. My…my mom always pulls me out for auditions and, you know, crap." Her tone was frustrated. It was something Leo liked about her. She'd been modeling for years but few people would even know if they hadn't been to her house and seen the huge blowups of magazine covers and catwalk shots her mother proudly displayed. He'd never been there but stories of lavish parties given for her birthdays and every other occasion were the talk of the school every year. "I miss at least two classes each week and I'm always behind."

"You're smart, Amy…we'll get you caught up in no time. You have cheer practice on the same days I have student government so we can meet here after. Is that okay?" She nodded happily and her smile caused a knife of pain in his groin, his will battling his physical reaction to her. Breathing through his nose he focused on the papers in front of him.

She scooted closer to him, "Leo, you're being really great about all this. I'm so, so sorry about my mother. Please forgive me. I know she's…horrible in so many ways. She didn't used to be like this. It was the lottery. She changed almost overnight. Dad tries to rein her in but…well, you see how she is. I admire you very much. I know you don't have time to tutor with everything you're involved in. You never tutor. I won't take advantage or…or take it for granted."

He set the books to the side and crossed his arms on the table. "Thank you, Amelia. I don't want you to worry."

They worked together three days a week over the next six months. Her test scores were outstanding; it was simply turning in the mounds of class work and homework that put her behind. A week before school finished, he helped her review for all her finals and she passed with a high B average for the year to the thrill of her teachers, her parents, and most importantly…herself.

He struggled every time he was around her but considered time with Amelia a good exercise in control. It was character building. She'd been reminding him about her end-of-year party for weeks and he hadn't decided if he'd be attending.

Since he'd opted out of the holiday party, her spring break bash, and the huge barbeque she'd thrown over Memorial Day weekend, she'd made it clear that his attendance at this celebration would mean a lot to her.

His hesitation wasn't due to Amy. The crowd she hung out with didn't usually take to people like him. In the end, he decided to go because seeing her outside of school seemed important. To see if she was less…*everything*…away from school.

Amy answered the door when he knocked and was clearly thrilled to see him. She wore a pretty green dress that matched her eyes but seemed too formal for the occasion. Leo gave her a gold charm bracelet that held symbols of the things he knew to be truly important to her and she teared up as she whispered, "Thank you so much, Leo."

As he watched, she pulled it from the velvet box and asked him to put it on for her. He was surprised she wanted to wear it *now*. Clearing his throat, he carefully fastened the clasp, marveling at the delicate skin of her inner wrist.

She took him on a tour of the house and blushed at the countless photos of her on the walls and the gaudy furnishings. At the threshold of the formal living room, she sighed at the French provincial décor and murmured, "My mother thinks it's classy. I know it's bad." Leo shook his head and gestured for her to continue. "You have very old world manners, Leo. It's very gallant, like you're from another century."

"My parents are very old fashioned. They come from old customs. I was born in Spain and lived there for many years. It is where I learned English before we moved to Scotland, near my mother's family."

"You speak perfectly…like a professor," she said quietly.

Giving her a small bow he continued, "I have no brothers and sisters but many cousins, aunts and uncles. There is a strict outline for my life at this point. I hope to break the confinement of their expectations as I get older. We shall see."

"I know a lot about being confined, about being forced into a mold you don't want to be in." He glanced at her, only a couple of inches shorter than he was and agreed she would probably know a great deal about how smothered he sometimes felt.

In her bedroom, he saw the simplicity of Amy as a person. The real young woman inside the perfect package her mother was determined to assemble. The room was done in varying shades of greens and decorated with furniture featuring clean lines.

He spotted the acoustic guitar and picked it up. Amy sat on the edge of her bed to watch him. Checking the tuning, he perched on her desk chair and played her a blend of Beethoven and Bach. When he started a rendition of *Spanish Romance*, she smiled.

As it came to a close, they didn't move. It was her mother's voice at the door that broke the spell. "Well, aren't you just so talented? Amy, you should take your lessons more seriously so you can play like Leo." There was an uncomfortable silence and Amy gave Leo a small shake of her head when he would have spoken on her behalf. "Honey, you need to be out here with everyone. Come on now, you can't be rude." Leo put the instrument away and followed Amy to the patio where the party was in full swing.

Amy was pulled from group to group, casually polite to all, her arm linked tightly through Leo's. He stayed with her, unsure why she seemed to want him beside her. She was popular, beautiful, wealthy, and talented. He was, for all intents and purposes, a nerd. Nothing else mattered when you were given that label in an American school.

Still, she wanted him with her so he stayed. Some of her friends gave her curious looks but didn't question her. Her position in the social hierarchy didn't permit others to question her.

As the evening drew to an end, he thanked her long-suffering father and obnoxious mother. Amy walked him outside and halted in surprise at the car and driver that waited at the bottom of her driveway.

"Wow, you weren't kidding."

He chuckled, "No, I was not. Amelia, thank you for a lovely evening. Thank you for inviting me."

She held up her wrist and watched as the charms on her bracelet sparkled in the moonlight. "Thank you for my beautiful present, Leo. I'll wear it always. And…thank you for braving my house as horrible as my mother can be."

Giving her a small bow he leaned to kiss her cheek and was floored when she turned her face at the last moment and his lips met hers. Startled, for a moment neither of them moved. Then Amy lifted her hand to the side of his neck and sighed against him.

The rapid fire of teenage male hormones tried to cloud Leo's mind but he gently lifted his hand to Amy's cheek and caressed her silky jaw with his thumb. He moved his lips over hers carefully, only for a few seconds, then pulled back and looked at her with a smile. "You taste like honey."

"You taste like cinnamon. Thank you for a beautiful first kiss, Leo." His eyes widened and she gave a self-mocking smile, "No, never before. What is that saying about perception?"

"Perception is reality," he supplied for her, still in shock.

"Exactly. People perceive me to be a certain way, so therefore that is who I am. It is very far from true." She brought his mouth to hers once more, kissing him more firmly, before turning and running back up the drive, her green silk dress shimmering in the moonlight. "Goodnight, Leo!" she called over her shoulder.

And that was how Amelia Whitehall, the most popular girl in the eighth grade, became his girlfriend.

# Chapter Two

*Senior Year*

Leo was racing from the house when his mother called him back, "Darling, it's supposed to rain, take your jacket. You're so distracted lately, Leo." Caressing his cheek lovingly, she said, "Bring Amy by one night this week. We haven't seen her in ages."

Bending to kiss her temple, Leo nodded, "She got back last night from the spring break photo shoot. I've only been able to talk to her on the phone. I'm dying to see her. Love you, Mother."

He ran for his SUV, throwing his books and jacket in the back before climbing behind the wheel and speeding toward Amy's house. He hadn't fully come to a stop before she was running down the driveway. He barely got out of the car before she barreled into him. "Leo, oh Leo…I've missed you so much."

He caught her up and hugged her tight, inhaling the scent unique to his beautiful Amelia. Opening the passenger door, he lifted her inside, resting his forehead on her shoulder while she stroked her fingertips through his thick black hair.

"You're hair is longer…it's starting to curl. So silky, Leo. Get me out of here, baby." He lifted his head and she kissed him lightly, "Get me away from here, Leo…*please*." He nodded and closed her door, running around the front of his car and climbing in. He put his elbow on the console and she placed both her hands around his large one.

Leo couldn't stop looking at her. They'd cut her hair a bit shorter. It fell just below her shoulders in pretty layers. She'd lost weight, as she always did when her mother whisked her away for modeling gigs. Her green eyes literally glowed from her face. Her breasts were high and firm, not very large but perfect. She'd grown taller and so had he, hitting a crazy growth spurt the year before and reaching six-three before he seemed to slow down. She was five-ten and stunning, long and lithe.

The charm bracelet clinked on her wrist, filled with many more charms than when he'd first given it to her. His family had insisted on taking her with them on their vacations over the last four years, assuring Amy's parents of the strict chaperoning they would receive.

As a result, they'd toured Europe, Great Britain, and Brazil together. This summer, when they graduated, they were going to Jamaica…just the two of them. At that point, there wouldn't be a damn thing either of their parents could do about it.

They were crazed for one another, unable to think most of the time if they were within touching distance. They'd spent so many years on kissing and heavy petting, they knew each other's bodies almost as if they had fully consummated their relationship.

Leo knew he could make Amy come within twenty seconds if he stroked her clit a certain way with the tip of his finger. Amy knew the exact length and width of Leo's cock and exactly how much of it she could take in her mouth. At eighteen, they were so tired of waiting, yet trying to respect the wishes of their parents.

Leo worked out constantly to relieve the stress of wanting Amy non-stop.

Two blocks from the high school, Leo pulled into the carport of a house that had been empty for years. "I need to taste you, Amelia. I can't wait another moment." Without waiting for him to put the car in park or detach his seatbelt, she had hers off and was coming over the console to straddle his lap. When her ass hit the horn, they both laughed and he backed up his seat. "I've missed you, baby."

Her kisses were aggressive, passionate and they were humping against one another in the dim light of the tinted vehicle. His cock was huge and hard, pressing against the cleft of her as she rode him. His hands were under her sweater, moving her bra and freeing her nipples to his fingers and mouth.

She clutched the back of his head in one hand as the other unbuttoned his jeans and slipped beneath the fabric to stroke as much of his cock as she could in this position. "I can't wait anymore, Leo. I can't. I need you so badly." She sobbed against his chest and he held her to him.

She was trembling in his arms and he struggled to settle his thoughts, to get his breathing under control. "Sweet baby, I know. It hurts all the time, the ache I feel for you…the need to bury myself inside you." He smoothed her hair and stroked his hands down her back. "I know a place on the lake. I can take you there." Pausing, knowing he had to tell her, "Amelia, there *will* be fallout. We'll have to deal with two sets of very pissed off parents."

She sat back and stared at him, "Take me there, Leo. Now, I want to go *now*." Wiping the tears from her cheeks, she whispered, "I can deal with anything that happens after. Please?" He nodded and set her back in the passenger seat. She fixed her clothing and buckled her seatbelt as he did the same. He left the driveway and got on the highway, heading in the opposite direction from their school.

It was the last few months of senior year. He'd tutored Amy every year, helping her stay caught up as her mother pulled her from school more and more frequently. He could have graduated two years ago but had chosen to take college courses in tandem with high school courses to stay with Amy. He'd already completed enough credits for his Associates and would have his Bachelors by the end of the year. He was the Valedictorian and the student body president.

But Amy…she was the light of his life. The reason he got up every morning.

He drove thirty miles outside their little suburb of Springfield, Illinois to the cabins he'd found when scouting for the perfect place to take her should their need overwhelm their reason. Walking into the small office, he emerged with the key in his hand and got back in the car, staring at her as intently as she stared back.

"Are you sure, Amelia? I worry about pushing you. I need to know you're sure. I won't be upset if you ask me to turn back. I love you with my whole heart. That won't change no matter how long we need to wait."

Leaning across the console, she stroked his face with her palm. "I need you, Leo. Four *years*, baby. You aren't pushing me. I don't want to turn back." Then she kissed him and he put the SUV in gear, driving through the maze of small roads until he came to the cabin he'd rented for the night.

Parking, she waited as he'd taught her and he came around to open her door, holding out his hand to help her from the vehicle. "That never gets old, Leo…how gentlemanly you are." He smiled and pulled her to him for a deep kiss before closing the door and taking her hand. They walked up the porch steps and he held the door as she entered. "It's so pretty here, Leo."

It was pretty. He'd made sure of it. He had no intentions of taking his beautiful Amelia to some seedy dive. Her first time had to be perfect.

The room was large and open. A huge bed stood in one corner, a large fireplace in another. A kitchen and living room between. The bathroom was modern with a large soaking tub.

He closed and locked the front door and she turned to him. Taking off her jacket and scarf, she dropped them over the back of the nearby sofa. Reaching down, she pulled off her heeled boots and socks. Standing barefoot on the soft carpet, she pulled her thick sweater over her head.

Leo had zoned on the vision of her removing her clothes and now shook himself to join her. By the time he had everything off but his jeans and boxers, she stood before him in her t-shirt and panties.

He opened his arms and she ran into them, loving the feel of his strength and warmth; she always asked him to let it seep into her. "Leo, I can't tell you how much I've missed you. How much I've needed you." Her hands went to his belt and she took her time separating the two halves, loving the feel of the thick leather in her hands.

The back of her knuckles brushed the skin of his abdomen as she moved to the button and he sucked air in hard through his teeth. She leaned forward and kissed his sculpted pecs. "Your body is so gorgeous, Leo. You were shorter than me for a little while in tenth grade then just shot past me. I dream about you."

She ran one hand into the waist of his pants, widening the opening as she ran the other over his chest and abs. "Your definition is insane. I have a personal trainer three days a week and work out six…I don't come close to this."

He put his fingers under the hem of her t-shirt and used the flats of his palms on her sides to slide it up and off. Her hair cleared the fabric and feathered around her face. She wore a beige lace bra that cupped her breasts and matching panties. He removed both and found himself speechless.

Her mound was bare and she moved her hands to cover herself, a lovely blush crawling over her chest and up her neck. "You've seen my body before, Leo. *What?*"

Leo took her hands and held them away from her body. "I've only seen *parts* of your body, never your entire body bared to me in all its beauty, Amelia. I want to sear this moment in my mind. The first time I've had a chance to take in everything at once." His large hands cupped her face gently. "I'm moved and honored and afraid I'll hurt you because I need you so bad."

In answer, Amy went up on tip-toe to pull him down for a kiss. The feel of her naked breasts against his skin was like nothing Leo had imagined. His hands stroked her, memorizing her. Sliding her hands down his back, she cupped her palms to his ass inside his jeans and pulled him to her.

"You won't hurt me. You couldn't possibly. You've been working to stretch me for months. I know how big you are and I know you're worried about me, Leo. I'll be fine, I promise. Please make love to me now. I'm desperate for you."

She pushed at his jeans and boxers, watching his cock spring free and immediately moving to take him in her hand. He held her wrist away, "I can't swear to my control right now, Amelia. Please baby."

In response, she dropped to her knees and took him to the back of her throat, sucking twice before sitting back. She pushed his clothes the rest of the way off him. Circling her fist around the base, Amy glanced up the hard length of his body.

"I've always wanted you naked while I did this, Leo. Come in my mouth...let me enjoy every moment without worrying about lights pulling up behind us." He stroked his fingers through her hair and she smiled, taking him deep and sucking him hard. His head fell back on his shoulders and he breathed deep, determined not to shame himself.

Over the last year, Leo had learned what Amy liked and she'd done the same for him. She sucked him for a long time, stopping him from coming and building him back up again as he watched her from above, his body locked to keep from falling.

Her eyes lifted to his and he watched the green darken with her passion. "Amelia, you look so beautiful. I want to please you, not take from you, baby. This isn't my time..."

Releasing him from the liquid heat of her mouth, she continued to stroke him as she said, "This is *our* time, Leo. As much as you ache to please me, I ache to please you. I want your come in my mouth, to drink you down and feed my body with yours. Give that to me, Leo."

She took him harder now, deeper; scraping her teeth lightly on the underside as she withdrew. Swirling her wicked tongue over him as he felt the back of her throat. She moaned and he watched her squeeze her thighs together, trying to get pressure where she wanted it. Her hands moved all over him, reaching around to grip his ass, massaging the tops of his thighs, kneading his balls, and stroking the portion of his cock she couldn't take.

When she closed her eyes in bliss, the climax hit him so hard he was almost unable to warn her. "I'm coming, Amelia. Oh baby, thank you. Yes, god *yes*, that feels so good. Take what you want, Amy. All I have, all I am is for you."

Leo worried his legs would buckle and she grabbed his thighs in her hands, adding her strength to his as the strong muscles of her throat milked his come from him. When she'd sucked him dry, she licked and kissed along his length. He took a moment to let his body settle back to earth, raking his fingers through her hair as she rested her face against his leg.

There was no more waiting. It was Amy's turn.

Dropping to a crouch in front of her, her green eyes met his dark blue ones. For the first six months, Amelia had believed his eyes to be black. Only when she'd kissed him after her party had she started getting close enough to him to figure out they were dark sapphire blue. He'd been surprised at how it had pleased her. She told him everyone would always think his eyes were black, but she would know because she knew everything about him.

Now his eyes bore into her, his hunger for her obvious as he stared at her like a jungle cat, poised to spring. Sliding his hands around her, he lifted her easily and carried her to the bed. Laying Amelia carefully in the center, Leo crawled up her body, settling in to kiss and pet her for a long time.

She'd always known touching her made Leo incredibly happy. It made him happier to touch and please her than receiving her attention in return. She knew how lucky that made her.

He wanted to move slowly, wanted to let her get used to the feel of so much of his bare skin against her. No matter how much they'd caressed one another, how well they knew one another, Amelia was still a virgin. He wanted everything to exactly right for her.

Slowly he stroked over her clit, something he'd done a hundred times. He knew she was familiar with his touch and Leo knew exactly what she enjoyed. Bending to take a pebbled nipple in his mouth, he worked her steadily, feeling her body tighten a moment before she gasped and sighed his name.

"You're so silky, Amelia. So beautiful inside and out." He traced the outline of her collarbone with his lips. "Baby, did they make you lose weight again?" She nodded and he gritted his teeth. This was what he hated most about her modeling and acting.

"You're *not* overweight. There's no fat on you, darling. I don't like that they make you drop weight. It isn't good for you, love. It scares me." She'd battled an eating disorder her junior year, refusing to eat so she'd be at prime photo weight. When he'd watched her eat lettuce and celery for a week, he had a complete breakdown in her lap, begging her to eat...to please just *eat*. They'd cried together and she'd agreed to go into therapy. "My loving Amelia. My precious baby. How I've longed to touch you, to taste you."

Moving down her torso, he touched her everywhere and licked a path to the vee of her body. Laying his cheek on her inner thigh, he took his time examining her up close, enthralled with her pale pink folds.

When he inserted one long finger into her pussy, she arched under him, bringing him close enough to kiss her mound. He felt her hymen with his fingertip and his cock twitched. On the next withdrawal, he added a second finger.

Grinding his hips into the bed, he moved his mouth over her in rhythm with his stroking fingers. Licking and sucking her while she writhed and begged him. "*Please*. Leo, please come here. I need you inside me. Oh god, baby, I'm coming again..."

Ignoring Amelia's demand was hard. Leo wanted nothing more than to be inside her. He refused to rush. Her first time had to be as pain-free as he could make it. For that, he needed her soft and slick. So ignore her was exactly what he did, bringing her up again and again, pushing against her virginal barrier harder and harder with each stroke of his fingers.

When at last he broke through her maidenhead, her pain was lost in the throes of her third orgasm and he smiled to himself. Leaving the bed, he pulled a condom from his jeans. She watched him roll it on as he came back to the bed and her eyebrows rose with a smile. His lips quirked, "Yes, I've been practicing. I didn't want to look like an idiot. It's my first time, too, remember?"

The knowledge seemed to hit them both at the same time. They had waited for one another for *years*; remained virgins though both had experienced opportunities with other people to change that.

Amelia smiled brightly and Leo returned it, the golden skin of his face making his teeth seem even whiter by comparison. He crawled up the bed, settling into the cradle of her body, their naked skin touching from breast to thigh.

"I love you, Leo. I've loved you so long that I can't remember what it was like before I did. I never want to know what it's like not to love you." She kissed him deeply, her hands in his hair as her feet stroked over the back of his legs, the short hair tickling her and stimulating her at the same time.

He lifted his face from her and set his cock at the entrance of her pussy, moving his arms around her. One around her waist; one behind her back gripping her shoulder. "I love *you*, Amelia. I remember what it was like before I loved you and it makes me appreciate how much life and color you brought into my world. Thank you for the gift you're giving me. I will cherish it always."

Then he surged to the hilt inside her as he dropped his mouth over hers. With a gasp, Amelia's thoughts split between the unfamiliar *pressure* and the familiar mouth loving her. She was so *full* with Leo. He was inside her body, being held by her. She stiffened for three beats of her heart and he held her, completely still.

When she released the breath she hadn't known she was holding, he smiled against her. "That wasn't as scary as I thought it would be." She gave him a huge smile. "You *studied*, didn't you?"

"Amelia, don't I always?"

She laughed and hugged him with her whole body. "Thank you, baby." Kissing him urgently she whispered, "Move now, Leo. I need to feel you move. You feel so much bigger inside me. I knew you were big but wow."

His laughter turned to a groan as she experimentally arched her hips into him. He started an easy rhythm, pulling out halfway before burying himself inside her again and again. The first time she came, he almost joined her, but reached between them to hold the base of his cock.

When she looked at him, still breathing hard from her climax, he shook his head. "You deserve more. I can wait." The tension etched into the beautiful lines of his face belied the control in his words.

Amy pulled her lower lip between her teeth, "Leo…" and sighed as he started moving again. When he knew the danger of coming too soon had passed, he pulled her knee to his hip and changed angles. Leo watched her face as he stroked steadily into the body of the woman he loved.

"That feels so good, Leo. This is so much more than I thought it would be. I wish we'd done this months ago. Yes, oh *yes*, Leo." He lowered his mouth to her nipple and sucked it to the roof of his mouth as she dug her short nails into his scalp and the back of his shoulder. He built her back up slowly; with the same assurance – some would call it arrogance - he'd exhibited his entire life. "I'm coming. Oh god, Leo, come with me. Please baby."

Amy's body tightened again, gripping his cock like a vice as her upper body left the bed and slammed into him while she screamed his name. Watching her in awe, he thrust hard three times and came with a groan, gripping her to him as he stroked shallowly, spilling his come into the condom.

He held himself off her by his elbows but she pulled him to her. "Amelia, love, I'll crush you." Shaking her head, she kept pulling until he flattened his body along her own, where she could wrap herself fully around him. "I need to pull out, baby. We'll lose the condom."

Shaking her head again, she whispered against his ear. "Nothing will ever compare to this, Leo. To the feel of your body against mine, the feel of you inside me. Knowing you love me as much as I love you. This moment is perfect and I want to hold onto it just a little longer. Don't leave me, please don't leave me, baby." He nodded against her neck, breathing in the essence of his Amelia.

For the next several hours, they were in their own world. When their second condom broke, they didn't stress because Amy had been on the pill for years. Alternating between making love, soaking in the tub, and sitting curled together in blankets in front of the fire, both felt at peace for the first time in a long time.

"You're going to be so sore, Amelia baby. I shouldn't be taking you so much." He played with her hair and let himself absorb the softness of her skin.

"I wish we could stay like this...just like this, Leo. Naked and fucking for the rest of our lives...only breaking for food and water. Reality will intrude all too soon and I have a feeling we're going to be grounded from one another for a while. Soreness is worth it." She glanced up at him with a mischievous grin, "I'll shore up memories for a little drought. Then we'll have Jamaica in the summer and I'll follow you anywhere."

Leo pulled her snugly against his chest, "Amelia, what about college?" She shook her head. "Baby, you're *so* smart...why?" He stroked her hair back from her face, watching the silken strands sift through his long fingers.

"I can't focus on school without your constant help, Leo, and I'm *done* using you like that. I literally don't have the attention span for reading anymore, writing anything longer than a paragraph. I have a few ideas for things I'd like to do. We can talk more after summer. You've worried about my work as well as your own for too long. I know you put off college for me."

"Amelia..."

"No, Leo. I *know* what you've sacrificed, baby. I've developed so many horrible habits. They're only going to get worse if I don't stop. I...I started smoking and doing energy shots to get through the sixteen and eighteen hour shoots on this last job. Soon it's going to be prescription meds and then coke or something. I'm so *tired*, baby."

For a long time he stared at her. "Amelia, how long are you going to let your mother live through you? You're going to end up so sick if you don't stop her. I can't bear what you're putting yourself through. What can I do to stop this, love?"

"Just love me, Leo. Love me through it and I'll come out whole on the other side." So he loved her until neither of them could think, until they were practically dehydrated. Then they fell hard into exhausted sleep, Leo's body curled protectively around Amelia's.

It was how their parents found them hours later. Having tracked Leo's vehicle GPS, the four adults used the manager's key to open the door, gasping at the vision of their children's naked bodies entwined, visible from the waist up.

Leo's eyes opened and he literally growled at them. "Get. Out. You have no right to see her this way." He pulled the blankets up and tucked her body closer to his own. Her eyes fluttered open to see Leo's feral expression above her and realized their peace had come to an end. "Wait outside, you will *not* humiliate her."

The adults backed from the room with stunned expressions on their faces. As the door clicked closed, he whispered, "I love you and it's going to be alright." She nodded and lifted her body, her palm on his cheek. They took their time showering and getting dressed. Before opening the door to their parents, he said, "No matter what happens I love you, Amelia. There are only a few more weeks until graduation. We've lasted so long...a few weeks is *nothing*."

"That was before I felt you inside me, Leo. I can never go back to *before* again. You're like a drug." She lifted up and kissed him deeply, thrilled when he gripped her body hard through her clothes.

They opened the door and all the so-called grown-ups were talking at the same time. He listened for thirty seconds and held up his hand to silence them. Four voices stuttered to a stop.

"First, you couldn't have called? Honestly, I'd love to hear the stories of your first times. I'm sure it was the night of your honeymoons, right? Each and every one of you was a virgin until then? Yeah, didn't think so. Second of all, we're *eighteen* and we've been dating for four *years*. We waited for one another and we used protection."

He tightened his protective hold around Amy's shoulders. She had her face turned into his chest, mortified. "We love one another and that should be all that matters. It wasn't the backseat of a car or one of us sneaking out a second story window. No danger, no fear. I drove Amelia here alone and I intend to drive her back *alone*."

Augusta was the problem, as always. "I can't believe you deflowered my baby! My sweet, innocent baby! You're a rutting animal!"

Leo whirled on her, years of pent-up fury at this ignorant and pathetic excuse for a mother spilling from his mouth, "How *dare* you pretend to care for her. She's a puppet to you, nothing more. You let her starve. You hop her up on caffeine and anything else you can think of that's semi-legal. She started smoking. She's working all the damn time. She's underweight *again* and you don't give a damn about the anorexia coming back. When she's away, she's depressed. When she's home, she strung out trying to readjust to her life. What do you *want* from her?"

Amelia's mother was sputtering and livid, her skin a mottled red, "If you got her pregnant, so help me God...*I won't have it!*"

Pulling himself up calmly, he towered over her and Leo spoke softly, his tone dangerous, "If all the protection we used didn't work and Amelia *is* pregnant, it will simply speed up our *wedding*. Don't make threats. I warn you, I wouldn't tolerate you trying to take that from us."

Looking at Amy's father, he added, "You need to grow a pair and stop letting her hurt your child. Have you no *pride?*" With that, he nodded to his own parents who had been mercifully silent. Turning, he led Amelia to his SUV, settling her on the front seat before going around and climbing behind the wheel.

Three of the parents watched them drive away, unsure what to do. Amy's mother simply fumed.

## Chapter Three

As predicted, Leo and Amy were grounded from one another but they spoke on the phone and sent text messages constantly. They saw each other in school.

The Thursday before graduation, he received a text from her phone that she was sick but Leo couldn't get another response when he asked what was wrong. He went by the house but no one was home. He called her phone repeatedly without answer.

Dozing off after midnight, he almost didn't hear his phone ringing since he'd fallen asleep on top of it. The screen showed an unknown number and he picked it up, apprehension curling in his gut. "Leo?" It was Amelia but she sounded wrong.

"Amelia...baby, where are you?" He was off the bed and slipping his feet into running shoes.

"I don't *know*, Leo. This is a *rotary* phone, Leo. I had to try five times 'cause I kept dialing the number wrong, losing my place. Leo, where *are* you?"

"I'm home, Amelia. Honey, what's the *last* thing you remember?" Pulling his jacket on, he grabbed his wallet, his keys, and tried to find the calm he'd always prided himself on.

"Going pee on a stick, Leo. Mom held a stick and I peed on it. I woke up here and...and it's really creepy and dark and *cold*. I don't like it, Leo. I'm scared to be here by myself. I don't like it here."

"I'm coming for you, Amy. I'll find you. Can you see anything with a name or brands or anything on it?" She was drugged heavily and couldn't read anything, couldn't think clearly, was getting to where she could barely talk.

"Gonna throw up...oh no..." The sound of Amelia getting sick was like a fist squeezing his heart. "Leo...Leo, I'm *bleeding*. I don't know where I'm bleeding. I...I can't...I feel so dizzy. *Leo...*"

The phone disconnected and Leo lost his fucking *mind*. Rousing his parents from their bed almost violently, he told them to come with him or prepare to bail him out of jail. They pulled clothes on hastily and met him in the driveway in less than five minutes.

Leo drove too fast across town to Amy's house. His repeated banging on the door finally brought a groggy Mr. Whitehall downstairs. Unable to contain himself, he grabbed the older man by his robe and slammed him against his open door. "Where is *Amelia*, Mr. Whitehall? Where *is* she?"

Confused, her father answered without hesitation, "They went to visit a new agent for Amy in the city. Augusta said they'd be back tomorrow."

Leo brought the man forward and slammed him into the door again. "Wrong, sir. You are so fucking wrong. I think your bitch of a wife just *aborted* my *child*. I got a call from Amy and she's puking and bleeding. She sounded drugged out of her mind."

He released him in disgust. "If I find out you had anything to do with this, I'll be back to beat you within an inch of your life." He watched as Daniel Whitehall clapped a hand over his mouth.

"She *wouldn't*. She wouldn't sink to such...*evil*. I know Augusta. At heart, she's still a good person. She wouldn't end a pregnancy when you're both so obviously in love and capable of taking care of a child. No, she *wouldn't* do that. I can't believe that."

Leo wanted Amelia and he wanted her now. His insides were boiling in barely contained rage. "Then find out where they are, Mr. Whitehall. Do it now. She was bleeding and confused and very afraid. Do it *right fucking now*."

Mr. Whitehall went to get his cell phone, dialing his wife as he returned to them in the foyer. Augusta picked up on the second ring. Calmly, he asked, "Honey, where are you?" He listened for a long moment and a frown appeared between his brows. "You're lying to me, Augusta. You just repeated the same sentence twice in a row. You're *lying*. Where are you? Where is *Amy?*"

There was unclear stumbling on the other end of the line as Augusta tried to explain. He listened for almost a minute and Leo watched with his parents as all the color drained from his face. "Tell me where to come get my daughter right now, Augusta. Oh my sweet Jesus, I want a divorce." They heard pleading on the other end of the line and he cut her off in disgust, "Tell me where you are or I'm calling the police, Augusta."

Another ten seconds and he disconnected the call. Then Amelia's father turned and threw up in the empty umbrella stand next to the door. Wiping his mouth on his pajama sleeve, he whispered hoarsely, "Let me get my wallet."

He rejoined them thirty seconds later and climbed in the passenger seat of Leo's SUV. "She's at an all-night clinic outside of town about ten miles." He gave them directions then began to sob. "I'm so sorry. I never thought…I've let it go too long. I kept thinking she'd come around; that she would see what she was doing to our child. Amy seemed not to mind most of the time. I…I can't ever make this right."

The rest of the drive was made in shocked silence. Leo found himself held captive between overwhelming rage at Augusta and terror for Amy, knowing she was bleeding and afraid. When he pulled into the parking lot of the rundown clinic, he was storming through the doors in seconds. "Amelia Whitehall, where is she?"

"I'm her father. I demand to see my daughter immediately."

The nurse looked terrified and led them back through double doors and down a hallway. The place *was* dark and cold. In the back of the building, there were several private exam rooms. A whimper then a scream had Leo shoving past the nurse and exploding through the doors of the only room with lights on.

He skidded to a stop as he took in the sight of his Amelia, bleeding out on a gurney. Nothing else mattered in that instant. He knew he had to get her to a real hospital. Moving further into the room, Amy was in so much pain she barely registered his presence.

His mother and father grabbed blankets from a shelf and spread them out on the other gurney in the room. Leo scooped his beautiful girl into his arms and placed her on the clean bedding, wrapping her snuggly in them as he held her tight to his body.

He whispered against her ear, "My sweet baby, I'm going to get you to a real doctor. It's going to be alright. I'm so sorry, Amelia." Having given his car keys to his father, he said dangerously, "Dad, drive it like you stole it. I have to get my girl to a hospital."

To a stunned and shaking Augusta Whitehall, he spit, "I'll deal with you later, you evil bitch." Striding from the room, he barked, "Let's get her out of this butcher shop."

He strode from the building and climbed in the backseat with his mother, Amelia held carefully between them. Blood was already soaking through the new blankets and it took everything inside him to keep from screaming in terror.

Surprisingly, Mr. Whitehall climbed into their vehicle as Leo's father got behind the wheel. He was on the phone with 911. "My daughter is bleeding out. I need a police escort to the nearest hospital. We're in a black Cherokee…" Then everything faded away but Amelia.

"Pretty girl…Amelia…baby, please stay with me." Her face was slick with sweat, her hair plastered to her skin. If he hadn't held her so firmly, the tremors rocking her frame would have pulled her out of his grip. "It's going to be alright, my sweet Amelia. Stay with me, sweetheart."

Her eyes were rolling back in her head but she tried to focus. "Leo…hurts. I'm tired. So tired. You *came* for me. You came for me, Leo."

Placing his forehead against hers, he fought tears and lost. "Of course I came for you, baby. I'll *always* come for you. I love you so much. I know you're hurting and tired, but you have to stay awake, Amelia. Stay awake and fight. Do it for us, honey. Stay awake and fight."

Her voice was weak and hoarse from her earlier screams. "I love you, Leo. You're the only person who ever really loved me. I'm sorry for always being a screw up. Loving you is the only thing I ever did exactly right." Mr. Whitehall was sobbing in the front seat and Leo was glad.

He smoothed her damp hair away from her ghostly face, "Amelia, fight for me, baby. We're almost there." Two state troopers pulled to either side of the Cherokee just then. One pulled forward and led the way going almost a hundred, full lights, and sirens blaring. "Dad, please get us there. *Please.*"

There was hospital staff waiting at the ER entrance when they pulled in. Amelia passed out with a scream as they lifted her to the bed that was already rolling inside. They were calling details to one another while a nurse stepped up to take her information.

Leo was covered in Amy's blood, as was his mother. She was holding his arm; in complete emotional shock with no clue what to say. Mr. Whitehall was giving them her medical history, explaining what he knew about how she'd come to be in her condition.

Leo said loudly and firmly to everyone in the hallway, "She's going to need blood. I have the same type. So does my mom. We're safe for her, take what you need."

The nurse led them to triage and Leo watched their fathers through the glass with the doctor and the police officers who'd escorted them to the hospital.

The next three hours passed slowly as a specialist was called in to try and repair the massive damage done to Amelia's womb when the supposed doctor who regularly *visited* the clinic had performed an antiquated abortion. She ended up needing two pints of blood from Leo and one from his mother.

Leo knew he would commit murder if the man was available. Head in his hands, he tore at his hair as he groaned, "If she was going to do this...take our child from us...there were *safer* options. She didn't have to go to some slaughterhouse in the middle of the fucking night. He might as well have used a coat hanger."

His mother rubbed his back. "I don't know, baby. Maybe she didn't want Amelia's modeling career affected. It didn't have to be this way.

It didn't." He lifted blood shot eyes to look at her and she smoothed his hair from his forehead. "Would I have been happy to have you taking on so much responsibility so young? No. I wanted you both to have a chance to live." She shrugged, "Things happen. You're in love, you're both smart. That baby would have been fine. I don't know, Leo. I can't understand."

Alternately pacing and sipping orange juice, Leo waited outside the operating wing. Mr. Whitehall came to sit beside him, his head low. "I know you'll never forgive me, Leo. I'm so sorry. I'll never let her down again."

Leo said nothing, not sure what he *could* say.

Augusta Whitehall swept into the hospital as if she owned the place an hour later and pretended as if this were nothing more serious than a sprained ankle. She had changed her clothes and freshened her hair and makeup.

Both fathers and an orderly had to physically restrain Leo from attacking her. Leo's mother, Sarabeth, walked passed them to Augusta and slapped the other woman hard across the face.

"You are a disgrace as a mother. Your daughter...sweet Amelia...could *die*. You already took their baby from them. They were old enough, with resources to care for a child. You had no right. You've used that girl since she was little. Sold one small piece of her at a time. You deserve to lose everything...absolutely *everything* that matters to you. Thankfully, what matters most to you has never been Amelia." Augusta's hand was cupped over her red cheek and Sarabeth reared back and slapped the hell out of the other side. "You sicken me."

With that, she walked over and sat down, shaking from head to toe. Leo and Alejandro sat on either side of her, holding her hands and glaring at the woman who'd brought them all to this place. Mr. Whitehall joined them moments later; sitting beside Leo as silent tears tracked down his cheeks.

When the doctor came out of surgery, he asked to speak to Mr. Whitehall, who stood and pulled Leo up with him. "She's going to be alright. She'll have to stay here for a few days to recover." Clearing his throat, he added quietly, "We couldn't save her uterus; it had to be removed to stop the hemorrhaging. We did everything we could to avoid it. I'm so sorry."

Leo took two steps and hit his knees, sobbing brokenly. His parents and Amy's father huddled around him. "She took our child...and all our future children from her...from us. Stole them away as if it didn't matter. A child created from the purest love on the happiest day of my life. A symbol of everything good between us."

Augusta Whitehall stood against the wall, shaking her head in horrified denial. "It was supposed to be safe," she whispered. "I didn't mean it. I didn't mean for this to happen." She started to cry but no one went to her.

# Chapter Four

Amelia was in and out of consciousness over the next day and Leo never left her side. When she finally woke up, she had disjointed memories, huge blank spots due to the blood loss and trauma done to her body. The first words she said were, "Leo, I...I think I'm pregnant."

Hysteria and agony crawled through Leo's chest. Soothingly, he whispered, "Baby, listen to me, I need you to focus on getting well. That's all I want you to do, Amelia. Focus on getting better. Then you're coming to live with me and my parents. We've already talked to your dad about it. He agrees that it's the best idea."

She rubbed her head, confused. "Why...why am I in the hospital? Leo...what happened?" Amy gasped and touched her stomach. "No, oh no...no...no, Leo." Tears were streaming down her cheeks and he held her, whispering how much he loved her and that everything was going to be alright. Feeling his tears in her hair, she asked, "Leo...tell me. Look at me."

He lifted his head and stroked her hair back from her face with his hands. She was so delicate compared to him. He'd never realized how fragile she truly was until this moment. "There's more...tell me, Leo."

"Baby. Please, baby, focus on getting well and we'll talk about everything when you're better."

"Leo, I know you're keeping something from me. You *never* lie. You *never* hide things from me. Tell me, please just tell me."

Taking a deep breath, he whispered, "There were drugs in your system, you were knocked out. You were checked into a clinic and...an abortion was done." The keening moan that left her throat at this news nearly broke Leo. He kissed her, loved her, and tried to absorb some of her pain into his own body.

She lifted his face so she could see his eyes. He realized she was waiting, shaking with the knowledge that losing their child was not the only blow coming. "What *else*, Leo?" The tears never stopped flowing down her cheeks; her hands were like ice on his overheated cheeks.

Leo didn't want to tell her. He wanted to hold her and let her get better first. He couldn't bear to hurt her anymore. When he tried to look away so he could tell her anything but the truth, she brought his face back and held his gaze.

She would accept nothing less, not from her Leo. He closed his eyes, gathering courage, inhaling a shuddering breath. "The...the procedure...it damaged your uterus. You were bleeding to death, Amelia. They had to...to take your uterus to stop the bleeding and save your life."

She went so still it frightened him and stared at him for a long time, as if not understanding what he was telling her. How much more pain could either of them take right now? "Leo, they took my uterus?" He nodded and held her hand against his heart. "I can...*never*...have children? This baby was taken and I can *never* have anymore?" He stared at her, his tears falling into her hair. "I can never give you a child? I can't have your baby?"

Amelia completely broke and he scooted her over carefully so he could lie down beside her. He held her gently, whispering. "It doesn't *matter*, Amelia. Oh baby, it doesn't matter. I love you so much. I will always love you, baby. We can adopt. You always talked about adopting a baby, helping a child who didn't have anyone to love them."

She sobbed against his chest, "That was after I'd given you children of your *own*, Leo. Oh god, Leo, you're an only child." It felt like she cried for hours. He held her through it, reassuring her, loving her. Before she drifted off to sleep, she murmured, "I'm not even a woman anymore. I have *nothing* to offer now." His heart broke for her as he told her it wasn't true. It would never be true.

They missed their graduation but the principal read Leo's speech to the graduating class and they said a prayer for Amelia before closing the ceremony. That afternoon, visitors began arriving and soon her room was filled with dozens of flowers and balloons.

She didn't speak but no one pushed. As the sun was setting, she said in disgust, "You've given up everything for me, Leo. You didn't even go to your *graduation* and you were Valedictorian. I'm like a cancer in your life."

Leo shook his head in disbelief. "Amelia, do you forget you missed *your* graduation, too? I'm right where I want to be, baby. You are *not* cancer. You are everything to me. I love you."

The next day, he was in the hall talking to her doctors with Mr. Whitehall when the nurse who stepped into Amelia's room behind them called a code. Amelia had taken a metal card holder from one of the baskets of flowers and sliced into her delicate wrists.

Leo stood at the door stunned and she stared at him as she passed out.

She was put on suicide watch and he sat with her constantly. She stopped speaking to any of them except to say it was time for him to let her go. "I *won't* let you go, Amelia. Baby, I love you and you love me. I know you're hurting but we can get past it together. You're strong. Don't give up. Please don't give up, Amy."

They took her home ten days after she'd been admitted. She still wouldn't speak, barely ate, and slept eighteen hours a day. One day, weeks after she'd been released, Amelia picked up her laptop and started writing. She sat on the back patio and typed furiously for hours at a time. Sometimes she smoked while she sat outside.

Leo worried constantly and didn't know how to bridge the painful gap that was opening between them. His heart ached for her; his soul called out for her. Only his strong belief that his love would be enough to pull her through kept him from giving in to despair.


Two months later, Leo woke in the middle of the night to see Amelia riding him. His heart soared at the sight of her, looking like her old self. He lifted at the waist and held her to his chest, touching her, loving her, everywhere.

When he realized he wasn't wearing a condom, he started to pull her away and she told him sadly, "No need now, Leo. We've only been with each another."

He stroked her face and hair. "I'm sorry, Amelia. We can be happy. Deliriously happy while we do all the things we've always dreamed about. I'll put everything I have into making your life all you want it to be. You'll never have a reason to doubt my love for you. You are everything to me, Amy. You *own* me. I belong to you and you belong to me."

She never paused in her movements above him. When she spoke, her voice was clearer than he'd heard it in months. Still, her question confused him. "Leo, why haven't you left for college? Your fall classes should have started by now."

"I wanted to be sure you were okay to travel, Amelia. We have to find an apartment and everything. Anytime you're ready, we can head up to Boston and scope out places to live. I put off classes for one semester. When I explained the circumstances, the dean was glad to give me the time I needed."

Amelia placed her palms on either side of his face, "You give up too much for me, Leo. Again and again you do it. One day you'll have nothing left. You care for me, protect me, rescue me over and over. I've become dependent on you to be stable. To help me get through one bad situation after another. When does it end? When is it *your* turn?"

"Amelia, I love you, baby. You give me so much; I don't know why you can't see that." He rolled her to her back and pulled her to him tight with his hands on her shoulders. "I *will* love you through this. We can get through it together. We can do anything as long as we're together, Amelia."

He made love to her for a long time. Only when the second orgasm crashed over her, when she was limp beneath him, did he allow himself to come. He held her to his heart as he told her again how much he loved her.

They fell asleep with him on top of her, eventually rolling to their sides.

The feel of her cradled in his arms again was pure contentment. Leo allowed himself to drift back to sleep, knowing things would finally be alright.

When the sun came up, he was in bed alone, a letter on her pillow. With dread, he opened it.

"My darling Leo…I've loved you forever and I always will. But I can't be with you anymore. It's too painful to know what I can't give you, what I can't be for you. Please don't try to find me. Let me go, for both our sakes, let me go. I need to start over, try to figure out who I am without your constant support. Learn to stand on my own feet without relying on your strength. Without my mother orchestrating every aspect of my life.

"I know you'll hurt. That you'll think you can save me again. I leave you with one promise…I won't hurt myself. I swear to you I won't. I realize now it was the coward's way out and it spit in the face of every single thing you've ever done for me. I've left an email address at the bottom of this letter and you can write me. I need time, Leo and you once said you'd give me anything I needed. This is what I need. I can still smell you on my skin. It comforts me to have that. You loved me so well the first time…even better the last. I have those memories to carry me through.

"Thank you for loving me. For always being the best man, even when you were just a boy. Keep being that person and maybe we'll meet again one day. I carry years of your strength with me, Leo. It will keep me safe. It's time to live your life, love. To start what I've delayed for so long. For me…do what you were always meant to do. Find love again, with a woman who is worthy of it. It will give me peace to know you have what you deserve. I love you, baby.

"Your Amelia."

Walking into the bedroom Amelia had slept in for the past months, every trace of her was gone. Downstairs, he handed his parents her letter as his heart shattered.

## **Chapter Five**

*Five Years Later...*

Leo graduated Summa Cum Laude from Harvard Law; the Valedictorian for their class and captain of their rowing team. In the beginning, he'd written Amelia every day, telling her about his classes and his life. A journal of sorts used to lessen his loneliness.

She rarely wrote back but when she did, it was like getting sunshine after weeks of rain. She kept it light, encouraging him, and wishing him all the happiness he deserved. Eventually, his emails to her dwindled to weekly, then monthly, until he only wrote a couple of times a year now. He couldn't bear the constant waiting to see if she'd reply.

During the first year, he didn't date. Then he saw a woman across the quad who could have been her twin sister. He ran toward her, realizing a few feet away it wasn't Amelia. She turned to him and smiled and he pretended it was his girl, the only woman he'd ever loved.

Stephanie was sweet and intelligent; Leo was achingly lonely. He dated her and bedded her, wishing she was Amelia or that he could look past the fact that she wasn't.

After nine months, she broke it off when she found a picture of Leo and Amelia from eleventh grade and realized she was a stand-in. It was amicable and she was better about it than most women would have been. He found himself telling her everything and she cried with him.

She told him everything happened for a reason and one day, he'd be with Amelia again. Then she kissed him gently and walked out of his life.

He found himself writing Amelia about Stephanie and she wrote back, confessing she'd dated someone, too. He found himself furiously jealous, thinking of her with another man. After he'd trashed his bedroom, he realized he was a hypocrite and tried not to dwell on it.

There were other women in his life when his loneliness got so bad he couldn't bear it.

Now, he cleared the last few personal items from his Boston apartment and thought how strange it was to feel like you were drifting when your life was so perfectly mapped out. He'd rented an apartment in Chicago to be near his parents and was entertaining several offers from local firms.

As he was sealing the last box, his cell phone rang. It was his mother. "Hi, Mom."

"Baby, Mr. Whitehall died of a heart attack last night." He met this news with silence, not sure what to say. He'd stayed in touch with Amelia's father over the years but the older man had never betrayed his daughter's location or her new identity. He heard his mother sigh, "His funeral is in three days. I think you should come."

"I don't know. I just don't know, Mom."

They talked for a few minutes and Leo struggled to keep it together…again. When would it feel like things were normal again? When would he be able to move on from the train wreck of emotion? Would there ever come a day when he could think about Amelia and *not* freak the fuck out?

Sitting on the edge of his bed, he rubbed his eyes and took a deep breath. Would Amelia talk to him if they ended up in the same place? Could he even *handle* seeing her?

With a groan, he finished what he needed to do and carried the few things to his old Cherokee. Loading everything in, he climbed behind the wheel and put on his sunglasses. His knuckles were white as he gripped the wheel.

He'd planned on unloading everything in Chicago and heading down to see his folks, he'd have to haul ass to make the funeral in three days. Attending might give him closure where Amelia was concerned. Maybe he could finally put her in his past and move on.

He glanced at his face in the rearview mirror and smirked. "Good luck with that."

Chicago was bustling; his apartment just outside the financial district was exactly what he needed. The view was stunning and he thought maybe he would be happy here. This was another fresh start for him. A way to fill his days with work instead of school and get some much-needed peace.

He'd always been a little stressed at college. Amy had talked about his education for years. Back then, the plan had been for her to be there with him. That she hadn't been, that he'd been alone, seemed to be in the back of his mind too often.

The furniture he'd ordered for the new place would arrive in a few days. The landlord was going to let the delivery men in; the list of where to place everything was on the fridge. He planned to bring back some of his personal boxes from his parent's house in Springfield.

Carrying up the last load from his SUV, he spent a few minutes packing a bag and a black suit. He was back on the road several hours later after a shower and short nap.

He was alternately nervous and angry, unsure what the next few days would bring. As he drove, he reminisced about the years he'd called Amelia his. When he'd planned that their futures would be braided together. He couldn't help but wonder how the years had treated the only woman he'd ever really wanted – who hadn't wanted him nearly enough.

Leo arrived at his childhood home, unsure if coming here was a good idea. Sitting in the driveway, he clutched the steering wheel and took a deep breath, fighting down the urge to turn around and drive back to Chicago.

"Stop being a coward," he muttered in disgust and opened the door. He took his time grabbing his stuff, locking the truck, and approaching the house he'd lived in his entire childhood.

Carrying his duffle and garment bags through the side door leading into the kitchen, Leo came to a dead stop when he realized Amelia was standing in the middle of the large open space with his mother.

# Chapter Six

The two women turned to him and he saw they'd both been crying. Amelia's green eyes were even more vivid than he remembered. Designer sunglasses perched on top of her head, pulling her hair back from her face. On her wrist the charm bracelet he'd given her so many years ago sparkled.

Leo hadn't had time to psyche himself up to see her; he had never dreamed she'd be standing in his *house*. In his kitchen...talking to his mother. Everything felt surreal. It was as if six years simply fell away. His traitorous mind gave him no choice but to drink Amelia in and just the sight of her woke every nerve in his body.

Her hair was shorter but her face looked the same. She was wearing low-hung jeans and a snug black t-shirt, black high heels that brought her closer to his six-four height, putting the top of her head at his nose. There was a black leather backpack over her shoulder. She was carrying more weight on her frame than he'd ever seen and it looked so damn good on her.

His mother came forward and pulled him down for a kiss, welcoming him home. His eyes never left Amelia, as if he was afraid she'd disappear into thin air. His mother patted his chest and left the room. He set his bags on the kitchen floor and they stood staring at one another.

Struggling for calm, he said quietly, "I'm sorry about your father, Amelia."

"Thank you, Leo." Hearing his name from her lips was a physical ache inside him. She didn't miss the flinch just below his eye. "Can we talk?"

He laughed shortly and gave a quick shake of his head. "Sure, why not? I'll just put my stuff down." The anger in his tone was impossible to miss. He grabbed his bags and carried them past her to the stairs.

Dropping them in the middle of his old bedroom, he was surprised to find her behind him when he turned. "O-*kay*…or we can talk here, too, I suppose."

Saying nothing, Amelia closed the door and dropped her backpack on the floor. He didn't move as she walked across the room and wrapped her arms around him, laying her face on his shoulder.

He tried so hard not to respond – to fight what she made every cell in his body feel – but this was *his Amelia*. His arms went around her back and into her hair, fisting it in his fingers. Leo pulled the sunglasses off her head and dropped them on her backpack.

When her eyes locked with his and she didn't try to free herself from his hold, he kissed her. Her hands moved up his chest, around his neck to the back of his head. Her fingers gripped *his* hair and Amelia pulled him to her aggressively. His hands acted independent of actual thought, tightening around her and plastering her snugly against him.

Then she licked into his mouth and both of them lost any connection to rationality or reason.

He backed her to the door, carrying her more than walking her. His hand reached out to turn the lock a moment before he slammed her against the wall beside it. He wanted her naked…now…and he rapidly yanked away her clothing, baring her body to his hands, his mouth. Separating from her mouth only long enough to rip his shirt away, he pushed away the rest of his clothes with a sense of desperation. The feel of her skin against his almost brought him to his knees.

Leo lifted her and felt her long legs go around his waist with all her strength. It was heaven.

He slid into the moist heat of her body without checking to see if she was ready. She was. His initial thrusts were deep and hard, punishing her for what she'd put him through. Amelia welcomed it, begging for more and when she came the first time, she moaned his name against his lips before she devoured him as if he were her last meal.

He pushed her up again and the feel of her pussy milking at his bare cock was so much better than he remembered. She tightened hard around him with her entire body. He watched her face as she climaxed then joined her after three more driving strokes, coating her welcoming body with hot seed that felt as if it was ripped from his soul.

They stayed where they were for several minutes, breathing hard; their hearts pounding against one another where their chests were sealed together. His face was buried in her neck, hers was buried in his. She felt so good. She felt like the only truly good thing in his life and the reality of that sent lancing pain through him, leaving him in complete emotional upheaval.

When she sighed deeply and began to stroke the back of his head with her fingertips, he pulled back to stare into her eyes. "*Why*, Amelia?" was all he could manage in a hoarse whisper.

Her half smile was filled with sadness and she shrugged one delicate shoulder. "Because I love you, Leo and you deserve more than I can ever give you." He started to disagree and she put her fingers over his lips. "Wait. From the moment my mother asked you to tutor me, you agreed because she humiliated me with her behavior."

Tears slid silently down her cheeks, "So many years you stood between me and disaster until the chance to be there was taken out of your hands. You blamed yourself for not protecting me. If I had stood up to her just one of the hundred times you begged me to, I wouldn't have been vulnerable that day. Making you hate me by leaving was nothing compared to how much I already hated myself for being stupid and weak."

"Amelia. You were so young. It wasn't your fault. None of it was ever your fault." He kissed her tears away and carried her to his bed. Still inside her, still hard, Leo stretched out on top of her. "Will you stay with me now, Amelia? Will you let me love you?"

She shook her head sadly. "I'm not right for you now anymore than I was six years ago, Leo. You're going to have closure now. We'll love one another for a couple of days and then you have to let me go. You have to find a woman who can give you everything you deserve. That will never be me, Leo. I wish it was. But I'll never be good enough for your life, for your future."

"Why do you punish *yourself*…punish *me*…for something you had no control over, Amelia? Stay with me and let me love you, let me heal you, baby. You *are* good enough. You're the *only* woman I want, the *only* woman I'm even able to love. Let me prove it to you."

Leo made love to her all afternoon, pushing her past one orgasm and into another. Making her come five times for each climax he allowed himself. He kissed, licked, and sucked every inch of Amelia's body. He took her in every position, keeping her mind unfocused and off kilter. He wanted her in complete chaos and he achieved it.

Hours later, he carried her to the large tub in his bathroom and soaked with her in the warm water. They were quiet as they reclined, her body stretched out on top of his. He touched her, learned her again, and Amy closed her eyes to soak up every sensation Leo gave her. He showed her how he felt through his fingertips, his palms, the beat of his heart and she took it as if she was starving.

When the water began to cool, he guided her into the shower and washed her hair, bathed her body as she held his shoulders for support. He wasn't going to talk her into staying with him. The time for talking and explaining was over. Touch was his only weapon and he planned to use it with no mercy.

On his knees, he kissed the tiny scar from her surgery, hugging her to him tightly as he stroked the backs of her legs. Her hands were in his hair and her eyes were closed tight against the onslaught of intense emotion being with him brought to the surface.

Amelia cried often through the day, certain in her own mind that their time together would end. No matter how much she wanted him, how much she needed him…and Leo could tell how much she did…she was determine to keep her heart locked away from him. It wouldn't matter. No matter the years since he'd held her, their bodies were *keyed* to one another. No one since Amelia had held anything more than his physical self. He would guarantee she'd experienced the same.

He wasn't letting her go again.

The next morning Leo drove her to her old house and waited as she slipped on a beautiful black dress and heels. She didn't wear makeup and she didn't need it; she never had.

At the funeral home, many people she'd never met and some she'd forgotten came to pay their respects to her quiet father. When she gave her eulogy, she stopped several times, catching her breath, stilling her emotions, before continuing.

Augusta sat in the back row, sobbing quietly and alone. Amelia hadn't spoken to her since she'd woken in the hospital six years ago. She was her father's sole heir and when his long-time attorney and best friend stood to say the last words, he informed those gathered that he had a letter Amelia's father had asked him to read on his behalf.

*"Frank, if you're reading this, it is because my heart finally quit on me. I expect it any day now. It's been coming for years and I won't prolong it, I'm ready to start fresh. Do me a favor and read this letter for me at my funeral.*

*"Augusta, I loved you the first moment I saw you behind the jewelry counter at Sears so many years ago. We were broke but we loved one another so well. When we had Amelia, I was the happiest man on Earth. I want you to know that despite your mistakes, I never stopped loving you, I never forgot the young woman I fell in love with. I forgive you and maybe one day you can find a way to make things right.*

*"Amelia, you were the light of my life from the day you were born and I'm sorry I didn't protect you. You are so beautiful, inside and out...you always have been. You are so much smarter than both of your parents. We didn't do our jobs as parents and I've run out of time to make my part in it right again. You were always the best of both of us. Don't lie to yourself anymore. Don't be afraid. Go after what you want with both hands and know you are good enough...you are perfect in every way that really matters. I'll miss seeing your laughing green eyes...you haven't laughed in so long. I'll be listening and watching for you to be happy. I love you, my precious girl.*

*"Leo, not a day has gone by that I haven't thought of you and what should have been. You loved her better than either of her parents and protected her more than we ever did. For that, I thank you. Don't let her get away again.*

*"For the rest of my friends and family, thank you for a life of memories. Most of them were happy. I'm not afraid.*

*All my love,*

*Dan"*

Leo and Amelia's hands were clasped tightly and both were crying jaggedly. His parents sat on either side, comforting them, hurting for them. They waited until the casket was lifted down and carried down the aisle to the hearse, rising to walk behind it to the waiting limo.

As they passed Augusta, Leo paused, taking in her sob-wracked frame. She was shaking, tears washing down her face. He bent and took her hand, gently lifting her from her seat. Amelia pulled her between them and they guided her to the car.

The moment they were closed inside, Leo's parents watched as Augusta sobbed over their children. "Please…if you only knew the regrets. Amelia, oh god, I know you hate me and I deserve it. Leo, I had no right…*no right*. I'll give you everything, *anything*, if you'll just let me see you sometimes. I know I don't deserve forgiveness but *please* forgive me, oh please forgive me. Please, I'm so sorry. You'll never know how sorry."

She was a completely broken woman and in an unspoken agreement, Leo and Amelia held her between them and cried with her. They held her and forgave her and let as much of the past go as they could. They had all paid. It was time to stop.

# Chapter Seven

The five of them stayed huddled together at the cemetery as the preacher prayed for the soul of Daniel Whitehall. Augusta's tears didn't stop as she mourned the man who had loved her despite her flaws. Amelia placed lilies on her father's casket and whispered her goodbyes.

Back at Amelia's childhood home, there were tables of food and people to greet. She stood with her arms wrapped hard around herself for a long time on the back patio.

Leo put his arms over hers and hugged her tight. After a couple of minutes of silence, he murmured at her ear, "I love you, Amelia. Don't leave me again. Don't make me beg you to stay." She leaned into him and his arms went harder around her.

"A man like you should never, ever have to beg, Leo." He wasn't sure what that meant but he didn't ask, giving her time to organize her thoughts. "There are so many things you deserve."

"You. That's all I want, Amy. It's always only been you. Losing you broke me, baby. I put myself back together but the pieces were jumbled up. I'm only whole, I'm only complete, with you."

"I'm afraid."

"You don't have to be. There should be nothing about us that scares you, Amy. I need you in my life. I'm weaker without you. I'm so alone without you. I've missed you and I've gone through the motions without you but it was never enough. Not once was it ever enough."

"Nothing could ever make you weak, Leo. *Nothing.*"

He held her close and inhaled the scent of her hair, of the light perfume that clung to her skin. "Being with you makes me strong, Amelia. I've always been a better man with you." It was nothing less than the truth. Since she'd walked out of his life he'd felt as if was on auto-pilot, not caring enough about anything.

She was quiet for several minutes and he simply held her, willing her to listen to her heart. She had to believe in what they had. Amelia had to realize for herself that they were always going to be better together than either of them could be apart. "You have to let me wrap up my life, Leo. Give me a few months and I'll come back if you still want me to." Her words slammed into him, rocking him to the core.

He turned her to face him and asked carefully, "Do you have a boyfriend where you live, Amelia?"

"No. I have a girlfriend, Leo." His eyes widened in surprise. "Women are easier and there are none of those pesky *do you want children* questions that I hate with everything inside of me. I also realized you are one of the few men in my life I actually liked. Most of the ones I met in the entertainment industry were cold and shallow." She tilted her head, "Do *you* have a girlfriend, Leo?"

He shook his head. "Not for a couple of years now. It was exhausting to keep from comparing them to you." She smiled and his heart tripped like it had that day years ago in the junior high library. Tightening his fingers on her upper arms, he asked her roughly, "Will you really come back to me, Amelia? Or do I have to do what my parents and your father talked me out of for years and track you down using private detectives?"

The smile she gave him this time was a little sad. "Dad said you'd threatened that weekly during the first year. I'm glad you didn't, Leo. I wouldn't have been able to handle it then." She laid her hand on his cheek. "Give me time to organize my business and say goodbye to Tara. I owe her a lot. She's put up with a ton of BS from me over the years, as a friend then as a lover."

Jealousy wasn't going to help convince her to come back so he shoved it deep and asked instead, "What do you do?" He was glad when she visibly relaxed.

"I run a photography studio for young women looking to break into the industry. I'm part of an industry movement demanding healthy models instead of anorexic ones. My girls are average weights for their body type. I also have great success with beautiful bigger girls. I love what I do."

His pride in her was overwhelming. "Protecting the next generation from some of what you went through. I'm so proud of you." The breeze lifted a stray curl to brush across her cheek and he tucked it behind her ear. "Where do you live, baby?"

"I have studios in Phoenix and LA. Are you still in Boston?" He told her about his recent move. "I like Chicago. I looked into opening a location there last year. I've been hounded for years about opening in New York but it was too close to Boston. I couldn't risk the temptation, being so close to you." She touched the hair at the nape of his neck. "I like your hair longer, Leo. It suits you."

Leo smoothed his thumbs along her jaw and leaned to kiss her. "Can you stay a little while?" She nodded and he cupped her head to his chest. "I want to make love to you over and over, Amelia. To make sure I'm imprinted on you so you remember how much I love you, how much I need you to come back. I want you to marry me and let me love you for the rest of my life."

She gasped and hugged him close, listening to his strong heartbeat under her cheek. "It was always about making you my wife, Amelia. I didn't want to ever let you go; I never doubted what I had with you. Never questioned how lucky I was to call you mine. No one will ever know you and love you as I do, Amelia. You're the other half of my heart. You make me whole."

Looking up at him, there were tears sparkling in her green eyes. "I love you, Leo. I've loved you since I was too young to even know what love was. I'm sorry that I left. I'm sorry I was a coward."

"No more wasted time, Amelia. We start over from now."

Nodding, she whispered, "Let's finish saying goodbye to Dad so we have the house to ourselves."

Leo kept his hand at her waist while she moved from one group to the other, accepting condolences and listening to stories about her father she'd never heard before.

His parents helped with the catering staff and when the last guests left after dark, Sarabeth and Alejandro made sure everything was back in order before kissing both of them goodbye, hugging them hard. Sarabeth whispered, "It's right that you're back, Amelia. We've all missed you so much, honey. Be courageous."

After Leo removed a small overnight bag from his SUV they sat together on the patio, talking about the years they'd been apart. When Amelia pushed her wineglass away, Leo picked them both up and took them inside.

He wasted no time in scooping his girl from her chair and carrying her upstairs to her bedroom. He peeled her clothing away slowly, savoring each section of skin as he bared it. When Amelia lay across her bed naked, he stripped for her before crawling up beside her.

"You're even more cut than you used to be, Leo. You're so beautiful."

"The three R's: rowing, running, and racquetball. Anything I could use to fill up my time, I used. I stayed as physically active as possible when I wasn't studying."

"I saw you took Valedictorian. You got to give your speech this time and I was really proud of you, Leo." He stared at her, his surprise clear. "Darling, I disappeared…*you* didn't. I've kept track of you through Law Review and your various activities. I wanted to make sure you were out in the world." Leo's brow furrowed with sudden stress and she smoothed it with her fingertips. "Yes, I saw your girlfriends. The fact that they could have been my sisters did not escape me."

"I…I'm sorry, Amelia. I felt like I was cheating…I *was* cheating."

"No. You were *living* and it changes nothing, not for me. I dated two men, slept with one of them, and realized that wasn't going to work when I was ready to book a flight for Boston in hysterics after I asked him to leave. I've been with Tara off and on for a couple of years. One other woman before her. I missed you every day and some days were much worse than others."

Ruffling her fingers through his hair, she added, "Now I know I can make it on my own if I have to, Leo. I can survive anything. I survived having my future pulled out from under me and I survived walking away from you. Perhaps not well, but I did survive. I needed to know I was strong enough to be alone, that I could stand without you holding me up."

"You've proven that strength to yourself but I *always* knew it was there, Amy. Now it's time for you to come back to me. I survived, too…but I *didn't* live, baby. Everything in my world was muted, colorless, and lifeless without you to share it with."

Leo moved over her, kissing his way to her breasts and taking each nipple between his lips, sucking firmly. Her hands moved through his hair, stroking and tugging. Her hands massaged his neck and shoulders until he was crazed with need for his beautiful Amelia.

"Please, Leo…I don't want to wait. I want you inside me. We can go slow later." He nodded and moved between her thighs, finding her ready and wet for him. She wrapped herself around him, pulling his mouth to her, and matching the rhythm he set in her body with her tongue. His hand cupped and squeezed her breast, his thumb flicking the taut nipple as she moaned into him.

"You are the only person I've ever loved, Leo. The only person I've said the words to. I couldn't lie to them, not even Tara, when I didn't feel it. I want you to know that."

He hugged her hard and whispered, "Thank you, baby. I couldn't pretend either. It felt like the ultimate betrayal of what I felt for you, what I've always felt for you."

Amelia rolled them over, thrusting her body over his and stroked her fingers over Leo's face. "I'm sorry…for so many things." She leaned down and ran the flat of her tongue over his nipple. His hands tightened on her hips and she smiled, moving to the other nipple. Bracing her hands on either side of his head, she said hoarsely, "Tell me you forgive me, Leo. I need you to forgive me."

He rolled them over again and took control. "There is nothing to forgive you *for*, Amelia. My love for you is unconditional. You did what you thought was right and maybe it was at the time. You've done nothing that requires forgiveness."

"I didn't protect...the...our *baby*, Leo." The tears welled in her eyes suddenly and he went back on his heels, taking her with him. "It was my *job*. I was supposed to protect our baby."

"No, Amelia...oh baby, *no*. You didn't know. You were drugged, honey. You were completely out of it when you called me from the clinic. You can't think I *blame* you? It *wasn't* your fault." He kissed her and hugged her until she was breathlessly sobbing.

"If you had been aware you would have fought like a hellion. Augusta knew that as surely as I know it now. It was why she knew she had to drug you. It was horrible but it was *not* your fault. I never, even once, thought it was your fault, Amelia. *Never*. You were a victim as much as our baby. So much more was taken from you."

Leo held her while she cried out all the grief and guilt she'd carried all these years. Why hadn't he remembered how sensitive Amelia was? Why didn't he realize she blamed herself? His hands stroked over her back again and again as she trembled in his arms. "I love you so much. I'm so sorry I didn't know why you were hurting. I should have known. My sweet, gentle Amelia."

Gradually her sobs began to ease and he could tell she was wrung out. He cradled her, crooning to her, smoothing her hair away from her tear-stained face. "Since the first time I saw you, Leo. I wished I could be more like you, Leo. I wished I could be strong and smart and perfect like you."

He shook his head, "I'm far from perfect, baby. At fourteen, most of my time around you was spent arguing with my erection." His chuckle made her smile. "It wanted me to listen to it all the time. You were the first girl I ever noticed had a scent. Used to drive me crazy."

"The pool party I held the summer after we started dating, I was bringing out a tray of lemonade and almost dropped the whole thing when you powered up out of the water to the deck. I remember thinking, *now I get what all the talk is about*. It was the first time I had to press my thighs together to ease the ache. It certainly wasn't the last." Amelia tugged her lower lip between her teeth then added, "Later that day, I watched you change in the pool house and you were hard. I masturbated later thinking about it."

Buried inside her body, his cock twitched firmly. He tightened his hold and stroked into her with everything he had, "Do you feel me inside you, baby?" She nodded. "I get hard for you instantly. I see you or smell you and every part of me wants you, needs you…loves you." His strokes increased and her eyes fluttered closed.

"Look at me, baby. Only *you* have this affect on me. You own me. Everything I am, everything I ever will be…it belongs to you, Amelia. Because you are the most perfect soul I've ever known." Her breathing was staggered now and he growled, "Come for me, pretty girl." She threw her head back and screamed his name as he rode her through the climax that stole her breath completely.

Laying her down, he never slowed. "Again, Amelia. I'm going to make you come until there is no doubt in your mind about how I feel for you. Again, baby." He drove her harder this time, pulling her onto his cock by her shoulders as he thrust up into her body.

"I need to go harder, Amelia…you're not hearing me, baby." He went up on his knees, laying her hips over his thighs, taking the bend of her legs in his elbows. "Feel me deep and know I belong to you. Only you, Amelia. As you belong only to me."

Her hands clenched the linens of the bed as her body arched hard, bowing her beautiful torso toward him as she screamed her release. "Yes, Leo…please don't stop." He pulled out and flipped her to her stomach, pulling her roughly into a kneeling position with her breasts against the mattress. His thighs outside of hers, he drove himself deep in one thrust.

"You're so wet, Amelia. I think you need to come again, baby. Come for me again. I love to watch it, to feel it." He gripped her waist, holding her immobile and submissive as he powered into her again and again. "We belong together, Amelia. Tell me. Tell me you fucking *know* we belong together."

"I belong with you, Leo. Only with you." She could barely speak as she gasped for breath.

"Tell me you'll come back to me. Swear it, Amelia." His own voice was low as he growled his command. "Swear it, baby."

"I'll come back. I swear it, Leo."

"Come for me, Amelia…come hard for me." She did and he watched the muscles of her body tense as he felt her pussy clamp around his cock like a wet fist. "Yes, pretty baby, come for me…I need to make you feel good. To give you good memories to replace the sad ones. Yes, Amelia…come here, baby."

He stroked into her several times and released his control, coming so hard it bordered on pain. His hands moved over her body, everywhere, through her hair and over her arms that were slick with sweat. Around to cup her breasts and down her belly to her clit, so wet and swollen as he played with her gently. He was still coming as he gently petted her mound, nuzzled her cheek.

"My beautiful baby. There is only you for me. Don't make me go back to being alone. I beg you to give me peace…no more pain. Please, no more pain."

She moved until he pulled away and gave her room to turn in his arms, kissing him as sweat dripped from their bodies. "I love you. Thank you for loving me, Leo. Say you forgive me."

"I forgive you for loving me more than you loved yourself, Amelia. There is nothing else to forgive you for. We start fresh from today." He pulled her down beside him and she plastered her body against him with a soft sigh. "Say goodbye before you leave. Don't make me wonder."

She nodded and they fell into exhausted sleep.

## **Chapter Eight**

They spent the next few days together, rarely leaving the bedroom, and having food delivered. Leo pushed Amelia, loved her harder each time he took her. Told her over and over and over again that she was beautiful, needed, wanted, and loved. He didn't let her rest, would not stop until she was too weak to stand, too weak to question what both of them knew she needed.

He rolled over, watching Amelia sleep as sunlight filled the room, knowing this was what every morning for the rest of their lives could be. He woke her gently and she stroked his cock in her sleep. Settling between her thighs, Leo thrust gently into her body until she was fully awake, fully engaged.

When she came, it was a gradual building that washed over her slowly as he kissed her, letting his own orgasm take him. "I'm going to make you raw, baby. I shouldn't be using you so hard."

"I love it. Please don't stop, Leo. There's so much time to make up for. So much I've missed." Her stomach growled and he laughed. "Yeah, you might need to feed me, baby."

They showered the sweat and sexual fluids from their bodies and made breakfast together. Sitting on the patio, he held her on his lap, feeding her. An hour later, the doorbell rang and Leo went to see who it was, grateful they'd thought to put clothes on.

Augusta stood in the doorway, framed by the morning light.

Her voice was quieter than he'd ever heard it, reserved in a way he imagined she'd been in her youth. "Good morning, Leo. Can I talk to you both for a few minutes? I promise not to stay long. I know you have five years to catch up on." Leo stood back and led her to the patio, asking if she wanted coffee or breakfast. She shook her head but thanked him. "Good morning, Amelia." Her heart ached to see the distrust in her only child's eyes, but she understood it.

"Good morning, Mother."

"May I sit? I have something I'd like to discuss with you both." Leo pulled out a chair and she smiled, "You always were such a gentleman, Leo. Always. It was one of the things I liked most about you."

Clearing her throat, she began in a careful voice. "I've been to my doctor, Amelia, and I think I can help you. You…you had to have a partial hysterectomy due to the damage to your…your womb. You still produce viable eggs. My doctor says I'm still young enough, in excellent health, to carry a child created from the two of you if you would allow me to do that."

"Wh…what? What are you saying?" Amelia's voice was barely a whisper as she stared at her mother with wide eyes.

"They would take your eggs from your ovaries, sperm from Leo and combine them. Then implant them to grow. It doesn't have to be me, of course. It could be any surrogate. I'd understand if you didn't want it to be me. But I…I had you so young; I'm only forty-one. I can do this for you. I know it isn't the same. It could never be the same. But maybe it will give me some peace…to do this…for you both." Silent tears tracked down her cheeks, "I want so much to help…to earn forgiveness for the horrible things I've done."

Leo stared at Amelia, seeing she was unable to find words, unsure what she wanted to say. Did she want to rage? Was she happy? "Baby, are you okay?"

"I…I don't know. I never even thought about other options. Isn't that *ridiculous*? A *baby*? A little baby of our own? I can't even think straight. We'd need to talk, of course…kind of hash out the pros and cons. Would that be weird? I don't know…" she trailed off and stared at the table top with her head tilted.

Then she stood and started to wander toward the back doors as Leo stood to follow, perplexed. "I have to pack. I have to get things tied up in LA so I can get back. So much to think about, so much to talk about. If I don't get there and get back, what then? More nothing on top of nothing."

She stopped and dropped, Leo catching her and scooping her up. He carried her inside and laid her on the couch.

Augusta came to him with a cool washcloth and he placed it on Amelia's head. "I'm sorry, Leo. Maybe I shouldn't have come so soon after...well, the funeral. Amy's dealing with having you back in her life, the loss of her father, me falling apart on her. I wasn't thinking. I came here straight from the doctor." She smiled wistfully. "I was so excited thinking I could help. I'll go. Give me a call if either of you need anything."

Leo touched her forearm. "Thank you, Augusta. I mean it. It is unbelievably kind of you. I know it will mean a great deal to Amelia once she can absorb things at a normal rate and process all the data flowing in. Why don't you give me a chance to talk to her?" She nodded and leaned to press her cheek against his.

"Thank you, Leo. Your kindness means more because of all people...I deserve it least from you." She kissed Amelia's hair and smoothed it back before heading out the door.

When he heard her car start, he crouched beside the couch, stroking the side of her face, and said, "Pretty girl...wake up, baby." Her eyes fluttered open and she looked confused. "There you are, sweetheart. Are you feeling alright?" She nodded. "You fainted, honey. Does that happen to you a lot these days?" Shaking her head, she moved to sit up and he touched her shoulder. "No rush, Amelia. Stay there and get your bearings. Can I get you something to drink?" She took the washcloth off her head.

"Leo?"

"Yes, sweetheart?"

"Did my mother come here and offer to carry a child for us?"

"She did."

"Leo, I'm really...overwhelmed about...well, just everything. I'm stressing a little bit and I'm really scared. I don't do well with scared, Leo. Please help me."

He scooped her up and settled her over his lap. "I don't want you to be afraid so let's take things one at a time. Your father passing is the most urgent because I know how close you'd grown over the last few years. You need time to grieve and settle his estate. I'm happy to help with anything you need, my parents too. You're not going to be alright with losing him overnight, no matter how much support you have." He stroked her face, kissing her temple.

"It will also take time to heal the relationship with your mother. I believe she is truly sorry, deep in her heart, for the heartache she's caused. I believe she wants to rectify it. The first step is admitting she was wrong and accepting responsibility. She's done that. Now she wants to make things right. If that is the path we choose together, so be it. If it isn't, I'm fine with that too." Amelia stared at him, as if seeing him for the first time.

"That brings me to us, Amelia. I love you…just exactly the way you are. I would have loved our child had he or she made it into our lives but I did not fall in love with you so you could bear me children. I loved you when we were little more than children ourselves. I love kids…but do not need them to feel complete or to feel our love is complete."

Amelia stared at him, fascinated with the movement of his lips as he continued, "If you get to a point where you want children, we have many options. I've usually thought adoption because I know we're in a position to change the entire course of a child's life if we take them into our home to love and raise. Your mother has given us another option, which I'd never consider with someone we didn't know. Or there is devoting our lives to charity and being content with one another. Whatever we decide, I have the ultimate faith in us figuring out the right path and loving one another through better or worse."

She sat up in his lap and wrapped her arms around him, laying her head on his chest. "My father told me once that yours was an old soul, Leo. A soul that had been through more cycles than most, who could see through to the heart of a matter, and see the clearest direction. I think I know what he meant now. I'm sorry I didn't trust you before. I love you very much." She leaned back to look at him. "I think we need more time together before we talk about all our options." He nodded and kissed her gently. "Make love to me, Leo. It always seems to center my thoughts."

With a smile, Leo stood with Amelia in his arms and locked the door before heading upstairs. "It would be my pleasure, baby."

He made love to her for hours and when she asked if he thought his mother would go with her to LA, his heart leapt for joy.

# Chapter Nine

*Seven months later...*

Leo was going out of his mind with worry. It had been three days since he'd spoken to Amelia and his mother was being far too vague for his comfort. They'd left together for LA three weeks after her father's funeral and his mother had been back twice. Amelia hadn't been back at all. He hadn't seen her, held her, or kissed her in more than half a year.

He was beginning to panic.

Their original agreement had been to speak once a day, in the evenings, so she could focus on running her business and transitioning work to Tara who would be taking over her LA branch. At first, his mother checked in constantly, talking about what a wonderful job Amelia had done with her clients and what an amazing life she'd built.

Two months ago, everything changed. He'd threatened to come out there and only his mother telling him it could sabotage everything kept him in Chicago.

He'd started his own practice in family law and was steadily building a client list for himself. He was also absorbed in several pro bono cases for impoverished families who'd appealed to him. He loved that he'd avoided the corporate and criminal law tracks, seeing the greater good he could do for children and families in his current path. He'd finished furnishing the large condo but was searching for homes outside the city where he could make his life with Amelia.

Leo was just walking in late on a Thursday afternoon when his phone rang. It was his mother and he knew instantly that something was very wrong. "Leo, I need to talk to you and I need you to not press for more information than I can give you. I've given Amelia my word and you know what that means to me. In certain things, my hands are tied."

"Mom, you're succeeding if your goal was to scare the absolute life out of me." He realized he hadn't put down his briefcase or taken off his coat. He did both and walked to the living room window with its view of the city. "Please tell me what's going on. As much as you can."

Clearing her throat carefully, Sarabeth De La Cruz simply said, "You need to come to LA. You cannot tell Amelia you are coming but you can't sneak up on her either. I'll pick you up at the airport and take you to her."

Sighing heavily, he could tell she felt the weight of her promise to Amy. "Leo, she's alright. She loves you more than her own life and I can tell you that with more belief today than I've ever had. She does not want you to come and you'll understand why when you get here."

Leo opened his mouth to question her further and she cut him off, "Please don't ask for more. Pack a bag, take a car to the airport, and fly out on the first flight you can get. Call me when you know it will land. You'll have to stay in a hotel tonight and I'll pick you up in the morning. Am I clear, Leo? I can't impress the urgency of this on you."

"I'll call you when I get to the airport."

"Good boy. I love you so much. Please don't be afraid."

"Too late to tell me that, Mom. I'll talk to you soon."

He disconnected and packed a bag as he called the front desk of his building and asked them to hold a car to O'Hare. Less than ten minutes after his mother's disturbing phone call, his apartment was locked and he was striding across the lobby to the waiting car.

An hour later, he was through security and waiting for his flight to board which didn't leave for two hours. He called his mother with the flight details and waited in silent dread.

The moment the plane landed at LAX and the caution lights went out overhead, Leo pulled his bag from first class storage. He was the first person off the plane and jogged for the exit. His mother stood beside a waiting car and waved him inside.

The tightness around her eyes and mouth attested to her tension. "Mom, you look more stressed than I think I've ever seen you. Is there nothing you can tell me?"

"I can't. I feel like I'm on the fence of dishonesty by bringing you here but I simply cannot bear the thought of something going wrong and you wondering why I didn't call you." They spoke very little since his control was precarious at best. He respected her need for silence but didn't like it in the least.

Leo stayed in a hotel not far from Amelia's studio and if he slept more than fifteen minutes at a time, it would amaze him. With gritty eyes and feeling like he had a hangover, he met his mother at nine the next morning in the lobby.

"Leo, you *cannot* freak out in any way. You must remain calm, calm as a still pond. *A still pond.* Do you understand me?"

He couldn't help the frown that formed. "Mom, since when am I the *freak out* type? I mean...really? Your own earliest descriptions of me were *calm* and *inquisitive*."

Giving a small snort of laughter, she retorted, "Oh honey, sometimes, one really can't *help* it. Even you, who still epitomizes calm and collected in any situation." She patted his leg and put her sunglasses over her eyes, staring out the window. Her banter had eased his mind slightly but he wouldn't fully feel better until he saw Amelia.

Sarabeth told the driver to drop them one block from the studio and to please be ready to pick them up when she called. They got out and walked; his mother's arm through his. Approaching the modern storefront, she held him back. "Deep breath, baby. This is going to blow the top of your head off."

She opened the door and Leo saw Amelia facing away from him on a stool in front of a huge digital camera attached to a tripod with an elastic cord. She wore a beautiful emerald green sweater with an empire waist and soft leather pants, flat boots. He smiled. He'd never known Amelia to wear flat shoes in her life unless they were sneakers.

Her hair was longer now, dark and silky in the set lights, and pulled back from her face with tiny clips. He listened to her laugh, encouraging the young woman in front of the camera to relax and be herself. She was doing headshots, something any aspiring actress, singer, or performer needed to break into the entertainment industry in LA.

"Kim, I want you tell me something funny that happened to you."

"Oh my god! I bent down to get something out of my locker in ninth grade and my pants ripped. Not a little bit, Ally…all the *way*. You could see my underwear with little green shamrocks over them. We were nowhere close to St. Patrick's Day. Mom hadn't had a chance to do laundry. I was thirty pounds heavier then. There was a boy I liked so I squeezed myself into my sister's jeans. It was such a big deal then. Now though…now I can laugh about it." The girl was lovely and Amelia took pictures throughout while she talked. A huge screen showed the results of her work and they were stunning.

"Oh, Kim, I think we have them. And let me tell you…if you have to squeeze into tight clothes for a boy, he isn't worth it. I promise the right man will love everything about you, no matter how flawed or bizarre."

"Do you believe that, Allison? Really?"

"I do. You'll believe it one day, too. Mark my words; you'll know the right man, the perfect man, when you find him. Your soul mate, Kim. The person you love more than your own life. That's the most important part. To find someone who thinks they can love you more than you love them. Happiness is sure to follow."

"Allison, you sound like you're in love."

"I am and he is so much more than I deserve." She stood up and Kim came to kiss her cheeks.

"I doubt that, Ally. You're spectacular. I'll see you next week when we go over the proofs." Amelia nodded and Kim jogged happily to the front door, smiling as she passed them. No one else appeared to be in bright, open space and Leo opened his mouth to greet her as Amelia turned.

His knees almost buckled. He blinked hard. He was sure it must be a trick of the light; he was experiencing jet lag, possibly suffering food poisoning. One by one, he checked off the possible explanations and took in the sight of Amelia from the front.

She was pregnant. *Very* pregnant.

"Amelia?" his voice didn't sound familiar to him, didn't sound like it was coming from his body. It barely carried but she heard him and glanced up. He tried again, certain the calm person he had always been was still inside him somewhere. "H…how is this possible? I…I don't understand." He felt lightheaded and stumbled forward, catching the side of the receptionist counter and leaning against it.

His mother was beside him as he sank to the floor. "Leo, I need you to take a deep breath. Ssh, darling. Breathe deeply and settle yourself for just a moment." Closing his eyes, the room began to spin and he barely caught himself before he passed out. "Leo, pull it together, baby."

He controlled his breathing, pulling air deeply into his lungs and out again several times. Amelia hadn't moved since she'd seen him, a look of sheer terror on her face. That snapped him into reality as nothing else could have. He got into a crouching position, and then pulled himself to his feet.

Rubbing his hands over his eyes, he asked quietly, "Baby…Amelia…honey, *are* you pregnant?" She nodded slowly. "Is that *our* little baby growing in there?" She nodded again. "How? Can someone tell me *how*? I was there when the doctor told us what he had to do. It isn't growing on your fallopian tubes, is it? That is so fucking dangerous for both of you." She shook her head and he walked closer to her. He flinched when she backed up a step.

"Amelia, Leo isn't going to hurt you, baby. You know that. He's just not sure what's going on. We have to explain it to him. His first concern is going to be *you*. It will *always* be you, Amelia." His mother turned to him.

"A couple of months ago, she was feeling pain, feeling achy in her midsection. With the scar tissue from her surgery, I was worried it was pressing on other organs. I took her to a gynecologist who told her she was pregnant. We both immediately assured him that was impossible. They've done multiple ultrasounds, Leo. Amelia *is pregnant* with your child."

"I don't understand…how? How is it possible?"

His mother smiled and he felt his heart calm a bit more. "Amelia has an extremely rare condition called didelphic uterus. She was born with two…both were attached to the fallopian tubes, each had their own cervix. When one was removed, the fallopian tubes simply used the other. The doctors never saw the second one; it isn't exactly something they look for. They saw the bleeding and stopped where it was coming from before removing the damaged tissue."

Leo whispered, "It's incredible…but is it *dangerous*? What are the risks to *you*, Amelia? I'm assuming that's why you didn't tell me." He closed his eyes, wondering why this beautiful woman thought a child was the only thing he wanted from her. "You're gambling with your own safety to give me a child."

"No risks…"

Sarabeth cut her off. "Amelia. You *cannot* lie to him. It isn't fair to keep him in the dark anymore." His mother moved to stand beside her, smoothing her hair.

Amelia sighed and gave Sarabeth a nod, facing him, "I…I could deliver normally but the risk of hemorrhaging would be higher since they're unsure of the strength of the uterine walls. I…I wasn't getting periods so there was no preparation for a baby to grow there. I'm supposed to be on bed rest but Tara came down with shingles really bad and I didn't want to cancel Kim's appointment."

Leo moved forward and scooped her up. "We can talk on the way to your house. And you *will* remain on bed rest, I don't care if the fucking world is burning, Amelia." Glancing at his mother, he added, "Shut this place down, Mom. All of it. Turn it all off and lock it up. Grab her backpack." He held Amy while his mother scrambled to close the studio then Sarabeth led the way to the front door where the car was waiting out front.

They slid into the limo and his mother told the driver where to go, climbing up front to sit beside him and closing the privacy glass. Amelia was perched on his lap. She looked nervous, twisting her fingers together. He wasn't sure when he'd get past terror enough to feel anything else.

She said quietly, "Leo, I was going to tell you soon. I wanted to wait, just in case he didn't make it. They want to take him in four weeks by C-Section. It will be six weeks early but they don't want to go past thirty-four, things get really tight, and the risks get a little higher."

He couldn't stop his frown. "What are the risks *right now*? If they take the baby ten weeks early? I want to know."

Amelia put her hands over her stomach, "No, Leo."

"Amelia, babies are born premature all the time. Medical science is not what it was even ten years ago." He knew he was pushing but couldn't seem to stop himself.

Her palms pressed more firmly around her stomach. "*No*, Leo. I'm not forcing him into the world a single day sooner than I have to. It's more dangerous for him than it is for me."

"Please, baby, please don't risk yourself. I can't *live* without you. I can live without a child but not without *you*, Amelia." He leaned his head back on the seat and took deep racking breaths. Amelia lifted his hand to her face, pressing her lips into his palm and kissing it gently. Then she placed it over her stomach and watched his face when he felt the baby move under his hand. He raised his head to stare at her stomach, his mouth slightly open.

"That is *our child* in there, Leo. By some strange twist of fate, we've been given a second chance. Leo, look at me...that is *your son*. Growing healthy and strong just under your hand. I've had every test done possible, checked for every known abnormality. Your poor mother has been out of her mind with worry. I kept the secret because I know you love me more than you love this baby." She put both hands on his face, "But Leo...I love *you* and *this baby* more than I love myself."

Both his palms were on her stomach, his eyes wide as he felt their child move again. He ground out hoarsely, "Amelia, I can't lose you. If I have to choose, *I will choose you*. Please, baby, please understand…I never thought this would be possible. I closed my mind to it."

Looking deeply into his eyes, she grinned, "Leonardo Stefan De La Cruz, you've never closed your mind to anything in your life." He gave her a small fearful smile and she turned more fully on his lap, gripping his shoulders. "I feel better now that you're here, baby. I was scared to tell you; I was scared not to tell you. I've missed you so much. But I've made it so *far*…I can go a little further. Say you'll help me, Leo. Give me this one thing…something I thought I'd never have after that horrible day so years ago. *Our* baby…from *my* body."

He was quiet for a long time. "It's a boy?" he whispered. She lifted his hands and put them on either side of her belly.

She nodded, "Oh, yes, Leo. And hung like his father already. The ultrasound wand was on me for like two seconds and the tech said *um, can't waffle on this one…definitely a boy*." Leo grinned and actually blushed. "Leo?"

He looked up and met the prettiest, greenest eyes he'd ever known. "Yes, precious Amelia?"

"I know you're worried. I know you're scared for me. But I need to know if you're maybe…just a little…happy, too?" She looked afraid to hear his answer and he realized he'd been wrong not to reassure her before worrying. He hadn't been able to help it.

He held her in his arms, kissing her until she was breathless. When he pulled back, he whispered, "Amelia, love of my life, I am so *happy*…so *awe-struck*…so excited to know that a child made when we came back to one another is growing in a *spare* womb you just happened to be carrying around. You are so beautiful. You truly are glowing. Please tell me you've been getting pictures throughout. I've missed so much."

Amelia nodded, "Remember, I didn't know myself the first few months. Had no clue. I haven't had a menstrual cycle since a week before we were together the first time. It's been so hard to keep it from you, Leo. I wanted to tell you but I knew you'd be afraid. I didn't want you to make me choose, Leo."

"Make you…? Oh baby, I wouldn't have done that. I wouldn't have asked you to end it. I would have carried you everywhere and refused to let you out of my sight. That you can fucking guarantee is what I plan on doing now." He stroked his palms over her hair, down her neck, over her shoulders and arms, lifting her fingers to his lips.

"God, Amelia. I'm scared and excited, I feel like my heart is going to explode." His hands roamed over her stomach gently and she placed hers over them. She moved them to her breasts and his eyes widened in surprise.

"Bigger…cool, huh?"

"Sweet Amelia, there is no *way* you're cleared for any sexual activity. I'm going to be a monk for the next few months, let's not discuss how much I want you right now…or that your breasts are fuller with the pregnancy. I'll die. I'm sure of it."

There was an evil look in her eyes when she leaned close to him and said, "I've always wondered what you look like when you stroke yourself, Leo. You could do that for me later and I could watch. That would make me very happy." She stroked her hand over the hard ridge of his cock beneath her thighs.

He jumped and she smiled, "Not funny, Amelia. I almost lost control just then."

"Since you never lose control in any situation, I might enjoy this very much." He pulled her to his chest and laid her head on his shoulder, one hand on her back, the other on the side of her belly.

"Baby, be still and very quiet for me. Let me calm down for a few minutes." She did, smiling against his chest and listening to his strong heart beat. Every time the baby moved, he made a little sound of surprise.

They arrived at her house and he thought it suited her. A pretty cottage on the ocean with lots of windows. She let him carry her inside like a child, laughing at his refusal to let her walk. She took him on a tour of the house and he marveled at the bright and cheerful space. The driver brought in his bags and his mother moved back to the guest room on the other side of the house.

When the three of them sat down to eat dinner together, Leo tried to figure out the next step. "No chance you should fly. I can't stay here for two months and I'm not letting you out of my sight. How do we do this?"

"We transfer my records to Chicago; I'll get a recommendation for a doctor there. How big is your apartment?" He told her it was three bedrooms and three baths. "Would you be alright with our mothers trading off to come stay with us? To help me while you're at work?" He nodded. "Then we should drive back. Shouldn't take more than a couple of days and we can leave right after my next doctor's appointment."

Sarabeth kissed them both. "I'm so happy you came, Leo. I feel so much better now that you're here. Amelia is in the best hands when she's in yours."

He cleared the table and carried her to the bathroom. Slowly peeling her clothes away, he took in the sight of Amelia's body, her rounded stomach clenching his heart in a vice of joy and fear. He whispered to the room, unaware he spoke out loud, "Please be alright. Please don't let anything happen to either of you." She touched his face and pulled him down for a kiss.

Bathing her in lukewarm water, then quickly bathing himself, he dried her and carried her to bed, tucking her in before turning off the lights and climbing in beside her. They talked for a long time, drifting off to sleep with Amelia's hands wrapped around his…which never left her belly.

Two days later he took her to her doctor's appointment and saw their child for the first time. He couldn't stop the tears that fell as everything sank in. They were going to have a baby. After all these years and so much sadness, they were going to have a baby.

They left the doctor and he rented a big comfortable car to drive them home, his mother beaming in the back. The look on Augusta's face coupled with the fact that Leo had to catch her when she fainted, was priceless. When she came around, she knelt on the floor in an expensive pant suit and heels and sobbed as she stroked her daughter's belly while Amelia smoothed her hand over her mother's hair.

# Chapter Ten

*Four months later...*

Leo left Amelia sleeping in bed and went to check on their son. Alejandro Daniel De La Cruz, Alex for short, was curled on his stomach with his legs tucked under his butt. He never tired of looking at their child or his child's beautiful mother.

Stroking his huge hand over the tiny head of curly black hair and down his back in the soft cotton pajamas, Leo knew there were no words to describe his gratitude.

Alex ate like clockwork so Leo scooped him up and nuzzled him close to carry him to Amelia. Laying the baby between them, her eyes fluttered open and she smiled. Curling one hand around Alex and tugging him to her breast, she used the other to pull Leo to her mouth. She kissed the father as she fed the son, feeling again the circle of completion she never thought she'd have.

Leo laid his head beside hers, watching as Alex breastfed. One arm moved under her neck and he stroked her bare back. He used his other hand to rake through Alex's hair, smoothing a fingertip over his cheek and smiling at the sucking movement he made.

His pink bow lips held her nipple firmly while his tiny fist opened and closed on the slope of Amelia's breast. He'd taken a thousand pictures of Amelia and Alex since his birth. He itched to get the camera and take another ten right now.

"He looks more like you every day, Leo. So perfect and tan. I'm jealous," she whispered, staring dazedly as she often did at their son.

"He'll have your eyes. I can't tell you how happy that makes me. I love your eyes *and* your flawless fair skin, Amelia." Already, the dark eye color Alex had been born with was getting lighter and the familiar green was beginning to show. "Amelia, thank you for being so brave and giving me Alex."

"You thank me every day, Leo. Thank you for loving me…for not giving up on me." He sifted his fingers through her hair, cupping the back of her skull and anchoring her for gentle kisses over her face. Pulling back, she asked, "Did you take today off, Leo?"

"Of course; you asked me to, baby. You never told me why."

"It's a surprise. Oops, he's done and sleeping." They looked down to watch as Alex barely had her nipple in his mouth, using it more like a pacifier. "He's so funny. Come here, baby boy." She sat up and lifted him to her chest, patting him gently until he burped. Laying him on his back between her legs, she checked his diaper. "Just pee. Aren't you so easy on Mommy first thing in the morning? Let's get you changed."

"You rest; I'll change him, Amelia."

"Um, Leo, you work. I don't right now. You should *not* have diaper duty, love." Alex opened his eyes and did a little raspberry sound. "Alex! You aren't on Daddy's side *already*?"

Leo chuckled, "He knows you're the one that keeps everything running. We can't wear you out. Besides, I love playing the *can I get the new diaper over him before he starts to pee* game. He hit the *wall* last time, Amelia. It was awesome."

She made a face and said, "Boys are gross. Yes, even you, Alex." She laughed and kissed both of them before standing and walking naked to the bathroom.

Turning back to remind Leo about Desitin, she caught him staring at her with his jaw clenched. "You need to stop torturing yourself by begging me to sleep nude, Leo. It shouldn't be too much longer."

Shaking his head as if to clear it, he said, "I'll wait as long as I have to, Amelia. The stress your body went through…we knew recovery was going to be longer than normal."

Two weeks before she was due to deliver, her uterus had begun to detach. She hadn't even been allowed to sit up the last few days. It was still unknown if they'd ever be able to have another child from her body but she was on birth control until an entire series of tests could be done in a year. Leo had been adamant: no more children until they could *guarantee* her safety and her body had been allowed to fully recover.

"You're so damn beautiful, Amelia. So long and sleek. I love looking at you."

"I'm roly-poly now, Leo. You're just biased. I love you. I'm going to shower. I have a follow-up with the doctor today. You'll be okay with the monkey?" He nodded and she grabbed a camera from the shelf over her chest of drawers, snapping several shots of Leo and their son in bed.

She'd discovered Leo was incredibly photogenic. The man simply didn't take a bad picture. Ever. Alex was of course the prettiest baby on the planet. She'd upload these to her computer later and add them to her rapidly growing collection.

Smiling, she put down the camera and went to shower; dressing in jeans and a t-shirt with sneakers. Checking on a sleeping Alex, she leaned in to kiss him as Leo came up behind her, wrapping his arms around her waist and guiding her from the room.

He leaned her against the wall in the hallway, sealing his chest to her back. He ran his hands over her sides, her hips, and her stomach. He stroked over the front of her body, his hands over her breasts while his thigh pressed up between her legs.

"Amelia, you smell fantastic. You feel so good and I miss you so much." She'd become so good at blowjobs she could make him come in seconds. He tried to keep her from doing it, feeling selfish when she hadn't been cleared for any kind of activity herself, but she often tackled him knowing he was afraid to hurt her.

Now he was rocking gently against her ass, watching as her face proclaimed her need. His voice was sensual in her ear as he said, "Tonight, I'm going to kiss and lick every inch of your body, Amelia, after I give you a massage. I want the taste of you in my mouth, on my tongue. I can't bear to be without you anymore. I'll be so gentle but I have to make you come. I can go without if I know you've come for me."

"Leo...?"

"Yes, baby?"

"I'm coming..." He felt her tighten under his hands, her body arching into the wall as he pressed into her back. He slid his hand between her breasts and up to cup her neck, feeling her pulse race beneath his palm, her breathing rapid against his wrist.

"Amelia, I miss you so fucking much." He laid his forehead on the back of her shoulder and she nodded with a whimper. He turned her in his arms. "A couple more months...we can do that, right?" She looked unsure and he smiled. "Remember senior year?"

Groaning, she wrapped her arms around him, hugging him tight. "Yeah, I know. But we made it through that...we can make it through this. God, baby, you really smell good." He pressed her into the wall and she stroked her hands up his bare back. He wore sleep pants and his erection was hard against her stomach.

Slipping her hands into the waist of the thin cotton, she stroked her palms around to his abdomen, dipping lower to reach for him. "No, Amelia. I can't bear it when you get nothing."

"Obviously, you don't *realize* what I get from it." She turned them, dropping to her knees and sliding his pants out of her way, nudging his legs apart as she took him to the back of her throat. Sucking him and stroking the base hard, she cupped his balls in her other hand and squeezed firmly, rubbing the patch of skin behind them with one finger, pressing in rhythm with her mouth.

"Amelia, oh God, baby." His hands were fisted in her hair as he watched her suck his cock. Her dark pink lips expanding to take him again and again. "Honey, that's so good. So fucking good. I'm coming, honey, I'm already coming."

As the first jet of hot semen hit her mouth, she increased the strength and speed she used on him, working with the rocking of his hips.

"God, yes, Amelia...oh sweet baby. Your throat is milking me so hard." She drank him down, swallowing around the head and feeling every throb of his cock against her lips and tongue. When he'd given her everything he had, she continued to suck and lick him, pulling back to kiss the head with a smile.

Rising to her feet, she pulled his pants into place and kissed her way up his stomach and chest. Stroking her hands over the hard lines of his abdomen, she pulled him down for a kiss and he tasted himself on her. He claimed her mouth aggressively, his hands wrapping tight in her hair.

Pulling her back, he asked roughly, "When is your appointment, Amelia?"

Glancing at her watch, she said breathlessly, "Forty minutes."

"Not enough time, damn it!" He kissed her again and moaned into her mouth. "I want to taste you so bad, baby. So bad it hurts. You need to get back soon. I'm stripping you down and eating your sweet pussy for hours, Amelia. I know I can't make love to you yet, but I can make you come until you're weak with it. Until you can't move from the exhaustion of coming, until I'm drunk from the taste of you."

She rocked her hips against him and he whispered, "Are you wet, Amelia?" She nodded. His hands went to the waist of her jeans and he had them undone, his hand inside her panties, in seconds.

Stroking into her cleft, he slid along her folds and slipped one finger carefully inside her as his thumb worked in small circles over her clit. "You *are* wet...dripping wet for me, Amelia." He growled from deep in his chest and watched her face as he touched her.

"I want you to come for me, baby. To feel you come for me. I need it more than air." She moved in rhythm with his hand and reached forward to stroke his cock through his pants. "I'm hard for you again, always for you, Amelia. I can't wait to bury my cock in your tight pussy and fuck you until you're screaming. Until then, I'm going to eat you constantly. Stroking into you with my fingers while I suck your clit between my lips. Every time I make you come, I'll fuck you with my tongue so I taste all of you. You're tightening, Amelia...are you about to come?" She nodded, her hand working urgently over his cock. "Tell me, baby."

"I'm coming so hard, Leo. I want your cock inside me so bad, Leo…*so bad*. Yes, god yes, I'm coming." He felt her go tight around him, felt the rush of her liquid heat over his hand, and arched into her stroking palm, coming with her as she collapsed against his chest. "Leo, I miss you."

Leo pulled his hand from her panties and sucked her juices from his fingers. "Amelia, you taste so good." He dropped his head against the wall and clutched her to him. "I loved you to distraction as a teenager and it boggles my mind how much more I love you today." He kissed her hair and strands clung to his morning stubble.

"You'd think it would weaken me but it makes me feel so strong. If I don't stand up and take my hands off you, Amelia, I'm not letting you out of this apartment. It's taking everything I have not to throw you over my shoulder and carry you to bed." He lifted her off him, smiling at the contented expression on her face. "You look so relaxed. Hurry back, Amelia. The car should be waiting downstairs."

Taking a deep breath, she said, "Pack a bag while I'm gone for each of us? We're heading to Springfield when I get back."

He raised his brows. "We're going to see our parents?" She nodded and he gave a deep sigh.

"Don't look so thrilled. They haven't seen Alex in two weeks. Do you know how much a baby his age changes in two weeks?" She went up on tip-toe and kissed him hard. "I won't be long."

Leo watched her leave with longing, wanting to keep her in the warmth and safety of his arms. There were days his protective instincts rode him hard and he could barely handle her being more than arms' length from him. They'd been through so much; fear of losing her or their child was his constant companion.

He checked on Alex and went to shower and dress. Peeking in on his sleeping son once more, he pulled their bags from the hall closet and went to pack. Leo had always liked packing for her. Amelia liked knowing that anything she took out of the suitcase was something he'd picked.

When his son woke from his morning nap, Leo brought him into the bedroom and worked with one hand while he talked to the tiny little person man-to-man. Unlike many young fathers, he didn't mind being left alone with Alex. He felt like they understood one another already. Serious eyes peered up at him as he spoke and Leo grinned.

"Your mom is the best and we're both very lucky to have her. When you're all grown up, I'm going to tell you the story about how much she risked so I could hold you in my arms." A small grunt followed by a familiar odor had Leo wrinkling his nose. "In the meantime, it seems *someone* has been only pretending to listen to me while concentrating on an important diaper development. May I simply say *eww*, little man?" After changing and dressing him, Leo finished and had the valet take down their luggage. Alex's diaper bag was waiting on the foyer table.

Two hours later, she walked in the door with a couple of bags and food for him from his favorite deli. His smile for her spoke loudly of the hunger he felt. She looked delicious and windswept. "You look like you've been getting into trouble, Amelia. That is quite the smug expression on your face, baby."

Allowing him only a small smile, she told him, "I plead the fifth. Tell me we're ready to go. I want to get there by the afternoon." She'd set down the bags from stores he didn't recognize and stood with her hands on her hips.

"Everything is already in your Volvo...except the baby, of course. In a rush?"

"Leo, I'm in such a rush that I plan on driving so you can eat on the way. Don't touch these bags. Surprises and you know how much I love surprising you." She reached down into the brightly patterned pack-n-play sitting in the middle of their stylish living room and came out with a cooing Alex. "Quick lunch for you, sweet baby, and then we are so out of here."

Leo watched as she settled in a thick chair by the window and breastfed their son. Grabbing the camera, he took several pictures. He busied himself checking the house and calling downstairs to remind the manager they'd be away for the weekend, to please keep an eye on the place.

When Alex was done, she made quick work of burping him. Glancing up at the man who never failed to make her heart race, she whispered, "Move, baby. I need you to hustle that fine ass to the car. Nope, take Alex; I'll get the bags, sneaky."

He laughed at getting busted and they were downstairs a few minutes later, pulling out of the parking garage as Leo ate his favorite Mediterranean sub from the best deli in the city. After it was demolished, he focused on trying to get details about his surprise out of her.

Amelia refused to budge and threatened to make him drive so she could put in her headphones if he didn't behave. He turned the conversation with a grumble and soon they were laughing and talking about everything and nothing at all.

Three hours later, they pulled into his parents' driveway and she grabbed one of the bags as well as Alex's diaper bag as Leo unbuckled the sleeping baby. Going around to the kitchen, he wasn't surprised to see Augusta waiting with his parents for them as well. Alex was immediately snatched from his arms and abducted to the living room by the grandparents.

Opening the larger bag, Amelia pulled out several bottles filled with milk. "Is that breast milk?" She nodded but offered nothing else. "Um, are we staying here while we're visiting?" Leo loved his parents but treasured the cocoon he and Amelia had built around themselves.

Turning to him, she answered, "Alex is. Mom is staying over here to help with him while we take a mini vacation. Since they're just up the road, it's close enough for me not to freak out." With a half-smile, she added, "I need to take baby steps, Leo. I'm not ready to be too far away." She didn't wait for him to process everything she was telling him.

He followed as she ran into the other room. She snuggled their son for a long moment and told him she loved him then kissed each beaming grandparent on the cheek, waiting for Leo to do the same before she dragged him out the door.

She drove like she was in a race to her old house and took out the bags she'd brought while Leo grabbed their one suitcase. "Listen, there are two or three things I have to do. Doctor's orders. That means I need some private bathroom time, alright?"

Immediate worry slammed into Leo's chest. "Are you alright?"

"I will be. It's just a precaution. We'll talk when I get out." She set a bag on the counter and said, "There is stuff to go in the fridge in this bag, will you put it away for me?" He nodded, feeling increasingly more confused and worried by the moment.

What could the doctor have found? Could she be sick?

He was trying to relax in the living room, watching football and pointedly *not* worrying before they could talk, when he heard a low whistle behind him. Glancing up the stairs, he was sure his heart stopped when he saw Amelia and absently shut off the television.

She wore nothing but a black velvet choker around her neck, black high heels, and a smile. As he moved toward her, he took in the sight of her long body, curvy in all the right places. She was stunning.

"Amelia, I'm only human." He was three steps below her when he bent to run his lips from her ankle to her thigh. His hands on her hips, he clenched his jaw in agony.

"Leo, honey, I have a prescription Dr. Evans gave me. Can you take care of it for me?" She held out a prescription pad from Amelia's OB/GYN and he took it, wondering if he was going to have to run to the pharmacy right *now*.

Turning it around to read it, he recognized the doctor's handwriting, "*Leo, all is well. Better than when we started actually. Not sure yet about future pregnancies but I can vouch for her good health and complete recovery. I'm proud of all the work you've both put in to keep her safe. Now, I need you to do something to ensure her mental state is as healthy as her physical condition. Leo…make love to your wife. She's driving me insane. Enjoy! Dr. Evans.*"

Leo looked at the paper, then at Amelia. He glanced at the paper again and she couldn't help but smile. "Leo?" He tilted his head as he stared at her. "Doctor's orders, Leo. I'm so not kidding." He let the note drift from his hand and swept Amelia into his arms. Carrying her to the bedroom, he stood her beside the bed as he stripped his clothes away faster than she'd ever seen.

Pushing her to sit, he knelt in front of her, his cock standing proudly erect between them and ran his fingers up her calves. At the backs of her knees, he moved to the front and ran his entire hands over the tops of her thighs before sliding them to the inside and nudging her legs apart.

He kissed her inner thighs, his hand pushing her back until she was propped on her elbows watching him. When his mouth kissed along the crease of her hip, she sucked air through her teeth and he smiled. Back and forth across her pelvis he licked and kissed her, watching her eyes darken with passion.

Amelia was most self conscious of the scars on her low abdomen, thinking they marred her and added to the overall softness she saw in herself. Her belly *was* softer, not hard like it was before she'd brought their son into the world and he loved knowing *why* she was soft.

"Amelia, you have the most naturally beautiful body I've ever seen in my life." He ran his hands over her legs, "These are the longest legs, so toned and flawless. Silken skin over every inch. I love these heels…that you can wear them with such grace as tall as you are and still be shorter than me." He moved the backs of his knuckles over her bare mound. "I love that I can see every inch of you, every fold of your perfect pink pussy. Nothing takes away from being able to worship you with my hands and mouth."

Leo set his lips against her, licking gently along the folds, using one hand to separate her and bare her clit to his attention. "I have *missed* you, Amelia. Do you realize it's been almost ten months since I've eaten this beautiful pussy? Since I've been able to lick and suck you until you're begging to be fucked?"

He ran his tongue from her pussy to her clit. "You showered…I can't taste your come from earlier. When I showered after you left, I rested my face on my hand so I could smell you while I stroked off, thinking about all the things I wanted to do to you. Remembering how well you sucked my cock before you left. I came so hard my legs almost gave out."

Leo slid two fingers into her rapidly slickening channel, feeling Amelia tighten around him. "You're sucking at my fingers, baby, trying to keep me inside you." He curled his fingers against the top of her pussy as he withdrew and watched her head drop back on her shoulders.

"I love watching you, Amelia. Watching you embrace the passionate person you are and letting your sensual side take over. Pleasing you, watching you enjoy it, means more to me than coming myself."

Setting a rhythm with his fingers, he matched it with his tongue over her swollen clit, swirling around the hard nub with the tip before sucking it between his lips. He felt her getting wetter, saw her entire body beginning to tighten. He increased his speed, licking and sucking her harder as he thrust faster into her body.

She climaxed hard, arching forward with her taut nipples thrust in the air, begging to be sucked. As she began to settle, she brought her face up to stare at him, breathing rapidly.

He smiled at her up the length of her torso, "Again, baby. Once is *never* enough." He pulled his fingers from her pussy and rubbed her juices over her folds before returning them to stroke more firmly as he licked every drop away.

Amelia watched him eat her, trying to bring her thighs together as the need to come built in her again. One of her hands went into his hair, tugging the strands before smoothing them back. When the orgasm crashed over her, spreading through her body like fire, she held him to her, working her hips against his mouth. He dragged it out for a long time, loving the way her body moved.

"Leo, I need you so bad, baby. Please, I need you inside me. I've missed you so much. Now. Take me now." She followed his hand as he pulled from her and stroked his cock, smearing her natural lubrication over the length with his fist. He rose over her, sliding his engorged length through the wetness gathered between her thighs.

Bending, he took her nipple between his lips and sucked, tasting the sweet milk she gave their son. His eyes widened in surprise as it hit him with an erotic punch. She saw the affect it had on him and looked surprised. "I thought that would gross you out."

"Would it gross *you* out if I did it *again*?" She shook her head slowly as he lowered his mouth to the other nipple and sucked her hard, swallowing the milk and tugging her with his teeth.

When she arched into him with a moan, he repeated the movement on the other side. All the while, he continued to slide the hard ridge of his cock along her wet cleft. He lifted his head to stare at her, "That is *crazy* hot. Is that weird?"

"It feels so *different* when you do it. It shoots tingles all over my body. Maybe it's because you have teeth and stubble. That feels *really* good, Leo. Does it…taste funny?" He lowered his head and sucked her again, moving to kiss her with the milk on his tongue.

She gripped the back of his head hard when he went to pull away, taking his lower lip between her teeth. He settled over her, her long legs going around his waist as Amelia's mouth made love to his. Grinding her hips into his pelvis, he positioned himself at the entrance of her pussy and slid carefully into the tight channel, slick and hot as it clamped around him.

"Amelia, how I have *missed* the feel of you around me." He moved gently, rotating his hips into her, the motion grinding his pelvic bone against her clit. Then she was coming, flooding him with her warm juices and gripping him with her entire body.

"Yes, honey, I have so much to thank you for…so many pleasures to give you for everything you've given me. Every time you've sucked me, I've wanted to return the favor, to make you feel as good as you've made me feel. At last, I can catch up. I can push you into one climax after another. It feels so good when you come with me inside you. You get so tight, milk me so hard. When you suck me and swallow around me with your throat, I think of so many things I'm thankful for. Buried inside your beautiful body is the only place I ever want to be. It's exactly where I belong, Amelia."

He extended one arm to lift from her upper body and pulled her thigh wider with his hand inside her knee. "Watch me take you, Amelia." She went up on her elbows, her eyes focused where they were joined, watching as he stroked deeply into her body, pulling out almost all the way – his cock slick with her come – before sinking into her again.

Five strokes, ten and she was coming, her hands on his hard shoulders as she collapsed against the bed. Tugging then, her arms and shoulders tight and toned, her torso snug where she bent to keep watching him fuck her. "You are so beautiful, it hurts, Amelia."

She raised her eyes to his and whispered, "Take me hard, Leo. I want to feel you come fucking me hard." His eyes glazed over and he went up on his knees, taking both of hers over his elbows and lifting her ass off the bed. He held her in place by the tops of her thighs. One leg was raised so he could kiss her foot, still encased in the sexy heels.

His eyes were pure desire as he anchored his gaze to hers. Moving only his hips, he powered into her, watching her writhe beneath him. "Play with your clit, Amelia. Let me watch you play with yourself while I fuck your sweet pussy." Her hand slid flat down her body, her palm on her low abdomen as she placed two fingers over her clit, stroking in the same tempo as his cock. "Oh my god, baby...*yes*, that is so beautiful. Come for me again, I can't hold back much longer."

She increased her speed as he did and she was climaxing from the dual stimulation, screaming his name, lifting her body higher from the bed as he plunged as deeply as possible and shattered, roaring, "*Amelia!*" to the empty house.

He continued to thrust and as the last of his seed left him, he released her knees and settled into the cradle of her body, still buried to the root. "I'll never be able to show you how much I love you. It keeps growing every day."

She cupped his face and kissed him with all the emotion inside her. "I love *you*, Leo. Thank you for giving me the life I thought I'd lost. Thank you for believing in me."

He stared down into the eyes of the woman he'd once thought was lost to him forever. Turning to his side he pulled her against him. As they both began drifting to sleep, he whispered, "Amelia, agreeing to tutor you was the most brilliant decision I ever made."

Leo heard two light thumps against the carpet. She laughed and whispered back, "My most recent brilliant decision was *definitely* buying these shoes."

# Coming Home

## *Novella Three*

### Chapter One

*Age Eighteen*

Rowan Foxe was sneaking out to see him at last. She prayed the dogs on the property bordering this one wouldn't start going crazy. Hounds could be heard for a mile. She'd gone out her bedroom window on the second floor and climbed the maple tree that grew along the back porch.

The scariest part was running across the cleared yard to the fence then crouching along that to the road. Once she'd made it to the road, walking the narrow two-lane track toward his property had taken time but it wasn't hard.

Gage Chambers had refused to sleep with her until her eighteenth birthday. With him being four years older, he said he didn't want to risk it. She'd been talking to Nina for weeks about how to get out at night, in preparation for this.

A few months older, Nina had seen it all and done it all. She was Rowan's go-to person on every topic and her best friend. She'd snuck out a couple of hours before, telling Rowan she'd see her in the morning and they would go together to the bus station. Nina never believed good girl Rowan would actually sneak out.

They both lived at the girls' home with other girls who had nowhere to go and were in danger of ending up on the back of milk cartons.

She'd just graduated high school and she planned on celebrating her embarkation into adulthood by giving Gage Chambers her virginity.

She'd worked her ass off to win a scholarship to the University of Texas. With her grades, a glowing recommendation from the woman who ran the home, and several charities she volunteered for – she was leaving tomorrow to get a college education.

On her way to a future she never thought she'd have when she was ten. Rowan had been found wandering the streets of Dallas with a major head injury. To this day she had no memory of anything before opening her eyes in the hospital.

Gage and his family volunteered time and money to the home – they had for decades. Fixing things, supplying necessary items like food and medicine, and bringing presents at Christmas were just some of the differences they'd made in the lives of the girls who lived here. The Chambers were good people, kind and generous, who owned Chambers Cattle Company a couple of miles up the road.

She had no illusions that Gage was going to marry her or give her a happily ever after. Rowan wasn't naïve. She just wanted this one memory to be with someone who knew what they were doing. Someone who wouldn't hurt her or make it awful.

She saw the gate to the Chambers' land and took the smaller of the two entrances, making her way along the cattle fence, thinking again how pretty it was here. The moon lit up the fields and gave everything a supernatural glow. The tree line was dark and she could see the huge main house standing bright and elegant two hundred yards away.

Her destination was the converted barn with lights glowing in the second floor windows. That was Gage's apartment. She made her way steadily, butterflies in her stomach, to the open doors of the lower level that still housed horses.

Taking the stairway in the back, she was quiet as she entered the open doorway and climbed the steps. There was noise on the second floor and she imagined him waiting for her, maybe thinking about her. Nothing romantic, he didn't seem the type...she really wasn't either. Just waiting for her, maybe watching television or...whatever else men did when they were alone.

At the top, there was a rail open to the main living area and music was playing. She didn't see anyone so she went all the way up. Rowan heard his voice and followed the sound to a large open doorway.

Nina was naked and riding Gage's equally naked body with his hands on her hips as he gave her soft encouragement. "That feels *so* good, Nina...so damn good. Oh, yeah, just like that, baby."

Nina's blond hair trailed straight down her golden back, brushing the top of her bare ass. She had a cute butt, small breasts, and a body that was long and lean. A couple of inches taller than Rowan's five-six, Nina still seemed more *delicate* somehow. It was a quality that drew boys and men alike to her like bears to honey.

The nervous butterflies that had been foreign to someone like Rowan evaporated in an instant and the sarcastic bitch that lived inside her, who helped her survive, came forward to save her dignity.

She said clearly and loudly, "Wow, *good form*, Nina."

Both of them jumped like a gun had gone off, turning to her with panic on their faces. Nina pulled the sheet over her breasts and whispered desperately, "Rowan, *please* let me explain. I *can* explain." Her chocolate brown eyes were wide with shock as she stared at her best friend over her shoulder.

With a grim smile, Rowan replied, "No need. I'm pretty sure I get the idea. I'm not *that* innocent, Nina." Gage kept his eyes on Rowan as he lifted Nina off him and set her to the side gently, standing to face her in all his naked glory. Six-three with a gorgeous sculpted lean frame, chestnut brown hair, and light hazel eyes. Putting on her most condescending expression, she told him, "Honestly, don't get up on *my* account, Gage."

"Rowan, let me talk to you. Let me explain this. I don't want bad feelings between us." His voice was like honey, flavored with the accent of deep Texas and calm from his years of handling skittish cattle. It was the wrong tone to use on a pissed off Rowan.

"Bad feelings, Gage? There would have to *be* feelings first, wouldn't there? Since you *have* none and mine don't matter, I don't think there's anything to discuss, do you?"

Sliding her gaze slowly down his body, she took in his rapidly deflating dick, though still much more than she'd realized he was packing, and said with a smug smile, "You're losing your condom, Gage. Funny I'd have *that* affect, isn't it? Sorry to make you waste one but it's good to know you're practicing safe sex. Y'all have a good night."

She turned to go and he grabbed her arm. "Get your hand *off me*, Gage. You *gave up* your right to touch me when you lied and pretended to be a man you so obviously are not." He dropped his hand as if he'd been slapped.

"Nina, let's say goodbye now, shall we? No need to go on pretending you're my fucking friend. How you both must have *laughed* at my stupidity. Mark my words; you'll never have reason to laugh at me again."

Nina had the grace to look ashamed. Were those tears in her eyes? Impressive.

"Rowan, we need to talk. Let me drive you back. Please. I don't want you walking the road. It's so late." He held his hands out in a supplicating gesture, trying to appear harmless.

Poisonous snakes were harmless compared to him. He'd hurt her more than anyone else could have. Though she knew she'd have never been good enough, that anything with him would have been temporary, she'd been in love with him for years. She would never tell him, never give him that power over her. He'd been her weakness and she'd just learned a valuable lesson.

"How the *fuck* do you think I got here, Gage? Please. At this point, I'd almost welcome some lonely man on the road. Virginity is highly overrated." He gasped and reached for her again. "Keep your fucking hands to yourself. You forget that I know where they've *been*, Gage. You *touch me* with that bitch's fluids on you and you'll never have to worry about condoms again."

She turned and ran as fast as she could for the stairs, reaching the bottom floor at her top speed which was something some of the best runners in the district had been trying to beat for years. As she exploded to the outside, she heard running down the stairs and put on an extra burst of power, thankful she'd worn sneakers. She ran for the fence instead of the road, vaulted the iron bars with one hand on the top rail, and hauled ass for the nearest tree line.

Gage began to call behind her, begging her to stop, but she never even slowed down. Entering the trees, she got into the deepest darkness she could and sat down with her head on her knees to wait him out.

He wouldn't look for her long. After all, he had a naked and willing woman already warming his bed. He didn't need her.

She underestimated his determination. He walked through the woods calling to her. "Rowan, I'm so sorry. Please come back. Let me talk to you. Please, baby. I fucked up so bad but I can fix it. I don't want you out here all alone in the dark. I know how you hate the dark, Rowan."

*Well, thanks for reminding me about that*, she thought snarkily.

"Rowan, I know you wouldn't have gone far into the trees. You wouldn't. I know you can hear me, sweet girl. Please let me at least drive you back. Don't sit out here like this." She listened to him move back and forth as he searched for her. She wondered how long he'd keep up the pretense of caring one way or another.

Then he shocked her by saying, "We were both waiting for you, Rowan. I…I've been sleeping with Nina for months. I was dying for you, trying to wait for you, and it just happened. She told me she's in love with you, Rowan. We didn't think you were coming. I'm so sorry, please forgive me." He mumbled something about her being in dark clothes and how black her hair was. "Please come out and let me take you home if that's what you want. Or you can stay and let us explain."

*Not on your fucking life*, drifted through her mind.

"I won't give up on you, Rowan. I need you. Please come out…" He continued to call for her, pleading with her to listen, to let him explain. He told her he loved her, that she was the one he'd always loved. She said nothing, letting silent tears fall on her raised knees.

# Chapter Two

The stress of sneaking out, the hurt from finding the two people she loved most together, and how hard she'd run from them had completely wiped her out. She didn't realize she'd fallen asleep until she was being picked up off the ground in the early dawn light.

Gage was carrying her out of the woods. "Don't run, Rowan. I've been worried sick waiting for light. I...I went back to shower and get dressed. Please don't run."

She kept her body stiff in his arms when only yesterday she would have given anything to find herself right here. "Put me down," her voice wasn't as strong as she would have liked but it couldn't be called weak either.

His arms tightened around her, "No, Rowan, you haven't eaten and you slept in the woods all night. You're a nervous wreck. I just want to help you. I'm not going to hurt you, honey." He stared into electric blue eyes set in a strong jawed face that featured the fullest red lips he'd ever seen. Long black hair and olive toned skin that he imagined covered every inch of her curvy frame. For a runner, she had more tits and ass than one would think. Considering how fast she was, the curves obviously didn't slow her down.

"Too late to worry about hurting me and don't *ever* call me honey again." She started to fight and he had no choice but to put her on her feet or risk dropping her. "Why are you even *here*, Gage? You have one idiot girl to fuck...two is just greedy."

She yanked her arm from his grasp and stormed ahead. Just before she hit open field, he grabbed her arm and spun her around, folding her in his arms and dropping his mouth over hers.

For one minute, she let herself feel what it could have been like, to experience what she'd been dreaming of for years. His strong arms around her, passionate kisses, the warm masculine smell of Gage's skin. It was her first kiss and she'd always wanted him to be the one to give it to her. He felt so good, so right, and she hated herself for still wanting him. Hated how much she loved the feel of his hard body against her and the warm cinnamon taste of his mouth.

When she sighed against him, he misunderstood it for giving in. In reality, she was letting him go. Letting her heart break in small pieces because she could never, ever keep him. She shifted and drove her thigh into his groin. Not hard enough to injure him but hard enough to double him over and give her a five minute head start.

Her voice was hoarse with the agony of heartbreak, struggling to hold back tears that wanted so badly to fall. "I told you not to touch me, Gage." As she stepped away, she wrapped her arms around her upper body. "I may not be much. I come from nothing and I have nothing but my word to my name."

Dropping her arms and straightening, she looked into his beautiful eyes. "I'm going to give you my word. I will never let myself *need* another man. I will never weaken my heart again. I will never allow another man close enough to me to hurt me as you have, Gage."

"Rowan, don't do this..." he said through teeth gritted in pain.

"I wasn't stupid, it's not like I expected you to marry me like fucking Prince Charming...but as white trash as I am, I deserved *better than this*. I didn't do anything to deserve being treated like the nothing I come from. I thought you were a better man than this and I was so wrong about you, about so many things. I'm through with you, Gage, before I ever had a chance to get started. I wish you luck in your life. I hope to hell you grow up."

She turned and ran hard for the road, cutting and heading for the home. By the time it came into sight, she ran an easy jog. Miss Jeffries stood on the front porch with her hand shielding her eyes from the first rays on the horizon. "Hey there, Rowan. You run so pretty. Have you seen Nina?"

Words coming in gasps from running and trying not to cry, she answered, "No ma'am. I'll run out to look for her if you like. I was going to shower and get ready for the bus."

The warmth of this woman's smile seeped through some of the hurt and the cold. She was deceptively soft and sweet; it hid a core of steel. "That's okay. Y'all are eighteen and startin' your new lives today. She'll be alright. If I don't see her by breakfast, I'll start to look around." The elderly woman turned to Rowan as she came up the porch steps. "Are you excited, Rowan?"

"I've never been so excited to just *get on with it* as I am right now, Miss Jeffries." As she said the words, Rowan knew they were true. She hugged Miss Jeffries tight. "I'll sure miss you and your fresh biscuits though, ma'am. I really will." One quick kiss on her wrinkled cheek and Rowan darted into the house before she started sobbing out her troubles to the one person always willing to hear them.

Heading to her room, she gathered her belongings and packed them in the large duffle bag provided to them – funny enough – by the Chambers family in order to start their futures. She worked quickly but methodically, folding each item neatly and packing it carefully because she had so few items to take with her. Stripping naked, she put her dirty clothes in a plastic bag and took a clean outfit with her into the bathroom.

Once she'd showered and dressed in jeans and a Texas Rangers t-shirt, she went over her half of the little bedroom she'd shared with Nina, the only other eighteen-year-old in the home. Leaving a letter that had made her cry while she wrote it on Nina's pillow, she said goodbye to the only home she remembered.

The next two oldest girls would get this room as soon as she and Nina were gone. Picking up the duffle bag, she went downstairs. Miss Jeffries handed her a plate with breakfast on it and she sat at the little table in the kitchen that was only big enough for three people. They talked about the other girls and Rowan felt the loving chatter smooth over her frayed nerves. She ate quickly and washed everything she'd used, refilling Miss Jeffries cup of coffee while she drank the last of her milk.

Taking a worn baseball cap from her back pocket, she pulled her long ponytail through it. From a small purse she'd had since she was fourteen, she pulled out her sunglasses and bus ticket, checking everything one more time before slipping the shades in place and bending to kiss Miss Jeffries' cheek once more.

Rowan lingered, inhaling the vanilla scent of the woman who'd raised, healed, cooked, and cared for young women her entire adult life. Pulling back to look at the only mother figure she'd ever known, she added, "I want to thank you for all you've done for me over the years. For the big things and so many little things. If you ever need me, I'll come back. I give you my word."

Miss Jeffries stroked a wrinkled hand down Rowan's face and smiled when the girl leaned into it, "You are so lovely, honey. I think you and Nina are the prettiest girls I've ever seen. You're the two I always counted on with the younger ones. The two who did the most volunteer work. I'm so proud of the young women you've become. I might hold you to that promise one day."

"Thank you, ma'am. I'll always come when you need me."

"Please be careful out in the world, Rowan. I've worked real hard to make sure you made it to eighteen in one piece. Don't make all my hard work count for nothin', you hear?" Rowan shook her head with a small smile and stood. "Goodbye, sweet girl."

"Goodbye, ma'am." Rowan picked up her duffle bag and backpack, leaving the kitchen. All the younger girls were away at church camp this week. She'd written notes for them yesterday and left them on their pillows with small gifts. Looking around her, she absorbed the feel of the place and her heart clenched in her chest, making her sigh.

Backing through the screen door, she bumped into someone and turned. Gage stood with a pained look on his face. "Back for more? *Move.*" He stepped back and she turned, taking in the sight of Nina on the other side of the porch. "Good luck, Nina. This fuck aside, I really loved you, girl." Slinging her bag over her shoulder, she added, "Y'all take care."

"Rowan, I'm taking Nina into town. Wait and I'll drive you. Please let me do that at least." Without turning back she waved at them and kept walking. "*Rowan...*" Gage whispered as he watched her get smaller and smaller on the road. When she disappeared, he pressed his thumb and forefinger into his eyes. "Gone. I was the first man she loved and

I broke her. I've lost her now."

"No less than you deserve, young man," Miss Jeffries said firmly from her position behind the screen door. Nina gasped and put her hand over her mouth as her guardian stepped out on the porch. They watched the older woman close her eyes and inhale deeply of the morning air, hands clasping one another.

When she opened her eyes, her voice was firm but not angry or judgmental. "Of course I know what you've been up to, Nina. You broke her heart as sure as Gage did. What did y'all think was gonna happen? That a virginal eighteen-year-old was going to say *sure let's have a threesome*? Nina, you're in a different place sexually than Rowan is but surely you know that would have scared her to death. Gage, you should have known better on *all* counts than to mess with either of these girls." Smiling gently at Nina, she said, "You're going to miss your bus if you don't get movin', honey."

The blond nodded and slipped past Miss Jeffries, going upstairs to shower, change, and pack. When she was out of hearing range, Annabelle Jeffries turned to the man standing on her porch with his head down and his hands on his hips.

"Gage, I've known you since you were born to two of the finest people I've ever known. You gambled and you'll lose them both because of it. They're too young for you and they've been hurt *enough* in their short lives. They aren't here on *vacation*, son." She patted his arm.

"Girls don't end up at my door treated either gently or well. For the last four years, since we got Nina, those two have been closer than any of my girls before. Figures it'd be a man who'd come between them. Let them get their educations, get their feet under them, and if someday you get another chance, treat them both better than you have today. Your life is charmed but you need to remember it is the *exception*, not the rule." Another pat and she chuckled, "I'm gettin' off my soap box now, Gage. Make sure Nina gets to her bus, please."

She went back inside and he listened as Nina came down a few minutes later and Miss Jeffries forced her to eat something. He could hear the soft sounds of them talking while Nina ate breakfast.

Nina was teary-eyed when she came out on the porch. She was so lovely, so broken on the inside, and he'd used her as surely as the men who'd come before him had. He wasn't in love with Nina but he liked her very much as a person. His decisions these past months would haunt him.

Gage took her bag and helped her up into his truck. When he climbed behind the wheel, she met his eyes and said, "We made so many mistakes. She left me a letter." He took it from her, noting his hand was shaking.

*"Nina…pretty golden Nina, by the time you get this, I'll be gone. I'm taking an earlier bus so there's no chance I'll run into either of you at the station. I've always loved you, from the first day you came to live with us. Girls like us react in one of two ways to our pasts, we get stronger…harder, I guess. Like me. The other reaction is you, Nina. Fragile and beautiful. Your heart is delicate and you love so easily. I can imagine how conflicted you were every time you went to Gage. Knowing I loved you…wanting him to love you, too. After what you came from, my only hope is he treated you gently and wiped away some of your painful memories. If he managed to do that for you, sweet Nina, I won't hate him. I'm sorry I called you a bitch. It was wrong and you deserved better from me.*

*"I fell in love with Gage when I was twelve years old. He was everything strong and beautiful I wanted to be myself one day. I thought he was a man of his word and it cuts deep to learn he's like every other man. I never imagined our time would last forever. I would never presume someone like me would ever be accepted in the life of a man like Gage. Honestly, I wanted him to love me once and love me well, to make sure I wasn't afraid…I hate being afraid, Nina. For him to have a part of me no one else could ever have because I admired him…loved him…long before I knew what it was to lust after him.*

*"I wish you only good things, Nina. Not because we're both so damaged but because I believe one day we won't be anymore. Find the strength in yourself, Nina. Don't give your heart away so easily or you'll get it broken again and again. While you find your strength, I'll try to find the softness I crush from inside myself so no one can hurt me.*

*"I ask one favor. Please leave me my dignity. I hate crying more than anything. Maybe one day, we'll meet again. I have a feeling I'm not done with the home…that it will figure into my future somehow. By the time that happens, Gage will be married to some pretty socialite and have six precious children. I think that will be*

*a relief actually. Go strong, Nina and maybe kiss him once for me. Sending you love from a tiny soft place I keep hidden behind the walls of my heart. Rowan"*

Gage handed back her letter with tears tracking down his cheeks. He stared through the windshield, thinking about Rowan. "I'm so sorry, Nina. This went so wrong. I damn well knew better." She nodded and he wiped his face, putting the truck in gear. "One day, I'll have a way to fix it. Until then, I'll try to become the man she always thought I was."

He took her to the bus station and Nina kissed him twice, once for herself and once for Rowan.

# **Chapter Three**

*Age Twenty-Two*

College was made for a driven woman like Rowan. She had no friends and she went out of her way to keep it that way. She bent all her focus, all her will, to getting her education. She had no intention of abusing the opportunity she'd been given. She wasn't going to disappoint people like Miss Jeffries who had made it possible for her to have a future.

Her formal graduation was in a week but she was done with her classes and her finals. Technically, she was already a graduate. Soon, she'd have her degree in finance and could start searching for a job that paid more than retail.

Her world was hers to command and that was just the way she liked it.

She regularly corresponded with Miss Jeffries, keeping up with what was going on at the home for girls. They actually wrote letters since the elderly woman didn't have a computer.

Gage and Nina sent her emails sometimes. Gage was running the cattle business for his dad and Nina was getting her degree in marketing out in California. She wrote them back but never told them anything personal about her life or asked them personal questions about themselves.

The four years since that night had given her some perspective. The three of them had been young and more than a little bit foolish. She didn't hurt as much as she had the first year when memories of Gage or Nina could bring on unexpected tears. Every year it got better but sometimes she dreamed about Gage and woke aching so badly in the morning she wanted to kick herself.

Rowan jogged from the campus bookstore along the huge box hedge that lined much of the property. She'd just sold back the last of her text books and was calculating her finances happily. As frugal as she was with every penny, her job at the local book store chain had provided a small nest egg that would let her get an efficiency apartment while she hunted for a permanent job. Leaving chaotic dorm life behind was going to be heavenly. She valued her privacy and quiet.

Running along the hedge, she was approaching a hidden drive when a limo pulled out directly in front of her. She was going too fast to stop and didn't want to take the hit in her legs. Twisting with a small jump, she slid over the hood on her butt and landed in a hard crouch on the other side. She could tell right away that she'd sprained her ankle and gritted through the sharp pain.

Car doors were opening and then two people were standing over her. "I'm fine, honestly. Please, I'm fine." Showing weakness *ever* was humiliating and grated against her fierce independence.

There was a small chuckle followed by a cultured voice saying, "Well, you just went over the hood of the car like a stunt woman. James, help her up please."

A very large golden man lifted her smoothly to her feet as if she was no bigger than a toddler and held her while she tried to stand. James was almost a foot taller than her, and his coloring reminded her of Nina. Both men watched as she tried to play off the sprain.

"Your ankle is injured," the driver pointed out. Rather unnecessarily in Rowan's opinion.

She took a deep breath. "It's probably just a *cramp*. Really, *no* reason to worry." She looked up and met the prettiest green eyes she'd ever seen in the face of an older man with black hair silvering at the temples. "You're Bennett Jefferson," she said in a quiet voice.

He nodded and waited for her to begin faking injuries left and right. She said instead, "I'm a big fan of your investment column. Wow, what a *thrill* to meet you in person. Honestly, a little bump was totally worth it for that privilege."

Looking up at the driver who still supported her elbow, she added,

"James, you're seriously strong, dude. I'm not light and you picked me up like a potato chip bag. I've got to get back to my dorm before curfew. Y'all have a great night."

She turned and started to limp away slowly. The investment banker and financier known to every person on Wall Street called out, "Young woman, what is your name?"

Over her shoulder she said, "Rowan Foxe. Don't worry, you won't see my name on a lawsuit, I swear. I'd rather swallow shards of broken glass than initiate another frivolous lawsuit in this country. I'll throw some ice on it and be good as new in a day or so. Again, really great to meet you in person. It was an honor."

She was really going to limp to her dorm after they'd nearly run her over. Unfamiliar surprise and admiration welled inside him. "James, please bring Miss Foxe back to the car so we can get her back to her dorm. She'll never make that curfew with a hurt ankle."

He watched as his driver and bodyguard walked to the stunningly beautiful young woman and spoke softly to her. Miss Foxe was arguing and shaking her head. Finally, James simply picked her up and returned her to the limo. She looked very annoyed.

"This is really unnecessary. I hate being an inconvenience second only to crying." Bennett chuckled. She was placed on the seat and he climbed back in. With a heavy sigh she answered James' question about which dorm she lived in and he closed the door. As he sat behind the wheel, she asked, "Can you stop a block or so away, James?"

"My goodness, may I ask why?" Bennett was more and more intrigued by Miss Rowan Foxe.

A small snort of laughter had him smiling. "Half the girls in this place come from extremely wealthy families, here to hook up with the next business mogul or oil man. It's beyond nauseating and I'm afraid I'm quite vocal about their complete lack of self respect. Selling themselves to the highest bidder and whatnot." Her eye roll emphasized her disgust.

"If they see me getting out of a limo, specifically *your* limo, when my Financial Analysis term paper was a study of your market strategies? It won't look good. I have to practically beat these silly bitches down half the time as it is." She looked truly frustrated and Bennett struggled not to laugh.

Controlling the smile in his voice, he had to ask, "Why?"

Affecting a stereotypical southern belle persona, she fanned herself and fluttered her ridiculously long lashes adorably, "Why, I declare, I don't know why they let these *scholarship* students in here. They should select applicants based on their level in the social and financial strata. Allowing *charity cases* into our hallowed halls is just plain *vulgar*."

"That bad, huh?" She nodded disgustedly and he gave her a grin that caused James's eyes to widen in the rearview mirror. "You seem grounded for someone your age. I wonder why that is, Miss Foxe. I'd imagine your attitude would be refreshing to other young people."

She waved him away, "Please, call me Rowan. I don't rate a 'Miss Foxe' in any company. I was found wandering in Dallas when I was ten. I don't remember anything before waking up in a hospital with a busted head. My name was on a set of dog tags around my neck." A little shrug downplayed the severity of an ordeal that could have broken most ten-year-olds.

"I spent the next eight years in a girls' home in a small town fifty miles from Dallas proper and don't regret one day of it. I'm here on academic scholarship and I work at Barnes & Noble. I buy my clothes off the rack…*gasp*…when I feel the need to shop once a year. I don't drink and I don't date ever. None of these people know how to deal with me and since I have no interest in dealing with them, it's just best if we avoid contact at all times."

James pulled over a block away from her dorm entrance and she moved to get out. Bennett put his hand on her forearm, "Please, Miss Foxe…Rowan. Allow me to assist you. You aren't going to be able to work for a week or two with that ankle and I feel horrible that I distracted James as he was leaving the parking lot. You must let me at least replace your wages."

With that, he pulled his wallet out of a suit jacket that probably cost more than every item she owned combined. Withdrawing a wad of hundred dollar bills, she thought there must be several thousand dollars there.

He tried to hand them to her and she laughed as she leaned away. "Um, no. Honestly, you don't know what someone makes at a bookstore these days, do you? I clear about a hundred dollars a week. If it will make you feel better, I'll take a hundred for this week. I'll push it for next week and be back at work, no problem."

Bennett quirked a dark brow, "I'm going to have to insist or I'll have James carry you to your dorm room and tuck you in, announcing to everyone that you're my new…protégé." Her mouth opened and closed twice before she snapped it shut with a glare. She took the cash, removed a single hundred dollar bill, and tucked the rest into a compartment beside the seat.

"I'm going to have to insist you be reasonable. You may be used to dealing with Wall Street but you've never dealt with me. I find you're much nicer than most people would think in person. Thank you for the ride. There are a thousand things I would have rather talked to you about; current interest rates and the depreciation of the American dollar, for instance."

James opened the door and helped her out, making sure she didn't trip as she hopped up on the curb. Bennett leaned out and said quietly, "It was a great pleasure to meet you, Rowan. Let me give you a signed copy of my book for all your trouble."

He removed a Mont Blanc pen and spent a moment signing the inside cover. James closed the door and went around to slide behind the wheel as Bennett rolled down the window. "Here you are. You're quite an enigma, Rowan. I hope we meet again."

She took the book with obvious excitement and thanked them again for the lift. She was limping badly and in obvious pain. They watched until she disappeared into her dorm. "James, remember the location of Rowan Foxe. I have a feeling I'll be coming back here."

"Yes, sir. I apologize for almost running her over, Bennett."

"Don't apologize, James. I think I've just found my third wife. Let's go."

# Chapter Four

Rowan made it to her dorm and collapsed in agony on the bed. Her ankle was so swollen she had trouble getting her sneaker off. The stairs had about been the end of her. She was sweating harder than when she ran. She felt like a wuss.

Picking up her signed copy of Bennett Jefferson's book – the one she hadn't been willing to buy but had checked out of the library twice – she opened it to read the inscription and was showered with dozens of hundred dollar bills.

"Sneaky bastard," she said laughing.

The inscription read, *"For Rowan Foxe...a stunningly beautiful woman with a refreshing take on the world I haven't heard in thirty years. You caught my eye and you have my interest. Expect to hear from me again. Bennett."*

His phone number was written under his name with instructions to call should she need anything. Her stomach tripped and she gathered up the money, replacing it inside the book and putting it on her closet shelf.

An hour later, a delivery man brought her a box filled with quick-freeze ice packs, Aleve, an ankle brace, and a collapsible cane. She had to chuckle. The lion of Wall Street was obviously a very nice man and didn't want anyone to know it.

The following day, she received a dozen Gerber daisies with a note. *"Rowan, you don't strike me as a rose woman, daisies are more down-to-earth and suit you, I think. Hope you're feeling better. Bennett."* Rowan managed to find a vase to put them in and sat staring at the vibrant petals for a long time.

When a huge order from a local Chinese restaurant arrived later that evening, it was enough for more than a dozen people. There was another note. *"Rowan, I can't imagine you're able to get around. I can't have it on my conscience if you starve. Bennett."* After she chose her favorite spicy chicken she gave the rest to the other people living in her building. It was strange how every bite tasted better than it ever had before.

The delivery of a gold anklet with tiny stars on it took her breath away. *"Rowan, it occurred to me that wrapping your ankle will detract from your amazing beauty. Please put this anklet on the other leg to insure my guilt is soothed for this gross oversight. Bennett."* The metal shimmered against her olive skin and she realized it was the first piece of real jewelry she'd ever owned.

Mexican food of every variety showed up just in time for dinner and people were starting to ask questions about her benefactor. She re-read his note as she moaned in happiness at the guacamole-drenched steak tacos she'd snagged before calling the other residents to enjoy what was left. *"Rowan, I can't help but wonder whatever you will eat if I don't send you something. Ramen noodles? Peanut butter and jelly sandwiches? I can't allow that. It wouldn't be right. Bennett."*

She dialed his cell phone from the common area phone and he asked what number she was calling him from. When she told him it was the lobby pay phone, he asked her to please give him an hour and he'd love the opportunity to talk to her.

Thirty minutes later, a Blackberry cell phone was delivered by a young man wearing a Verizon polo and a huge smile. The moment she had it in her hand it rang. "Hello?"

"Rowan. Bennett Jefferson. Are you still in the common area?" Bennett.

"Um, yes. I am, why?" Rowan.

"Are you dressed?" Bennett.

"I'm dressed in a t-shirt and leggings. Why? Is this one of *those* calls?" Rowan.

"I *do* like your spunk, Rowan. Please stay there." Bennett.

As he said this, James appeared at the main doors and headed in her direction. "Ma'am, will you allow me to carry you to the car?" He smiled, "I don't want everyone to think you're being kidnapped but I need you to come with me." When she said nothing, didn't move or have any clue how to react, he chuckled and gathered her in his arms, lifting her as if she weighed nothing. Again.

Putting the phone to her ear as people in her dorm stared in awe at the huge man carrying Rowan out of the building, she asked quietly, "Why…exactly…am I being carried out of my dorm?"

"No one is going to hurt you or take advantage of you in any way, Rowan. You have my word," Bennett's voice was calm and she found it strangely soothing. "Ah, there you are. James is thankfully very strong."

"Is that a fat joke?" she asked with a smile in her voice.

"Not in the slightest. You're…curvy. Solid but far from fat. What I personally feel embodies the very essence of all things feminine." James carried her to the limo where Bennett stood waiting in the open door. "Hello again, Rowan."

"Honestly, I was just calling to say thank you. That's all," she told him nervously.

James deposited her carefully on the seat and Bennett slid in beside her. As the door closed, Rowan found herself cocooned with one of the most powerful men on the planet. Her eyes clearly telegraphed her wariness and confusion.

"Rowan, what do you know about me…other than professionally?" She shrugged her shoulders delicately. "You've done no research on my personal life?"

Clearing her throat, she replied, "I know what's in your public bio. I didn't go digging if that's what you're asking. I just needed basic facts for the introduction of my paper. I didn't examine your blood type or sexual kinks, for goodness' sake." He chuckled softly.

"You know I've been married twice before?" A curt nod. "That I have three children from those marriages?" Another nod. "Do you realize my ex-wives, in all their gold-digging wisdom, are partnering with my children to have my competence questioned in order to seize control of all my holdings?" Rowan gasped and shook her head firmly. "Does this surprise you?"

"Unfortunately, no, it doesn't, Mr. Jefferson," she told him honestly.

"Call me Bennett, Rowan. Why does this not surprise you?" he asked her quietly.

"Because powerful and successful men, while attracting the best the world has to offer in professional relationships, tend to also attract beautiful women who are willing to trade themselves as currency in exchange for the lifestyle to which they wish to become accustomed."

Refusing to look away no matter how awkward the topic, she continued, "Since these relationships are built on the superficial, often primarily financial, they're doomed to failure. Whether due to boredom, lack of common interests, horrible behaviors, or plain greed…they don't tend to last very long. I've also noted women like this try to get pregnant as quickly as possible in order to increase their earning potential when things head south."

Rowan folded her hands on her lap and regarded him carefully. He was breathing rapidly and his color wasn't good. "Sir, you don't look well. Are you alright?" Sitting back against the seat, he removed a small bottle from his jacket and took one of the pills inside. He sat silently for a long time before turning his head on the leather.

"No, Rowan. I'm not alright. My heart is failing."

"I'm sorry, sir. I'd think that would be the worst organ to fail. I haven't used mine but you're welcome to it if I'm a donor match or something." He stared intently at her for a moment before reaching out to take her hand.

"Rowan, of the many regrets a man of my age and position has, I think not being in prime health when I manage to find the one woman guaranteed to keep my attention may be the worst of all." He smiled gently, "Did you just offer me your heart?"

"I'm assuming that's what this is about. I'm sure a new heart would allow you to live another twenty years and you have much more responsibility than I do. I have no family. No connections to anyone really. How can I help you?"

He stroked her hand with his thumb and whispered, "I have no intention of taking an organ from you, love. Unfortunately, a new heart isn't an option in my condition. That I will never *truly* have you causes me untold pain." His eyes closed and she watched as he focused on his breathing.

"Listen to me, Rowan. I'd like to discuss a personal and business venture. It is unorthodox, I grant you, but I ask you to consider everything I have to say before you reject me. Are you willing to listen with an open mind?" She nodded. Lowering the security glass, Bennett told James to take them to the house.

"Yes, sir."

"Please tell me you spent the money in the book on something frivolous, Rowan."

Smiling cheekily, she replied, "Not one dime. Had I known I'd be abducted, I would have brought it and hidden it somewhere in the limo."

Chuckling, he said, "Exactly why I didn't give you an opportunity to plan. You are the most enigmatic woman I've ever had the pleasure of speaking with, Rowan. Your beauty was, naturally, the first thing I noticed. However, your plain manner of speaking…your outlook on life and your place in it…were so strikingly different from any female I've ever known, I decided I had to know you." His hands cradled hers between them and she was enthralled by how warm he was.

"I've run intensive background checks on you. I find you to be exactly as you've portrayed yourself to be which is yet another shock to my system." He stared into her blue eyes and he was unable to hide the primal hunger in them. "You could prove to be the most outrageous experience I've ever known. And yet, I feel I must be completely honest with you from this moment. I cannot exert myself in any way, Rowan. The slightest rise in my blood pressure could send me into cardiac arrest." She wondered at the expression of disgust that crossed his face, "It is why I am unable to even assist you from the car. A pathetic end for a man who has lived his life as I have."

"You could *never* be pathetic. You've lived every moment of your life balls-to-the-wall and though slowing down so drastically must be agonizing to a man's man such as yourself, I hope you find comfort in the great memories you've accumulated over your lifetime. I would hope that provides you comfort. I'm sure there are few things you haven't seen or done."

Rowan placed her other hand over his and he was struck by her compassion almost as much as her beauty. "As far as sex, I'm afraid you picked the least experienced person on the planet to discuss *that* with." Her small shrug brought his attention to the lovely breasts that pressed against her soft t-shirt. Then her words penetrated the gradually building lust.

His eyes snapped to hers, "Rowan, are you telling me that with your looks and at age twenty-two you are a virgin?"

"I am. Does that bother you?" she asked him with small tilt of her head.

He strangled the laugh that bubbled up his throat. "Rowan, I can tell you in all honesty that I've never in my life wanted to make love to a woman more than I do you at this moment. I beg you to call me Bennett." He pressed his eyes with the fingers of his other hand and took several deep breaths. "If I were to ask you for an examination to confirm, would you think me hideous?"

"No, but you should know I don't have insurance."

This time he did laugh and Rowan felt her own heart stumble a bit in her chest. "Do men ask you often for proof of your virginity?"

"Of course not. I don't interact with people. I told you that. I assume if you ask, there's a reason. I'm not offended; there are so many women in my dorm that actually *convince* their dates they're virginal to extend foreplay. Ridiculous." Clearing her throat, she asked quietly. "Sir…Bennett, what is it you need from me? You don't need to talk in circles. I promise I'll listen to everything you have to say before I give you my answer."

"I want you to marry me, Rowan." His voice was matter of fact and her mouth dropped open.

"Wh…what? S…Bennett, you don't even *know* me," she whispered incredulously.

He tugged her and she came closer, drawing her feet up on the seat and laying her head on the back. "On the contrary, Rowan, I'm an excellent judge of character. Usually only in regards to business...never usually when it comes to women, I admit."

He stroked one finger down her petal-soft cheek, "But you, Rowan, you are different than anyone I've ever met and I need your help. I need someone who will fight *with* me and *for* me, Rowan. If I were to tell you my beneficiaries were trying to take everything I've worked for, sell it off piece by piece, and split the profits...how would you feel about that?"

"It makes me mad. I would tell you to hire one thousand of the most aggressive shark-like lawyers in the United States and rip them to shreds. Everything...from their personal lives to their acquaintances to their work history and academic performance and show them you are willing to keep them tied up in court for the next hundred years. I would evict them from any properties and cut off every single line of credit paid for by you. I would *then* draw up reasonable, realistic settlements and present them once they were broken and begging for mercy."

Her eyes were lit with fury on his behalf. "But you do not need to *marry me* for my advice and I'm sure there are hundreds of people willing to fight for you, Bennett. The last damn thing you need is another wife and believe me, your family would pounce on me as a gold digging bitch."

"Five more minutes with you and I will be completely in love for the first time in my life." His words weren't meant to stroke her ego and she was unable to formulate a thought. "I'm fifty-eight, Rowan. It is unlikely I will live another year. I will never be able to make love to you and the realization of how many times I've fucked casually, taken women simply because they were available and willing, has never struck me until this moment."

He stroked his fingers through her hair. "Your hair is like spun silk." Placing his hand flat on her chest over her heart, he said, "Your heart is pounding, Rowan." She didn't know if she was supposed to say anything but found she was beyond speech.

"Marry me. Fight for me. Help me and let me love you in the only ways I can. When I die, you will never have to worry about working another day in your life." Had any man's voice ever sounded so hungry for her?

"I'll fight for you, Bennett, without becoming your wife and without taking a dime from you. From everything I've learned about you, I already hold you in high regard as a philanthropist and as a businessman. No one gives to charity like you. I don't require a piece of paper or money to do the right thing. Refusing to allow you to be stripped of your accomplishments is the least I could do."

He had spent his entire life knowing when his goal was in sight. "Let's compromise. Allow me to draw up agreements protecting you. I'll make a statement to my attorneys and publicist about your place in my life. If you feel I've treated you fairly, we marry and you become my sole heir. You agree to spend whatever time I have left with me; talking to me, sharing your spark."

She was destined to surprise him again. "Bennett, allow me to make a counter-offer. Let me help you fight your family and when it's over, if you feel the need to marry me on an emotional level, we can talk about it then." Her sigh was sad. "I'm afraid to fall in love with you, Bennett. Love is *painful* and you would be *very* easy to love, I think." Far too easy, she thought to herself.

There was such sadness in her eyes. "Did someone break your heart, Rowan?"

"Many years ago. Allowing myself to be fooled was a harsh lesson. If I love you, Bennett, and you are taken from me, it would be more pain than I could handle." His eyes were so green, so filled with life. It wasn't right that he was facing his own mortality so young.

He settled his head beside hers on the leather. "I'm going to teach you about it being better to have loved and lost than to never have loved at all. That will be my goal, Rowan – a lesson for both of us." She nodded slowly but looked afraid. "You are young yet so solidly *in* the world. I think we will enjoy our time together. You will learn about yourself and I will learn to use a part of my heart I have never engaged before. Perhaps the exercise will do it good."

Over the next week, Rowan was indoctrinated on the inner workings of Bennett's world. In the second week, the process began of introducing her to the world and removing all doubts as to her place by his side.

An interview was being arranged with Barbara Walters, who'd been trying to gain access to the reserved Forbes 100 alumnus for twenty years. He hired more lawyers than she could keep track of to review every document ever signed by him or his current beneficiaries.

He hired a team of doctors and psychologists to interview both of them, to attest to Rowan's purity and Bennett's current health, mentally and physically. He called in every favor he'd ever been owed by politicians to have his assets blocked from seizure by his greedy ex-wives and children.

Then he created a new will in the presence of ten witnesses, judges from all over the state, who were also asked to interview Rowan and attest to her honesty and solidarity. She submitted to lie detector tests by three of the best technicians in the country to vouch for her lack of ulterior motive.

In the end, Rowan was spending twenty-four hours a day with Bennett and her heart opened to him, inviting him into the warmth and comfort he found there. Their time together seemed to fly by.

# Chapter Five

*Age Twenty-Four*

After two months together, Rowan still refused to marry him and Bennett found he had never wanted anything more in his life. When he'd asked her several times, with a ring worth millions, he finally became desperate and arranged a July Fourth ball.

He had his assistant invite more than a thousand of his closest friends and associates. Seated at a table placed near the top of the ballroom at his country estate, he asked for a microphone and carefully went on bended knee to propose.

Rowan's eyes were wide with fear and she whispered he did *not* have to do this. She told him she didn't need his money and that she only wanted him. Then one of the most powerful men in the world proceeded to beg, on his knees, in front of every person he knew.

"I cannot survive another day without you agreeing to marry me, Rowan. It is the *only* thing I must have before my illness claims me completely. I need to know you share my name, that you are protected by it. I want to show you the respect and the love you have shown me these past months."

"Bennett..." her eyes filled with tears.

"You have asked for nothing, refusing to sign documents granting you access to my money, fighting by my side every day, and talking me to sleep every night. There are so many things I can never give you, Rowan but I can give you the part of my heart that beats only for you. Marry me, Rowan."

She sank to her knees in front of him and nodded against his neck. He gripped her to him accompanied by the cheers of their audience. "Bennett, I love you and it doesn't hurt."

His arms tightened around her with a small gasp and when she moved to stand, only James, standing closest to them, knew how Bennett leaned on her, relied on her to help him up. He took several discreet deep breaths as James moved imperceptibly closer. When he placed a ring on her finger with a diamond so large the refracted light from it was blinding, she sobbed against him, her arms wrapped around his waist.

Calling a local judge to the front of the room, he said, "I have all the documents ready to go. I'd like you to marry us immediately." And so they were married ten minutes after their engagement. They were congratulated by so many people their faces began to blend together.

She and James guided him into his den and gave him a pill when there was simply too much activity and stimulation for his heart to handle. She refused to go back to the party and put Bennett's longtime assistant in charge of overseeing the rest of the evening.

James carried Bennett to the rear elevator and they settled in their rooms for the night. When she removed his clothing she saw the man he was now as well as the man he'd once been. Unable to overexert himself over the last several years, his once powerful frame had softened a bit.

Pulling sleep pants over his lower body, she stripped out of the designer gown he'd given her and wore one of his shirts to sleep in. He watched her, his breathing rapid, until she was covered.

Crawling up beside him, she curled her body around his, talking softly until he went to sleep. As she watched his breathing level out, her fingers stroked his salt-and-pepper hair and loved him with everything inside herself.

Ten days later, his ex-wives and children caved to the unbelievable pressure Bennett's attorneys had applied. Each of his children was set to inherit twenty-five million in cash while his ex-wives would inherit ten million as well as the homes he'd purchased for them.

His total estate was worth a thousand times that and he'd put Rowan in charge of his charitable organization to distribute funds as she saw fit.

Other than the bequests to his relatives and retirement packages for his staff, he left every last dime to Rowan. So many fail safes had been put in place that if his family thought to dispute her rights after his death, they would receive nothing. Lawyers would file on behalf of his estate and Rowan wouldn't even have to show up in court.

Their life settled into a routine of conversations with her snuggled against him. She asked him about every second of his life that had been filled with adventures and moments of brilliance. Once a month, she agreed to one event, typically a charity, and they would attend together with James always close at hand.

Bennett passed his fifty-ninth birthday and the world seemed to hold its breath. When he made it to his sixtieth, the media swore Rowan had given him a new lease on life. She held a huge gala, so thrilled at the additional year they'd had together that she wanted to share her joy with every person he knew. As a testament to everything he'd accomplished in sixty years.

Every charity he'd donated to over the years was asked to send a representative, paid for by the charity fund Rowan managed. Each was asked to bring a story, a photo, something showing all Bennett had done to touch other's lives.

By the end of the night, there were thousands of framed photos and letters, plaques signed by children, and trophies in thanks of his years of dedication to those less fortunate on display along the walls of the grand ballroom.

It was a physical representation of how many lives Bennett had truly touched. She instructed each item be handled carefully. She planned to choose a few to place in their personal rooms while the rest would be shipped to organization headquarters.

There were speeches from children who had once been homeless, women who had been trapped in abusive relationships with nowhere to go, and businesses that credited him for saving their families. Many of the stories began in tragedy but all of them ended with sincere thanks to Bennett for caring, for putting his money into the preservation of people he never thought to meet.

Rowan cried more than once and proudly held Bennett's hand as he thanked all of the guests for coming, for validating his life-long stance that wealth was useless if it wasn't used for the betterment of society as a whole.

He lifted Rowan's hand to kiss it. "I'd also like to thank my stunning wife who has taken over the running of the organization that has meant more to me than any other. She reminds me daily that she is even more brilliant than she is beautiful." He winked and added, "I didn't even know that was possible." She blushed and he kissed her cheek. "Thank you again for coming. Enjoy the rest of the evening."

They walked from the stage and when they were in the private hall, James carried him the rest of the way to their rooms. For the first time, she saw tears in the eyes of the big man and it caused her chest to ache painfully.

## Chapter Six

When Bennett was settled comfortably, James joined her in the sitting area and took her hand. His voice was quiet and he looked as though he was struggling to speak. "You have been so good for him, Rowan. No matter what, never forget you've given him two years of peace and unconditional love he would *never* have had without you."

She nodded and willed herself not to cry. Not to be weak when her husband was always so strong. She took time to compose herself, waiting until she heard the sound of their suite door closing before she finished undressing.

When she climbed into bed beside him, Bennett's arms wrapped around her firmly. "Thank you, oh my god, *thank you* for loving me so well, Rowan." She turned into him and sobbed brokenly while he held her as tight as possible. "Tell me why you're crying, my precious darling who fears weakness in herself above all things?"

"You're *preparing* me. I can *feel* it. What's happened? Did the doctors say something?" She looked up into his face, cupping his cheek and kissing him with all the love in her heart. "Please don't leave me. I can't live without you now, Bennett. Please, baby, I'll do anything to keep you with me."

"Will you truly do anything, sweet Rowan?" She nodded. "Will you bear our child…when I'm gone?" She went up on her elbow to stare into his face with undisguised shock. "Rowan, I sense your pending devastation. I need to know you have someone to give your love to when I'm not here. If you have our child, I know you'll pour all the love you've given me into them. I'll know you aren't alone. That you aren't dwelling on my death."

Bennett's child growing in her body filled her with happiness. With deep longing. "But our children would never be able to *know* you, Bennett. They wouldn't have your love and attention. They wouldn't know the magnificent man you are as I do."

His green eyes sparkled with love for her. "Of course they would, love. They'd have you to tell them all about me. You've taken thousands of pictures in our two years together. A day by day documentation of our life." He slipped his hands into her hair, "I've had sperm extracted and frozen for you. But Rowan, what I want more than to continue living is to make love to you."

"No...*no*, Bennett. It will *kill* you. I'll be your *murderer*, Bennett. I couldn't bear to be the cause of your death." Tears were suddenly pouring down her cheeks.

He pulled her close. "Rowan, my beautiful darling, you would deliver me from one adventure to the next. I've left documents with the attorneys and doctors stating I can no longer live without consummating our marriage. That I'm insisting on it and will wear you down as long as it takes."

He angled her face to him for an aggressive kiss and she responded immediately before pulling back. "Bennett, I'm afraid. Please don't leave me, Bennett. Not yet. Please not yet." She held him tight and he stroked his hands down the body he'd ached for nightly for two years. "It will be like living without the sun."

"Darling, you're twenty-four and have never been made love to. For two years, you've given me everything I've asked. Lived for me and fought for me and cherished me as no one, not my parents, my previous wives, or my children have ever done. I knew you were the right choice the day I asked you. You've proven me right a thousand times since then."

Her sobs sank to the bone but he needed her, he needed this. "You know I'm getting weaker; every day I struggle a little more. I'm so tired of being trapped in this frail body, Rowan. If there is one thing I must have, it is to feel you naked against me, letting me make love to you before I die. I beg you to look into my eyes and know I need this one last sacrifice from you, this one last request."

"Bennett...oh my god, baby...making love to you isn't a sacrifice. I've wanted you so badly since our second day together." She stroked her hand over his bare chest.

"Do you know how many times in the two years you've slept beside me that I've woken with your fingers wrapped around my cock, Rowan? My need to come so great, my heart pounding. Having to pull you away and take the frustration over the release? Do you know how many times I've watched you touch yourself in your sleep, stroking your clit as you rock your hips against your own hand…sighing *my name* when you come before you drift away again?"

Her face blushed hot and tears continued sliding over her cheeks. "I've *driven* you to this."

"Baby, *no man* could lie beside you and not want to possess you. You're a sexual creature, as I was once, and you *need* release. It's physical, Rowan. Though I wouldn't have blamed you, I know you've taken no other lovers."

Her face set, she whispered hotly, "Bennett, I would *never* do that to you. It would be a slap in the face of my love for you, of yours for me. I can go without it forever if I have to. I don't care as long as I have you. I don't *need* sex, Bennett."

Bennett gave her the truth that had grown more and more real over the past year, "Rowan, I *do* need it. I need you so badly I can't sleep anymore because of it. I can't focus when you're near me, the scent of you, the softness of your skin, how your black curls shimmer in the sunlight…all of it has me crazy with need. I'm dying for want of you as surely as my heart is taking me by inches."

Her eyes were wide and frightened. "Before I met you, the longest I'd ever waited to make love to a woman was two *weeks* and I didn't love any of them. I *worship* you, Rowan, and have slept beside you for two *years*. I'm insane with my need for you. *Love me*, Rowan…then let me go."

She leaned away and wiped the tears from her face, taking a deep breath. "Bennett, I am more afraid than any virgin has ever been in all her life."

He opened his arms and she curled into them, "I know this is so much to ask of you, pretty girl. I know I'll probably scar you for life. Losing your virginity and your husband croaking on you. I get it." She gasped against him and fresh tears fell on his chest. "No, no more tears, Rowan. Please, baby, give me this one thing and I'll *never* ask for anything else."

"God, Bennett, your attempt at humor is horrifying." He gave her time to calm down, to try and stop the tears she shed for him. More tears than anyone had ever cried for him. "Is there no way to talk you out of taking this risk, Bennett?"

"Rowan, I *will* make love to you. I can't go on like this anymore."

She closed her eyes and couldn't stop the tears that flowed from under her lashes. Leaning up to look at him, she asked hoarsely, "Should I touch you, Bennett? I've been so careful all this time and I don't know what will…affect you. I want to be careful, to go slow…maybe we'll get a miracle."

"Yes, Rowan, we might get a miracle." Both of them heard the lie he told her. "Take your shirt off, baby. Lie here beside me." She pulled it over her head and lay on her side next to him. He nudged her to her back, stroking his large hands through her hair, over her face, her neck, her shoulders, her breasts, and her upper body bowed up into his hand.

Bennett watched as her nipples pebbled tautly beneath his fingers. "You're so responsive, Rowan. I always knew you would be." Bending, he took her nipple in his mouth with a low moan and her hands caught in his silken black hair.

"Bennett, oh my god, it's so much *more* than I ever imagined."

He slid his palm over her stomach and into her panties, one finger sliding along the cleft of her. She whimpered as he brushed over her clit and he sighed, laying his cheek against her abdomen. Her hands never stopped working, massaging his scalp and neck as her hips moved with him.

Dipping one finger carefully into her pussy, he began to stroke her, feeling the tight walls flex around him, sucking at him as he withdrew. The tip of his finger bumped against her hymen and he pressed against it.

Moving down her body, he laid carefully over her torso as he began to lick her clit. Rowan's body bucked beneath him and she climaxed so quickly his heart started to race in reaction. His name was a sigh from her lips.

Lying down again, he moved more firmly inside her, his thumb circling on the little bundle of nerves while he settled his pounding heart. When she came again moments later, her entire body going tight beneath him, he felt her hymen tear but not completely.

Again he worked her up, wanting and needing her to be ready. "Play with your beautiful breasts for me, Rowan. I can't be everywhere at once like I want to be." He was propped beside her on his elbow, watching her.

She continued to work her hips against him and blushed hotly as her trembling hands moved to her breasts. "That's it, love. Take your nipples between your fingers. Ah, yes, Rowan. God, how beautiful you are." He kissed the skin of her belly and watched a shiver work over her torso.

"Bennett, I didn't know everything would feel so good. I love you so much. More than I can possibly tell you," she whispered.

"Oh, Rowan, I know, baby, believe me. I've never once doubted your love for me. I can't do the things to you I want so badly to do, darling. There is so much I wish I could show you, to make your first time everything it should be."

Bennett kissed her belly again as he stroked hard into her. He felt her barrier give completely as he pressed against her clit with his thumb. One small gasp of pain was all Rowan gave him to let him know she'd felt it. He pulled his fingers from her, sucking her fluids and the bit of blood from his fingers. He wasn't about to waste any part of this experience.

He stretched out beside her, his fingers returning to her clit. Rowan's hips rocked reflexively to him in rhythm with his movements. He stared at her face, watching as she came again, pinching her nipples firmly between her fingers. "You are so fucking beautiful, Rowan." He closed his eyes, willing his heart to ease again.

"Bennett," she said breathlessly, "When I was very young, I fell in love with a man. I'd planned on him taking my virginity when I turned eighteen because I didn't want to be afraid. I found him with someone else and I swore to never need or want another man so badly."

She turned her tear-stained face to him and cupped his cheeks in her hands, "You have taken my fear of the unknown and given me pleasure I didn't know existed. My fear of the known, I can't stop. Part of me wants my heart to stop beating when yours does, Bennett." She sobbed against his neck as he held her.

"Rowan, you would destroy what I love most if you wished to die. Your love of life, your spark, is what drew me to you. I need your vow that you will continue to live…that you will love again, Rowan. You love with every part of yourself and you *need* to give love to survive."

He stroked her back, aching for what he was doing to her. "Swear to me you will go on and try to find someone worthy of your love." She shook her head and cried harder. "Swear that you will, Rowan. That you'll try."

"No. No, no, no, Bennett. I'll keep going to bring our child into the world and hold you with me always. I can't promise to love another man, Bennett. Please don't ask it of me." Her voice broke and more tears tracked into her hair.

He pulled her into their usual sleeping position, ready to talk to her until she was calm again. Making this as painless as possible for her was critical. "Beautiful Rowan, I have to ask it. You're too young to remain a grieving widow. You *always* keep your word. If you swear to me you will try, truly try, to find love again…I know you won't break your vow to me. I know you'll be hurting but, Rowan, I *need* you to be open to love if it comes to you." He dried her tears, stroked her hair back from her forehead, and smiled at her.

She nodded despite her sobs and he kissed her.

His hand was touching her folds again and his kiss turned possessive, hard. Rowan glimpsed the lover he'd been before his heart began to fail on him. He kissed her for a long time, making love to her mouth in the same tempo his fingers made love to her pussy.

Finally he pulled away with a growl of need, "I need to be inside you, Rowan. To feel your slick heat around me. You'll have to be on top. I'll show you." She nodded, dazed from his touch, and he rolled to his back, watching as she moved to straddle his hips.

"You need to slide along my length, get me wet so I cause you as little pain as possible, Rowan." Going forward on her hands, she stroked her cleft along his cock while his jaw clenched and he took deep steady breaths.

When he was slick with her juices, he lifted her slightly and set the throbbing crest at the entrance of her body. "I don't want you to feel pain, baby. I need this to be as good for you as I can make it."

Rowan was kneeling above him and she kissed him slowly as she carefully lifted and lowered again and again. She was *so* tight and he wished again he'd had more patience, more time, to prepare her body for this first full penetration. He could tell she was forcing her body to accept more of him than she was ready for and he slowed her down.

When he was fully seated inside her, Rowan's eyes locked with his. "Bennett…" Her walls tightened around him and they moaned. "I feel like you're everywhere inside me now." Taking her lower lip between her teeth, she stared at her husband and placed her palm over his chest fearfully.

He removed her hand and kissed her palm. "Don't think about it, Rowan. Are you alright, baby?" She nodded. "You feel more spectacular than I ever dreamed, Rowan. I've wanted you, had to deny us both, until my mouth watered for you." She kissed him again, sucking his tongue between her lips in an erotic rhythm that shot straight to his cock and made him jerk inside her wet heat.

His heart started to race and he grabbed his pills from the bedside table, placing one in his mouth. She didn't move. Terror was etched clearly on her features as she waited. "Rowan, my love…the *only* woman I've ever loved. Ease your thoughts, baby. Let me have this pure memory of you, this one part of you that no one else will ever have."

Staring into his eyes for a long time, she stroked his face and started to move over him. He watched as her body learned by instinct and moved over him carefully, then more smoothly as she figured out the rhythm. Rowan drove herself over her first climax and Bennett watched and felt her muscles tighten inside and outside as she rode him through it, forcing him past tension of her body.

He put his hand over her breast, the other dropping to circle over her clit. She responded with her entire body. Moaning his name and still moving, trying to control her urge to move faster. When she came a third time, both of them were slick with her fluids and their combined sweat.

Bennett gripped her hips and released his control, coating her with his seed as he roared her name into their silent bedroom. Still she moved, watching his face and waiting for a sign that she should stop. His heart was like a hammer in his chest but he wouldn't let her stop.

Because she never slowed, he never softened and hardened completely again moments later. "Yes, Rowan, yes. Please don't stop, baby. Love me through it all. I'll take your love with me, pretty baby. Your love will be like armor around me." She came twice more before she felt him tightening beneath her, expanding inside her. "I love you, Rowan. You saved me."

He came high and hot in her body a second time and she saw when his heart began to seize but still she moved. She knew this was what he wanted, what he had planned. To let go of his life in her arms. "I love you, Bennett, more than myself. I love you so much." She could be strong enough to give the man she loved the choice of when and how he would leave his life.

His voice was strained now, "Yes, Rowan, love me through it…I'm not afraid. I love you…thank you so much for loving me." So she moved, his hands stroking her thighs, and when his heart stopped completely, he was smiling softly at her.

# Chapter Seven

Rowan stopped and dropped over his chest, clutching him with her entire body and sobbing until she thought her own heart would stop. "Bennett, I'm not ready. Please wait...don't go. I love you. I love you. I love you. I'm not strong enough. Please don't leave me, Bennett. I'm not ready."

Suddenly James was beside the bed, pulling a robe over her nakedness as he cried with her. He knelt on the floor beside the bed as she wept brokenly; he'd stopped his watch when he heard what Bennett had told him to listen for.

Finally, he moved to lift her from her husband and Rowan fought him violently as he'd known she would. "No, Rowan, you can't go with him. You have to live. He wanted you to *live*, Rowan. You promised. Remember your promise to Bennett, Rowan."

She shuddered once and leaned forward to kiss Bennett's lips once more. "I love you, Bennett. I love you and I miss you already." Then she went limp and James pulled her away, her soul wrenching in denial as their cores were separated from one another. He wrapped her more tightly in the robe and pulled the blankets over Bennett to his chest.

Carrying Rowan like a fragile doll, he called in the doctor who'd been standing by. They gave her a sedative and James carried her to the sofa in the small seating area. Tucking her under several blankets, he stood guard over her as she slept, watching the hustle and bustle happen around the single best man he'd ever known. Paramedics removed Bennett's body and everyone was silent, afraid to wake the woman who'd loved him enough to let him go.

James instructed the maids to change the sheets but leave the old pillowcases on the pillows. They went to grab the dirty clothes and he told them to leave the shirt Bennett had worn the night before. They nodded in understanding and completed their tasks quickly.

When the bed was made, he called in the nurse who had been hired to watch over Rowan. He instructed her to bathe and dress her charge in soft pajamas. When she was ready, he moved her back to the bed and tucked her around Bennett's pillow.

The next few days were the worst of James's life. Rowan would not eat and the nurse finally resorted to an IV. The bright and happy Rowan that Bennett Jefferson had fallen so deeply in love with within moments of meeting her was broken.

Almost a week after Bennett passed, Rowan turned to James and said weakly, "I...I have to lay him to rest, James. It isn't right to keep him waiting. He wouldn't like that." With a careful smile that looked as though it physically hurt her, she added, "Powerful men never like to be kept waiting." She stood and he guided her slowly to Bennett's assistant to make arrangements.

Three days later, they filled the largest church in Austin to the brim and put up speakers for those people outside who couldn't fit in the church for Bennett's memorial. For almost an hour, his closest friends talked about Bennett's life, his legacy, and the young bride who made his last years happier than anyone had ever seen him. They thanked her for showing him what real love was before he died.

At last, Rowan stood and went to the pulpit to speak. There were dozens of glass displays along the stage holding all the gifts he'd received the day he died. Everyone could see she'd lost weight and looked ready to fall over.

She tried to speak and broke down, turning away and waiting a moment before starting again. James handed her a crisp handkerchief and she nodded in thanks. Surprisingly, she started with a chuckle, likely more for herself than anyone else and James cheered for her silently.

"My husband, Bennett Jefferson, was larger than life. He was already very sick when I met him. And still, he was able to completely run me over. Even ill, he was enigmatic, powerful, and so, so beautiful in every way.

"He didn't care where you came from, how much money you had, what race, color, or religion you were, he looked you in the eye and saw an equal. For all his success, all his money, he wasn't a snob. He was loved by tycoons and little children alike. Adored as much by celebrities as well as those people he made sure had heat in the winter."

She paused to clear her throat and gestured to the displays. "These mementos you see are the thanks he received from thousands on the day he died. Their love and devotion is clear in every photo, every award, and every letter written in crayon. He was a man who gave everything of himself to his work, his charities, his friends, his family...and to me."

Stopping again to pull herself together, she closed her eyes a moment. "Bennett gave me *everything* I never realized I needed. Gave me love so pure I could become drunk on it. He lived his life hard and he loved hard. I will miss him. He carries my love and a piece of my heart, like armor, into his next great adventure. I love you, Bennett. I will miss you...so much."

Rowan took two steps and collapsed, James catching her and carrying her to the first pew. By the time they lifted the coffin, she was coming around and sipping water James held for her. He guided her behind the procession and she walked in a daze with a small veil pulled over her eyes.

Nothing could hide the tears pouring freely down her face. Acting solely as bodyguard, he climbed in back of the limo with her and kept her tucked into his side until the coffin was loaded into the hearse and the funeral procession got under way. Bennett was being interred in a large mausoleum built in the back garden of his estate home. By the time they were turning onto the property, Rowan had calmed enough to walk to the giant marble tomb.

Family and closest friends watched as Bennett Jefferson was laid to rest. Rowan whispered, "I'm going to fall apart. I'm going to be sick. I...I can't let anyone see me, James. Bennett would be so disappointed." He hustled her to the limo and she was completely hysterical as he held a little bag for her to throw up in while he rubbed her back.

There was to be a reception at the house and when she got out of the limo she was swaying dangerously. James tightened his arm on her low back, holding her other arm to keep her steady. Leading her to

Bennett's den, he settled her in one of the large sofas in front of the fireplace and brought her a cup of tea, watching as she sipped it.

Ringing the bell, he ordered light food be brought to her. A soft knock on the door brought him to his feet in front of Rowan as she stared into the fireplace. Rowan didn't respond the first few times her name was spoken softly. Only when small hands began removing her hat and veil did she glance up to see the kind face of Miss Jeffries sitting beside her.

"Hello, sweet Rowan." She didn't see the other people in the room as she allowed the woman she privately thought of as her mother pull her snugly against her chest while she sobbed her broken heart out. It was several minutes before she could speak between her sobs.

"It's my fault. It was the only thing he wanted…what we couldn't share in all this time. We knew it would be too much for his heart. He was getting weaker, worse every day. He wanted to give me one thing before he died. For my first experience to be what I'd always hoped it would be. To love me through the beginning so I wasn't afraid. To have me love him through the end so he wasn't afraid. We both knew it would kill him but he said he wasn't afraid…he wasn't afraid and he loved me. But now I'm *so* afraid. I don't know what to do." She clutched the older woman around the waist, her cheek on her lap as she was held and Miss Jeffries stroked her hair.

"Rowan, that man loved you with every single ounce of his being. You eased the end that would have come for him either way. He was able to choose his method, choose his time because he needed to love you just once. And no matter what happens, you will always have that."

Rowan raised her face and Miss Jeffries wiped her tears. She whispered brokenly, "I'm pregnant. The doctor confirmed it this morning."

"What a *beautiful* final gift he gave you, Rowan. It isn't what you're used to anymore, but you always have a place with me, honey. I'm very good at easing young women through all sorts of heartache. No one would bother you. It's quiet…peaceful. Why don't you unplug for just a little while, Rowan?"

Soft hands smoothed her hair again and cupped her cheeks. "Settle your urgent business here and we'll get through it together. I only have two very little girls right now. I'm getting too old not to place them if they can be placed. They won't be any trouble, Rowan."

With a small nod, Rowan hugged her. "Thank you. James is my only friend. There isn't anyone else. He has to come with me. Bennett would have a fit if our child were left unprotected."

"We'll make up the downstairs office for him. How's that?" Rowan nodded and Miss Jeffries added, "I brought two old friends with me, Rowan. Right now, you need as many friends as possible. Maybe six years is enough to heal old wounds."

Rowan turned her head and took in Nina and Gage standing in the corner. After a long moment, she smiled sadly and they approached her, kneeling at her feet. Both of them had been crying. "You look the same, Nina...so beautiful. Gage, your hair is longer...it looks good that way."

Then she buried her face in her hands and wept as they leaned forward to hug her.

# Chapter Eight

*Eight months later...*

It was time to start lessening her workload with the charity committee. Rowan was due in a few weeks. Every time she tried to cut back, another needy family or shelter on the verge of closing was sent to her email. Her staff knew her pet projects and forwarded non-association charity requests directly to her.

Every morning for the past six months she'd awakened in the only house that held childhood memories for her. She did her stretches before showering and getting dressed. Heading downstairs, there would be a new FedEx package from the office and at least a hundred emails in her inbox.

She opened her laptop on the same small table in the kitchen and started responding to requests for assistance. Sitting in the same wooden chair she always had, now sporting a soft cushion, she glanced out the window and watched the sun come up.

Her hands moved ceaselessly over her round belly; the happiness was bittersweet. She was carrying Bennett's son and he would never know his father. Patting her belly, she told the baby good morning and how much he was loved.

Right after the funeral, she'd closed up the house for a while and moved into a hotel suite with a single bag and Bennett's pillow while she settled things that had to be done. James was her constant companion and made sure she had everything she needed, sometimes before she thought to ask.

She gave him a huge raise so she'd know he'd never have to worry. God knew he'd gone above and beyond in every way for Rowan. They talked about Bennett a lot and he helped her remember all the good things instead of dwelling on the devastation of losing him. James had been with Bennett for twenty years and loved to regale her with tales of his hell-raising days.

"Good morning, Rowan. How's your little passenger today?" James asked her cheerfully as he mixed up protein shakes for both of them. It turned out James was a great cook. He often took over for Miss Jeffries and whipped up food for all of them. "You're still not eating enough, young lady. You're carrying a *boy*; he's going to eat his own face."

Rowan chuckled, "I'm eating more than a human being should physically be able to consume, James. I mean…really." Rubbing her belly gently, she asked, "What are your plans today?"

"Well…I'm taking you to your ultrasound appointment. Then when the house isn't empty later, I'll go running." He grinned at her over the blender.

"Is Nina going running with you, James?" she asked sweetly and watched as James bobbled the milk jug. "I take that as a yes. Hmm…why so nervous? What exactly are you *waiting for*, James?"

He poured ingredients and sighed dramatically. "First of all, I'm *way* too old for her, Rowan. I'm like…grizzled. She's so fresh and young and pretty. Second of all, I tend to be cranky."

"You realize you're twenty years *younger* than Bennett was and that Nina and I are the same age?"

Every time Bennett's name was mentioned, she rubbed her belly. It made his heart hurt for her. Since the day he'd met Rowan, James had thought of her as a younger sister. He'd been awed by her all-consuming love for a terminally sick man.

Bennett had been not only his employer but his friend. When he'd come to James, explaining that he couldn't bear not making love to his wife anymore, Bennett had been very aware of the mess he'd be leaving behind.

Rowan's body would essentially be the instrument of his death and she'd have to live with that.

He'd been determined to leave her with a child if he was able to the old-fashioned way; medically if his time with her hadn't taken. James had pleaded with him to take a suite in the hospital, to have doctors on call.

Bennett told him he was going to love Rowan as hard as he was able one time, her first time. He was determined to make her first sexual experience safe and loving, to show her how much he loved her and how much he appreciated how she'd changed his life simply by loving him in return. Then he was going to give her back her youth.

If he'd still had his health, their age difference probably wouldn't have bothered Bennett as much as it did at the end. He'd told James that being old enough to be her father was bad enough but having the stamina of a great-grandfather was something he could no longer live with.

Now he looked at the young woman he admired more than anyone else and hid his own cowardice. "Rowan, sixteen years is a huge difference in age. She deserves her youth...as you now deserve yours." Rowan's eyes filled with tears and James moved to crouch in front of her.

"Honey, after the baby is born, you have to go back out in the world." He brought up what he considered the white elephant in the middle of the room. They all saw how Gage felt about Rowan but none of them talked about it. "You know he waits for you. I think he learned his lesson. He isn't going to hurt you again. I'd have to shoot him if he did and none of us wants to deal with that."

Gage cared for her gently. He visited her every day to check on her health, both mentally and physically. When James came down with a painful sinus infection, it was Gage who'd taken her to her doctor's appointments with his sworn vow to James to keep her safe.

Rowan shook her head slowly, "I don't think I can open my heart to someone else, James. Bennett is...*was*...my husband. I'd feel like I was cheating. I waited until I was twenty-four to lose my virginity, losing the man I loved at the same time. It's hard to move on from a man like Bennett."

It was hard to argue with a woman who was pregnant with his best friend's child. "Agreed, he was a leader among men, Rowan. Loving again won't be forgetting him. It will be sharing the love he taught you to feel."

She stood and hugged him, her huge belly getting in the way. "You are such a very good man, James. Has Nina said anything? Given any sign of her thoughts?"

James shook his head and allowed the topic change. "It's been so long since I had a normal relationship I wouldn't even *know* the signs, Rowan. But I doubt there are any. Old…grizzled. Young…fresh." Before he could prepare, she hit his stomach with a one-two combination…and Rowan did *not* hit like a girl. He *oomphed* out a breath.

One of her rare laughs filled the small kitchen. "Yeah, you're *grizzled*. Give me a break. You're like a brother but I'm not blind, James. You're like…hot and stuff."

"Please, I beg you to never say those words to me again. I just aged to a hundred." He tweaked her chin and she grinned.

"Why do you feel like you're a hundred?" Nina asked from the screened back door. James groaned silently as he took in her cutoffs and tank top, flip flops on her pretty feet. Her straight blond hair fell loose except for a little clip holding two pieces away from her face. She set a small duffle bag on the floor by the door. "Running clothes…so, why do you feel like you're a hundred?"

"Just the woman I want to see. I need a second opinion. James thinks he's old and grizzled. I just hit him twice in the torso and there was no give." Rowan's smile was smug as James glared at her. He started slicing bananas.

"Oh, yeah, James is *very* hot." A thump and muttered *fuck* behind them had them turning.

James held his hand in a paper towel and it was filling with blood. Rowan rushed to the sink and threw up. Nina stood between them, unsure who to tend to first. Rowan waved her off and Nina unwrapped the paper towel while holding the back of James's hand in one of hers.

"Damn, its deep, James. You're going to need stitches in your thumb." Glancing up, she said softly, "Sorry." The slight tilt of his head made her smile. "Come on, I'll drive you."

Rowan finished rinsing her mouth and said, "Sorry, James, blood *never* freaks me out." Facing them both, she asked weakly, "So, what's the verdict?"

"James is going to need stitches in his thumb. Up for a little drive?" Nina asked. Rowan shook her head and propped her upper body over the sink again. "Alright, let me see who's around. Miss Jeffries is in Tyler at the Girl Scout Jamboree until Monday. No way should James drive himself. We can't leave you alone…Gage it is."

Without waiting for Rowan's response, Nina dialed and Gage picked up on the first ring. "Hey there, can you sit with Rowan while I take James for stitches? 'Kay. See you shortly." Turning to James, she suddenly realized he was in sleep pants and a t-shirt. "You need clothes, James."

He turned to head into his room and Nina followed. Realizing she was behind him, he gave a little jump and said, "Nina, what are you doing?"

"Um, you're gushing blood from your thumb. If you're going to cover your clothes like wardrobe from a crime scene, just go in your jammies." Her fingers tapped on her hips. "*Or*, you can be a big boy and let me help you."

Rowan watched from the sink as she struggled to settle her stomach. Shrugging at James, she turned around and got sick again.

Nina muttered in frustration, "Dear lord, I've seen men naked. I think I can handle you in your boxers." She took in the expression on his face and grinned. "Ah, a commando guy…edgy. I like it." Walking past him, she called, "Come on Rambo."

One hand in a bloody wad of paper towel, the other rubbing down his tension filled face, James sighed and followed.

*Damaged*

# Chapter Nine

Nina was going through his closet. She pulled out worn jeans and a clean t-shirt, dropping them on a chair. Approaching him, she put her fingers under the hem of his t-shirt, raising it slowly up his torso. Several times, her fingertips brushed against his skin and he stared at a point above her head, gritting his teeth.

Since James was at least six-five, she leaned close to pull it over his back, her breath going over his nipple. Every muscle in his body reflexively locked and Nina went still. "That was very pretty. Do it again." When nothing happened, she licked the nipple in front of her and his pec jumped. "What a nice reaction. I wonder if the other side does tricks."

She blew on the other nipple and he went tight. When she licked it the muscle jumped. One of her hands was tangled in the fabric of his shirt at his back, the other tangled in the front. Both of his arms were raised and he had his fingers pressed hard to the bridge of his nose.

Taking his hand, she let go of the shirt and tugged him into the small attached bathroom, unwrapping his hand over the sink. Opening the medicine cabinet, she found an assortment of emergency supplies as she'd known she would. Miss Jeffries was predictable like that.

It was still bleeding but not as bad. He watched as she rinsed his thumb with cold water, pressing gently. "Bend it for me." He did and it was a relief that he could. Rinsing it again, she dried it carefully and took out butterfly bandages. Criss-crossing them over one another, she pulled them snug. "Again." He bent it again and there was some seepage. Wrapping gauze firmly around it, she covered it with medical tape. Pressing carefully, he watched her smile from the side as she grinned.

He moved to leave the bathroom and she grabbed his shirt. "Where are you going, James?"

"To get dressed, you have it all sealed up now," he said in confusion.

"I'm not done. Give me a second." He watched her clean everything up and put the supplies away. Then she pulled him near the toilet and held his shoulder while she climbed up on the closed lid.

Turning, she slipped her arms around his neck and wrapped her legs around his waist tight as he went rigid from head to toe. Taking his face in her hands, she lowered her lips and kissed him. Sliding one hand into his hair, she pulled at the strands he'd let grow longer since they'd moved here. He growled against her mouth. Smiling, she pulled it harder and moved her other hand to pinch his nipple through his shirt.

Pivoting them smoothly, he slammed her back against the wall by the door, devouring her mouth as she gripped him with her whole body. The uninjured hand slid down her side and clenched her ass. When she rocked her body against his cock, he lifted his mouth and stared at her.

Her brown eyes stared into his lighter ones. Her blond hair was a bit lighter than his and both of them had golden skin. "You realize everyone is going to think you're my daughter, right?"

"Not if I fuck you in public."

He ground against her with a low growl. "I'm sixteen years older than you, Nina."

"Think of it this way, you're going to be fucking a twenty-five-year-old."

"Nina, I'm serious."

"James...*so am I*. I look at you and I see a man, not an older man. Just a man. A man I'm insanely attracted to and have been since I saw how you protected a shattered woman who could do nothing to protect herself." She raked both hands through his shaggy hair.

"As big as you are...as alpha male a figure as you present...you can be so gentle. I need someone who won't hurt me. Who can understand I have nightmares sometimes. A strong man who will take me hard when I want it and love me softly when I need it. Right now, James, I'd like you to do either because I've wanted you so long I can't think clearly."

"Both." He lowered his mouth to hers and loved over her lips slowly. She parted them on a sigh and he licked into her mouth, sucking her tongue. His forearm went beneath her ass as support so the other hand could slide along her neck and cup her jaw.

He ate at her mouth, nibbling her with his teeth and she held him tighter, moaning. Pulling her away from the wall, he carried her into the bedroom and lowered her to the bed, stretching out over her with his cock notched against the seam of her shorts, grinding against her clit with just enough pressure to make her crazy.

She wrapped her legs harder around his waist and he groaned, loving the feel of her in his arms.

He reached up and removed the clip in her hair, running his fingers through the silken length as he stared into her face. "You're so beautiful, Nina. So young and full of life. You make me want things I've never really thought about before." His hands stroked down her sides and went to the hem of her tank top, pulling it up and over her head.

His palms settled on her breasts, his good thumb flicking over her nipple as Nina took her lower lip between her teeth and arched more firmly into his grasp. He kissed down her neck and over her collarbone, licked her upper chest until he sucked a nipple firmly into his mouth. Her hands moved to the back of his head, fisting in his hair and holding him against her.

Nipples that tasted like warm raspberries became his entire world. Releasing her with a soft pop, James raked his teeth over the tip and blew across it, watching it draw up even tighter. He took turns licking and sucking them until her hips began to thrust upward, stroking along his dick and sending chills down his spine.

He went up on his heels and moved his hands to the waist of her cutoffs, watching her suck in a hard breath when the backs of his knuckles brushed her taut abdomen. Separating the fly, he flattened his palms on her hips just inside the denim, lifting her and pushing down the shorts and her panties at the same time.

The short golden curls that covered her pussy came into view and his body tightened in vicious hunger. Nina pulled her legs up, walking her bare feet up his chest as he pulled the clothes away.

James lifted her under her arms and moved her further across the bed, separating her legs and settling his shoulders between them. As if he had all the time in the world, he explored her. Raking his nails gently through the curls again and again had Nina clenching the bedding with both hands.

When he flattened his fingers and traced them over her outer lips, she bucked under him. He smiled and trailed one finger into her cleft, circling over her clit before continuing down and tracing the entrance of her pussy again and again.

Nina's head was moving from side to side and her breath was racing. He stared at her face as he stroked deep inside the tight warmth. Her upper body surged off the bed and she moved her hips, rocking them toward him, inviting him.

Unable to deny himself another moment, he separated the plump lips and licked through the slick sweetness from her pussy to her clit. One of her hands went into his hair, the other over her breast. On the next stroke out, he added another finger, wanting to stretch her for him.

As he worked over her, getting into a soft tempo of licking her clit while he fucked her pussy with his fingers, he realized she was rolling her nipple in the same rhythm between her fingers. She came hard and suddenly, her pelvis jerking upward as she pinched her nipple tight and he continued moving until she began to loosen.

"James. Please come here."

"I'm far from finished with you, Nina. You're delicious and I need more."

She sat up and lifted his face to her, "Then strip and change positions, James. I want to play, too." His eyes went hungry and he pushed himself off the bed. James pulled his t-shirt over his head then hooked his fingers in his sleep pants, pushing them off his hips and kicking them away.

"Oh my god put your hands on your hips. You're like a fucking *Muscle & Fitness* ad." With a half smile, he did and watched as she scooted off the bed and stood. The top of her head came to his shoulder. Then her hands were everywhere and he closed his eyes at the sweet torment.

Walking around him, Nina stroked down his back and across his ass. When she was standing in front of him again, her hand circled his cock. Her fingers didn't meet as Nina stroked his length and earned a low growl from James. His body was achingly taut and she said, "You certainly take care of yourself, James. I've never had the urge to lick anyone from head to toe before. My mouth is watering."

His hand went in the hair at the base of her neck and he pulled her head back, kissing her aggressively as her fingers tightened around his cock. He ate at her mouth with his lips and teeth and tongue until she was whimpering. Her other hand went into his hair, gripping it as he gripped hers and holding him to her possessively.

James tackled her to the bed and powered them across as he continued to devour her. Her knees were tight at his hips and she worked her wet slit against him. He manhandled her, pushing and pulling at her body and sucking at her mouth, then her nipples, then her mouth again until Nina was begging, pleading with him to fuck her.

Rubbing her clit along his cock made her come. Reaching between them he placed the head at the entrance of her pussy, powering forward and burying himself to the hilt as she bit his shoulder and held him against her with surprising strength. One fist wrapped in her hair, holding her in place while he fucked her harder than any man ever had before.

"Yes, James, yes...*please don't stop*. I want all of you. Fuck me hard and make me yours, James. I need you to take me hard...I need to belong to you." Going up on one hand, he pushed her knee out from her body and watched his cock disappear inside her.

He was slick from her come and when he slammed her into another climax that bordered on pain, his eyes roamed over her body. Both her hands went to her nipples, cupping her breasts as she pinched and pulled them away from her.

He went harder and she stared at him in wonder, nodding her head. "You won't hurt me. No one else would ever take me like this, James. They were afraid to hurt me but you know I'm not weak. You know I'm stronger than I look. I need it hard, so hard. You feel so fucking *good*, baby."

James went back on his heels and lifted her feet over his shoulders. Bracing one hand on the bed, the other held her shoulder as he drove down into her with his full strength and watched as she climaxed screaming his name.

Driving down into her, letting everything go for the first time in his sexual history, he felt the come leave the head of his cock with enough force to have him gasping for breath. He forced every drop into the depths of her spasming pussy until he'd dragged another orgasm from her.

Releasing her legs, he collapsed on his forearms and kissed her long and slow. Her hands roamed him, strong fingers kneading into the muscles of his arms and back. Her narrow foot stroked over his ass and down his legs. He didn't remember a woman ever touching him so much.

He was staring at sunlight-gilded strands of her hair when she said, "James, I've done so many things I'm ashamed of. So many things I regret. You make me feel different, like I'm brand new…just washing away all the horrible things I've done." She hugged him with her entire body and he pulled back to look at her face, watching as tears slipped from under her golden brown lashes.

"Nina, you're so young. There's nothing you could have done so very bad. Your entire life is ahead of you, honey." He stroked her hair back from her face, his fingers lingering over her skin.

Her small laugh held no humor. "You have no idea, James. I'm probably the worst person you'll ever know." She turned away, unable to look into his eyes, and he brought her face back to him.

"Why don't you tell me why you're such a horrible person, Nina? I don't see it."

She took a deep breath and stared at his shoulder as she gripped him hard, "It was my fault…with Gage and Rowan. I was scared to lose her. She was strong and I needed her so I didn't feel weak. I thought I was in love with her for a long time. I would have been with both of them to keep her, scared her sweet innocence out of her."

Swallowing hard, she whispered, "I went to him, drew him to me physically, James. He was desperate for her, waiting until she turned eighteen. I knew it and I used it. Used my body to get my way. I'd learned to do that really young." A small shudder worked its way over her body and James held her tighter.

"It was how I ended up here. My crack-head mother sold me to a child porn ring. The FBI found me when I was twelve. Kept me in custody for two years because I…I was the oldest girl and fit to testify. Most of the other kids were so broken, so destroyed they couldn't function."

Shaking her head, she said in disgust, "Not me though. I was cool as a cucumber. They changed my name and put me here with Miss Jeffries. I was so cold, so hard inside when I met Rowan. You know how she is. She loves so well, so beautifully. I felt cleaner just being around her."

James stroked a strand of her hair between his fingers while she talked. He could tell she was waiting for him to get disgusted, to pull away from her. She might not know it yet but every word only made him more adamant to keep her, to heal her, and to love her.

Fresh tears coursed down Nina's cheeks, "She saved me and I needed her. I seduced the man she loved and I broke her heart. Since then, whenever I've been tempted to use my body as a tool, I remember her face when she caught us. I will never forget that look as long as I live." Her voice hitched on a sob.

"I've been a horrible person, James. I've committed more sins in my life than you have. I *feel* older than you. I can never have children because of all the…the physical damage done when I was little. I have nightmares and wake up fighting. There are days I have so much anger

I run until I fall down. I know, without a doubt, you are too *good* to be with someone like me, but I've never wanted anyone or anything so badly in my life."

James slid his hands up her back and hugged her to him with all his strength. "Nina, precious Nina. If it takes every day I have left of my life, I will convince you there is nothing bad, unclean, or damaged about you. You were hurt and taken advantage of. All your innocence and childhood stripped from you by force. That doesn't make you a bad person."

A low moan vibrated in her chest and he kissed her gently, easily. He drank her down and let her absorb the feel of him holding her. He planned to hold her a lot. "I already knew about you and Gage. Nina, you were eighteen with a bad childhood behind you and the unknown ahead." She shook her head and he kissed her silent.

"You tried to hang on with both hands…it was just a mistake a lot of people have made. Do you know how Rowan views it? That it had to happen so she could meet Bennett and have the ability to love him…a love that bettered both their lives." Bringing her hands up to cover her face, she began to cry harder.

James lowered his body weight more firmly over her and put his mouth close to her ear. "She said Gage would have helped you then, treated you more gently than you were used to. That you needed him more than she did. And she was right. Everything happens for a reason, Nina." He nuzzled his face in her hair. "All those pieces falling together brought you to me. Embrace it. I'll never let anyone hurt you again, Nina. I'll only love you and protect you for the rest of my life."

He angled his mouth over hers as he started to move inside her, loving her with his body as he had with his words. Stroking her up slow and easy, he held her as she came sobbing in his arms. When she calmed, he brought her up again…then again…until she was weak with sexual satisfaction.

"I love you, Nina." She moaned against his shoulder. "I accept you unconditionally as the person you are because everything that happened to you brought you here, to this moment, so I could give you all the love I've waited all my life to give to the right woman." Then he pushed her up again and watched her as she watched him.

When she came, she whispered fiercely, "I love you, James. I won't let you down."

"I won't let *you* down, Nina. Your heart is safe with me." Then he released his control and coated her body with his release. He hadn't used protection and he didn't care. As their pounding hearts began to slow and their breathing returned to normal, he moved to lift his body off of her. She held him tight with her arms and legs.

"I'm going to crush you, sweetheart, I'll lay right beside you and snuggle." She shook her head and held him tighter. He kissed her neck and settled his weight over her carefully, not surprised when both of them dropped off to sleep within a few minutes.

It was the best sleep he'd had in years and he drowsily wondered where he could buy her a ring.

# Chapter Ten

Gage came through the back door and went directly to Rowan's side, pulling her long hair out of the way and holding it back for her as she got sick again. "Are you alright, Rowan? What can I get you?" She wore a loose sundress and stood in her bare feet.

Cupping water in her hands, she rinsed her mouth and washed her face. "Give me just a minute." She went into the small half bath in the mudroom and he heard her brushing her teeth. He waited with his hip against the counter. When she reappeared, she look fresh and beyond lovely. His heart slammed into his ribcage as it always did. "James sliced open his thumb. The sight of the…the blood hit me wrong. I'm *never* sensitive to blood. Pathetic."

"You could never be pathetic." He looked around for James and Nina. "Where are they?"

"Nina is helping him, um, get dressed and we're going to be silent as church mice and leave them alone," Rowan smiled to herself as she started gathering up her laptop and files. Pausing for a moment, she giggled. "I just thought of the funniest thing. It takes so little to amuse me apparently. I'm barefoot and pregnant…in the *kitchen*. That is hysterical."

He laughed softly with her. "Where are you going with all your stuff?"

Rowan met his eyes and cursed the physical reaction she was beginning to feel against her will around Gage. "If I was reading the situation correctly…and since I'm barely non-virgin, I could be wrong…what I've seen brewing for months is about to culminate into either a fight or a sexual attack. Initiated by Nina, not James. I'd rather not be working ten feet away. I'm sure I'd be scandalized." Her face felt too hot as she tucked her stuff into a small bag and walked out on the front porch, leaving him staring open-mouthed behind her.

Settling into one of the wicker chairs, she sat back for a moment with her ankles crossed and her hands over her belly. Gage came out, catching the screen door before it banged shut, and sat in the chair beside her. They enjoyed the silence, watching the clear hot day. Birds played in the little statuary bath. Bugs hopped in the grass. A stray cat stalked along the fence looking for prey.

Rowan wasn't necessarily uncomfortable around Gage. It was more…on edge. For almost nine months, they'd pointedly avoided discussing their past or the last day she'd seen him before leaving for college. He checked on her, helped her, talked to her, and kept her company.

He avoided touching her if possible and she did the same. They had a lot in common and knew many of the same people since they'd spent so many years of their youth together. She knew his family and they knew her.

A month after she'd arrived she had a visit from Gage's mother. Two years after Rowan left for college, Jennifer had lost her husband, the father of her four sons. A year ago, she'd remarried his friend and business partner. She seemed very happy.

Rowan had been to her doctor's appointment earlier in the day and he had confirmed what she was positive she'd known from day one. Bennett had given her a son. By the time Jennifer arrived, Rowan had barely been hanging on.

The older woman had taken one look at her and guided her to sit on the couch. She held her there while she cried, simply stroking her hair and murmuring softly. "What I want you to know is that it gets better, Rowan. I swear to you it does. I still have moments when something reminds me of Greg and it makes me laugh; sometimes things make me cry."

"It doesn't feel like it will ever stop. Not ever," she had whispered through her tears.

"I know, honey. Greg and I had many years together and a full life. You had to force a lot of life into so little time with your husband but you have those memories. He'd want you to heal, honey. For you to find happiness again someday. I was too young to spend the rest of my life alone and I was nearing fifty."

Easing Rowan back, she'd smoothed her tears away with a small smile. "I know right now, your heart is hurting. But one day, you'll begin to hurt a little less and you'll think more of the memories than the loss. And little by little, the pain will begin to fade. Not all of it but most of it. Your late husband would be so proud of you. He's waiting for you to get past your grief and remember the person you were before the sadness. The person he fell so famously in love with."

Since that day, Jennifer called her often and Rowan valued the woman's friendship and her singular understanding of all the people in her life of what she was going through.

She could feel Gage watching her and she turned her head on the back of the chair to look at him. He said quietly, "You're so very beautiful, Rowan. Pregnancy takes your normal beauty and pushes it over the edge, making it almost painful to look at you."

"Thank you, Gage."

He stared at her for a long time before standing and moving to kneel at her feet. This close she couldn't ignore how gorgeous he was and it frightened her. "Close your eyes, Rowan." After a long hesitation, she did as he asked. He placed his large hands on either side of her pregnant belly, leaning forward to lay his cheek against her. The contact startled her but she kept her eyes closed.

Gage's deep drawl pulled her into a strange disconnection. "I think if Bennett were here, he'd touch you often, Rowan. He would love on you gently as you both waited for your child to be born. He'd want to soothe your fears and he would remind you often how much he loved you." Rowan felt hypnotized by the picture he wove for her.

"I know you miss him so much. I know you'd rather he were here and able to touch you. I want you to pretend, Rowan. Clear your mind and imagine Bennett is here right now in front of you. You can talk to me as if I'm him and let me help you, Rowan. I want so badly to help you."

He stroked over her belly, over her sides, down her legs and up again.

Slipped his palms across the tops of her hands on the chair, up her arms, over her bare shoulders, and cupped her face with his fingertips in her hair. He smoothed his thumbs over her jaw and up to wipe the silent tears from her cheeks that slipped from her closed eyes.

Then he gently pulled her to him and cupped the back of her head against his chest as he stroked her hair. He moved closer to her and held her tightly as her arms went around him. He kissed the top of her head and rested his cheek there.

She began to cry brokenly and he hugged her harder. "Tell me, Rowan."

She whispered through her tears, "I'm so sorry you were sick. I'm sorry you felt less than the man you were. It wasn't fair after the life you lived to be weakened that way; to have your strength and vitality sapped from you one drop at a time day after day."

Her arms tightened at his back and she gasped for breath, "I'm sorry I wasn't able to love you past it, couldn't love you every day as I did our last day together. That I was the…the *reason* you died. I didn't want you to be afraid so I tried not to be afraid. Even though I knew I was killing you, knew I would have to live with that the rest of my life. I deserve the pain and the guilt because I killed the only man who ever loved me."

She was shaking and hurting. "It wasn't your fault, Rowan. He needed your touch more than the next beat of his heart. I completely understand." Gage tilted her head back and kissed her, stroking her face and moving his lips over hers until she opened for him. He made gentle love to her with his kiss for a long time, his hand smoothing from the back of her head to her low back again and again. One of her hands came up to rest on his chest, over his heart and she sighed into his mouth.

Breaking the kiss, he told her, "Rowan, open your eyes." When her blue eyes were staring into his, he whispered, "Bennett was the *best* man who ever loved you, Rowan…but he was *not* the only one." Then he kissed her again and felt when the tension eased and she accepted him. Her hands drifted around his neck and her fingers stroked through his hair.

He pulled back and she stared at him. "Let me love you, Rowan. Let me give you peace for a little while. I won't hurt you, I expect nothing. I know you won't be thinking of me. You can close your eyes. Let me do this for you."

When she nodded, he lifted her in his arms and carried her inside, up the stairs to her bedroom. Standing her on her feet beside the bed, he whispered, "Close your eyes, Rowan." She did and he pulled the soft dress over her head. Going to his knees, he pulled her panties away and drank in his first sight of Rowan in the nude.

He hadn't exaggerated. She was so beautiful it was painful. That she was pregnant with another man's child hurt his heart. If he'd been a better man, a stronger man, it could be his child growing inside her. His pain, his regrets were not important anymore. Only what Rowan needed mattered.

He pulled his shirt over his head and lifted her hand to place it over his heart. He wanted her to feel him, to know she wasn't alone. That she never had to be alone again. He steeled himself for her to whisper another man's name, knowing it would cut deep, and that it was what he'd earned for betraying her and breaking her young heart.

He stripped his clothes away and gathered her in his arms. Lifting her, he placed her carefully in the center of the bed, lying down beside her and kissing her until she was breathless. For ten minutes he kissed every inch of her face, made love to her mouth, and kissed her face again.

Only when she was moaning did he move to her neck, giving her little sucking kisses down one side and licking into the hollow at the base of her throat. The fingers of one hand went into his hair while the other clenched the sheets with white knuckles. Moving over her collarbone and across her shoulder, he moved slowly, relishing the feel of her at long last.

When his mouth closed over a nipple, her upper body arched into him and he caressed the other breast as they pebbled harder with his attention. Plumping and squeezing the far breast, his hand drifted over her pregnant stomach, his palm warm as he explored all of her.

Gently tracing the tops of her thighs before raking his knuckles over her bare mound, he watched her hips thrust instinctively against his hand. The flat of his palm stroked her, one finger pressing into the cleft of her and pulling a whimper from her.

He kissed down her body and settled in the cradle of her thighs. He left one hand flat on her stomach, gently stroking back and forth as he used the other to separate her folds so she was open for him to lick through the slit of her body to her clit.

With his first taste, Gage groaned against her. He moved his other hand to the entrance of her pussy and slipped one finger deep into the slick warmth, licking her clit in a matching rhythm. She came quickly the first time, lifting her hips to him, and fisting her fingers in his hair.

He didn't stop, wanting her to feel everything she deserved, bringing her up and over twice more and loving the soft sighs and moans she gave him in return. Her inner walls were warm and pliant now; he knew he wouldn't hurt her.

Reaching beside the bed, he picked up his pants and removed a condom. He rolled it on and crawled up the length of her body; kissing her mound, her belly, her breasts before claiming her mouth again. He stretched out beside her and rolled her carefully to her side.

Lifting Rowan's leg to his thigh, he set his cock at her pussy and sealed himself to her back, his arm beneath her head, and one hand cupping her breast as he gradually entered her. When he was fully seated in the closest version of heaven he'd ever experienced, he tugged her back against him more firmly and squeezed her breast before sliding his hand to the center of her and stroking over her clit as he began to thrust carefully.

Her hand closest to the bed held his and her other was over his wrist, caressing him as he moved over her and inside her. Gage watched her breasts tighten further over her shoulder as he kissed her neck. She began to meet him, thrusting her hips back as he moved forward and when she came, her nails left marks on him. Rowan's pussy clenched so tight around him and small vibrations shuddered over her body.

He kept moving, pushing her through one climax and on to the next.

Over and over, he loved her with everything he had, every skill he'd ever learned, refusing to let himself come, focused only on what Rowan needed, what she deserved.

He was careful not to speak to her, though there was so much he wanted to tell her. When he felt her beginning to tighten again, he exerted what he had left of his control to keep himself from going over with her. She came harder this time, locking around him and gripping his hands with all her strength. "Oh Gage, how I wanted you. So very long I waited to know you like this. Thank you."

Gage's heart stuttered in his chest and he came moaning her name over and over in the hair behind her ear. He thrust shallowly until there was nothing left to give her, exhaling so many years of regret against her neck and pulling her to him, hugging her tight.

"Rowan, forgive me for being stupid." She nodded and tightened her arms over his. "I love you. I've loved you for so long. I don't remember what it was like not to love you. To hold you at last is…thank you. I don't expect anything. I know what you're going through. I just…I needed you to know."

They lay in silence for a long time and when both of them felt her water break over them, they went utterly still. He pulled from her carefully and rolled her to her back.

"Weird but fitting, don't you think?" she asked with her hand on his cheek. "The first time I took a life…the second, I get one back." He kissed her palm and lifted her to the edge of the bed.

"Are you alright, Rowan? Did I hurt you? I put you into labor, Rowan." He was scared to death.

Rowan shook her head, "I'm at peace. I need to shower and dress. You'll have to take me to the hospital." He carried her to the bathroom and climbed in with her, helping her wash herself before quickly washing his own body. Holding her hand, she stepped from the shower and he dried her, being achingly gentle.

When he knelt to dry her legs, she put her fingers under his chin and raised his face to look at her. "Gage, I *loved* Bennett and there will *always* be a part of my heart that belongs to him. Just as there was *always* a part of my heart that belonged to *you* while I was with him. He knew that and he loved me anyway. He would have liked you, I think. I love you."

He stood and took her face in his hands, "You shouldn't feel guilt about Bennett's death, Rowan. He knew what would happen and chose to leave this life with you in his arms. I know it would be my choice if I had it." More tears slipped down her cheeks and he wiped them away.

"You are the strongest woman I've ever known and I'm so sorry for hurting you. I think you had to have Bennett love you first. To let him show you exactly what you were worth. I was too young to love you the way you deserved then, to treat you as you deserve to be treated. He loved you perfectly and gave me an example to follow that I'm grateful for."

He lowered one hand to her belly, stroking over her skin gently. "I will love this child as if he were my own, Rowan. He will never doubt my love for him. As long as I live, I will never let you regret letting me love you. For giving me another chance to be the man you needed me to be." He kissed her deeply and held her. "I love you…let's get you to the hospital before I pass out from stress."

Chuckling, she let him lead her back to the bedroom and when she pulled out panties and another sun dress, he dressed her. Slipping sandals on her feet, he insisted on carrying her downstairs. Walking through the house, he tapped on James's door, "Wrap it up. Rowan's water just broke."

There was frantic scrambling inside and when James opened the door shirtless and looking panicked, he took in the sight of Rowan in Gage's arms and smiled. "Rowan, do I…do we have five minutes?" She nodded and he slammed the door hard unintentionally.

Gage sat on a kitchen chair and held her through a small contraction, checking his watch. They listened as Nina and James took a thirty second shower and made all sorts of noise getting dressed.

When the door opened, it bounced back hard and slammed against the wall behind it. James flinched as he heard the knob damage the wall. "I'll fix that. I promise."

Nina pushed past him and crouched in front of Rowan. "Are you okay?" Rowan nodded and suddenly Nina seemed to take in the fact that Gage held Rowan on his lap. A huge smile broke over her face and she nodded, "It's about time. Alright, what do we do?"

James had Rowan's bag and the SUV keys in his hand. "People, do you need an invitation? You're cordially invited to get the hell in the car before we're delivering this baby ourselves. Damn…hustle, hustle." He held the door as Nina went out giving him a wink followed by Gage looking freaked out and carrying a calm Rowan.

When everyone was in the car, James gripped the wheel tightly. "Honestly, my brain has gone totally blank. I forgot where the hospital is. Fuck."

"Just drive, baby. I'll tell you where to go," Nina told him laughing.

# **Chapter Eleven**

*Rebirth...three months later*

Rowan tucked her breast into the nursing bra and pulled Bennett Jefferson the Second up on her chest to burp him. They called him Benji and he was the best baby on the planet as far as his mother was concerned. It looked like he'd end up with his father's green eyes and black hair. He rarely cried, seeming to stare at her with such intensity she often zoned while he was nursing.

Over the past months, Rowan found herself wondering if Bennett hadn't placed his own soul inside their son as he'd died. In a fit of nervous energy, she'd had James help her request photos of Bennett throughout his life and organized them chronologically, staring at them constantly...especially his baby pictures.

She had dreams that verged on nightmares almost nightly. Guilt was rearing its ugly head at every turn and every day since Benji's birth she'd had a crying jag.

Gage was walking on eggshells around her, knowing she was having second thoughts about them. He'd held her hand through delivery, his eyes on her as Nina recorded the entire thing. She hadn't handed him the baby in all this time, worried to push the issue.

Gage hadn't taken the baby from her since he was unsure of his place in her or Benji's life. He was desperate to hold both of them and ready to crawl out of his own skin. Whenever the cattle business didn't need him, he stayed close.

When he was working, Rowan found herself questioning everything silently. She'd bought a piece of land further down the road and was considering having a house built. She felt caught in stasis.

Benji burped and fell immediately to sleep on her breast, his little hands opening and closing on her. She stood and placed him in his bed, watching as he settled comfortably. Grabbing the baby monitor, she headed downstairs and Miss Jeffries stood with Gage in the small kitchen.

"Hey there. Where are the girls?" Miss Jeffries had taken in two five-year-old sisters, twins who were just adorable, a few months before Rowan had come back. Their mother had dropped them off at the local fire station as she was heading through town with her boyfriend. Apparently, he thought they were a pain in the ass. She was hoping for a family to place them with but intended to keep them until that happened.

Smiling softly through the kitchen window, she said, "Nina is playing tea party with them in the side yard. Come take a look." Rowan stepped up beside her and stared through the window at Nina sitting with the two red heads around the picnic table set with one of Miss Jeffries's old tea sets.

Nina was in running shorts and a tank top, sneakers on her feet. The girls were barefoot in cotton sundresses. They were all three holding teacups with their pinkies up daintily. A soft breeze was blowing Nina's long ponytail and she looked incredibly happy. Rowan removed the camera she kept in her pocket at all times since Benji was born and took pictures.

Suddenly, a stiff breeze lifted the napkins and scattered them across the backyard. Rowan continued to take pictures as Nina and the girls ran around dizzily trying to catch all the paper birds. When she went down on one knee to pick up two near the fence, the little girls tackled her to the side and jumped on her.

She quickly gained the upper hand and had them giggling insanely from being tickled. Collapsing back on the grass with her arms out, she was obviously startled when the little girls curled into her side on the soft grass. They couldn't hear them, but it was obvious the three of them were talking.

When Tia and Tara fell asleep on her a few minutes later, Nina made no move to get up. They watched for another ten minutes and realized Nina was asleep as well. "That is the most beautiful sight I've ever seen," Rowan whispered with tears in her eyes. "She looks so…peaceful."

James came in the front door and saw them all standing at the kitchen window. "Who looks peaceful? What's going on?" He stepped up beside Rowan and took in the scene. Tilting his head to the side, he had a soft smile on his face. He motioned to Gage and they went out the screen door. Picking up both the girls carefully to keep from waking them, he knelt to smooth Nina's hair back from her face.

When her eyes opened, she was confused but she focused on James's face and broke into a smile. She saw one of the twins in his arms and her smile turned sad. She stood up and kissed his cheek before heading to the picnic table to clean up their tea party.

James and Gage brought the girls inside and laid them end to end on the couch in the living room. Gage went back to the window as James went out to help Nina clean up. He tugged her down beside him on the bench and leaned back casually, his arm around her.

After several minutes, Nina tried to get up and they could see she'd started crying. James tugged her back down on his lap and her hands went over her face. He forced her to look at him. They spoke quietly for a long time and she kept shaking her head.

She yelled the only audible sentence from their entire conversation, "Because I'm not fucking *good enough*, James. That's why!" He pulled her face to him and kissed her, leaning her back in his arms until she went limp.

Miss Jeffries whispered fiercely, "Everybody scatter."

Rowan sat down at her laptop and Miss Jeffries went into the laundry room as Gage walked to the living room to check on the twins before heading back out to the fields.

Ten seconds later, the back door slammed open and James entered, carrying Nina in his arms. She was crying against his chest and neither of them said a word as he went in his bedroom and closed the door with his foot.

James toed off his shoes and laid Nina across his bed. Pulling off her sneakers, he crawled up beside her and took her in his arms. "You're an amazing woman, Nina. You would make a wonderful mother and I think it's something you want very much. Why do you think you aren't good enough?"

"I didn't help them."

"Help who, baby?"

"The other kids…with me. I didn't stop…what was happening to them. I even…I even had to do stuff…perform with them. The people who had us, they kept talking about how I was getting too old for some of the films, I was so tall. They started bringing in more full grown adult men to…be recorded with me. They were worried that my boobs would get too big. I cannot be trusted with the safety of children, James. I'd fucking contaminate them."

It was very rare that James had cried in his adult life. When he lost his mother, then his little sister a year later, when the towers fell on 9/11, when Bennett died and Rowan was so broken, and now. Now he held Nina and sobbed for the childhood that had been ripped from her. He sobbed for the way she saw herself when he knew how purely good she was.

He crushed her to him and then she was crying, too. They clung to one another and wept openly for several minutes.

When his tears slowed, he told her achingly, "Nina, I want you to see that you are kind and beautiful inside and out. That you have so much love to give…*so much*…you overflow with it. You couldn't help those other children any more than they could have helped you…because *you were a child*, too. You didn't do anything wrong. I'm so glad you survived so I can love you as hard as possible and one day convince you of what I see when I look at you."

He stripped her of her clothes and pulled his away, taking her in his arms and loving her slow and easy. As James moved over her, he whispered, "You saved me, Nina. From spending the next forty years alone and lonely. Now I have you beside me and my life has so much more color. Your love was exactly what I needed, baby."

He stroked one hand through her hair while his other held her knee to his hip. She stopped crying and ran her hands over him. James kissed her fingers as they smoothed over him. "Tell me what you think about me as a man, Nina."

"What do you mean, James? I think you're the best man I've ever known. Good and strong and kind. You protect everyone around you and make the world seem safer, more solid. You love me so well, James, in so many ways." His thrusts into her body were slow, pulling almost all the way out and stroking steadily until his pelvis bumped against Nina's gently and his cock was nestled firmly at her womb.

"And if I, with all my goodness and strength…after so many years spent alone when I had *so many* opportunities to give a woman my love but didn't…if I chose you, *out of everyone* to love…what do you think that means? You can't have it both ways, baby. Either I'm good and practical or I'm a blind fool to the imagined evil you see in yourself."

He watched the conflict begin in her eyes as her body took over and shoved her hard into a climax she simply couldn't fight. Nina's pussy clenched along the length of him, milking him inside her as her thighs pulled in and her upper body slammed into James. He never slowed, pushing her higher and she moaned low in her throat.

He stroked his palm along the side of her face, down her neck, and across her collarbone to cup her breast. Squeezing gently he lowered his mouth to suck her nipple and her hands went into his hair, holding him against her and running her fingers through the strands.

"James…how much I love you."

James lifted his eyes to hers, "I love you, too, my precious Nina. I don't think you realize how much I love you, how much I believe in you as a woman, as *my woman*, Nina. I need you to see yourself as I see you, baby. Look at me, honey. See what I see." He loved her up and over the next peak and she was breathing hard.

"Again. Keep looking at me, baby. I *am* a good man, Nina. I've worked hard my entire life to make sure I was. See yourself…your true self, Nina…as the man who loves you more than he loves himself sees you. See the woman I love and accept that image as the truth because I would never lie to you, I would never hurt you. See the woman I love, Nina."

Over and over he pushed her, talking to her and loving her until she was sobbing and clinging to him as he held her, both of them slick with sweat.

"My woman is a survivor. My woman loves others to the point of pain. My woman protected enough of her heart to give it to me so I could protect it and help it heal for the rest of my life. My woman is good enough, kind enough, loving enough to stand up to anything. My woman deserves every chance to share all the love she has to offer."

Going up on his heels, he pulled her with him. She wrapped her body around him and rested her forehead on his shoulder. "Look at me, Nina baby." She lifted her head and her tears trailed down her cheeks. He kissed her deeply, lifting and lowering her on his cock as she moaned into his mouth. "Nina...tell me, honey." She clutched him hard around the neck and buried her face in his hair shaking her head. "Nina, *tell me*...I need you to, honey."

Taking a deep shaking breath, she whispered, "I want them...so bad, James. I want those precious little girls so bad."

His arms locked around her hard and he said, "I want them, too. For them and for you, my pretty baby." Then James slammed her to the bed and began fucking her harder than she'd ever begged him to. "Who *are* you, Nina?"

Gasping and moaning, she managed, "Your woman, James..."

"And what does that mean, baby?"

"That I...I'm good enough and you couldn't love me if I...if I wasn't."

"Come for me one more time, baby...oh God...I love you so much, Nina." He powered into her body and watched as the orgasm scratched and clawed its way through her, exploding in liquid heat that traveled over every inch of his cock.

Before she'd finished trembling, he groaned her name against her mouth and pumped his seed deep into her body. The climax went on forever, dragging both of them through a physically exhausting experience.

James cupped the back of her head in his palms and she was staring at him in wonder. "You are going to be a perfect mother, Nina. Just as you'll be a perfect wife. Marry me, Nina."

"Are you…?" she started to ask him and his eyes narrowed making her smile. "Yes, James. Absolutely yes." James hugged and kissed her until she was laughing then moved to the edge of the bed with her still connected to him and opened his nightstand drawer.

Pulling out a box, he handed it to Nina with a smile. She opened it and gasped at the large princess cut diamond inside set in gold. "James, it's so gorgeous…my God, you didn't have to…nevermind, thank you," she told him with a smile when he lifted his brow.

"I bought a house on the other side of the property Rowan bought. It's being repainted and getting new floors. It has plenty of room for your marketing business and the girls. I think you're going to love it, Nina…close your mouth, baby." Nina was staring at him in stunned disbelief.

"You…you bought a house?" He nodded. "You want me to live in a house with you…and the girls?"

Chuckling, he said, "That's usually the way it works, Nina love. You'll get used to being settled and loved, I promise." James took the ring from the box and slipped it on her finger. She stared at it for a long time and kept touching it with her other hand. Then Nina threw her arms around him and hugged him with all her strength. "Oh, sweet baby, I love you, too."

James carried her to the shower and they bathed together, taking their time getting dressed. Nina had clothes in the bottom drawer of his dresser and he watched as she pulled on jeans and a t-shirt, padding to him barefoot and wrapping her arms around his waist with her cheek on his chest. "James. I want you to know I'm going to try and be everything you see in me. I might mess up sometimes so I apologize in advance."

"Nina…messing up is part of life, honey. We'll get through it together."

They went out to the kitchen and Miss Jeffries was folding laundry. She glanced up and smiled when Nina held up the ring James had given her. "Oh, Nina, that is wonderful. James is such a good man. He certainly chose wisely, honey. I'll contact the state to start the paperwork on the girls." Nina's eyes opened wide.

"Sweetheart, you've been spending a few hours every day with those little girls for months. I know love when I see it." Nina hugged her hard and asked where Rowan was. "You know she won't leave the house. She's upstairs with the baby."

Grabbing James's hand after he kissed Miss Jeffries's cheek with a wink, they went upstairs to the little room that had been converted into a nursery for Benji. Rowan was sitting in the rocking chair staring out over the back fields.

Nina approached when she saw the baby was sleeping soundly in the crib. Kneeling in front of Rowan, she showed her the ring and her eyes widened before a huge smile broke over her face.

She stroked Nina's cheek and whispered, "He could *not* have chosen better, Nina. You're the perfect pair and I'm so, so very happy, honey." Nina laid her head in Rowan's lap and cried softly. When she whispered she was sorry, Rowan stroked her hair.

"Gentle Nina, oh honey, there is nothing for you to apologize for, I promise. Everything happened as it was meant to. Look at me, Nina." When the blond head lifted, Rowan wiped her tears. "Never again are you to think of that time with sadness, Nina. We were so young and so desperate to be loved. It pushed us in the direction we were meant to go, I think. Don't think of it sadly. I don't."

Nina stared at her oldest friend for a long moment, "Rowan, honey, what's going on? Why won't you leave the house? Why won't you talk to Gage?" She picked up Rowan's hand, "Please let me help you, Rowan."

Her blue eyes went wide then filled with tears and she shook her head,

"Nina, I'm losing my mind. Really and truly losing my mind. I…I think Benji is Bennett reincarnated. He's so…still sometimes, staring at me. He knows…what I did. I shouldn't have cheated on him."

James gasped behind her and came to kneel beside Nina. "Rowan, don't you do this to yourself. You *did not* cheat on Bennett. He would have wanted you to be happy, to be loved, and protected. For Benji to have a man to look up to, to teach him how to grow into the man he's meant to be."

He leaned forward and kissed her cheek, stroking her hair as tears fell silently down her cheeks. "Oh, honey, I was *there*. I know how pure your love was for Bennett. I know how much he loved you. He wouldn't *want* this. He'd ache to see you like this."

"I have no right to be happy…"

"Rowan! Bennett would flip out if he heard you say that and I never even met the man in person," Nina said incredulously. "You *have* to know that isn't true. You have to know he'd want your happiness more than anything else."

"But…Benji…" Rowan whispered.

With a smile, James went to pick up the baby, coming back and kneeling in front of Rowan. "He's a beautiful baby, isn't he, Rowan?" She nodded and stroked Benji's face. "If this is Bennett reincarnated, you couldn't have a better man to call your son."

Her eyes lit up at the thought. "I think if that is the case, he's waiting for you to be happy. Benji is so precious and he rarely cries. He also rarely smiles, Rowan. Either this is Bennett or it isn't; either way, this baby can sense your sadness. I don't believe this is Bennett, I believe this is Bennett's son, who will look at the world just as his father did, hoping most for the happiness of others."

Nina continued, "You can't keep grieving, Rowan. It isn't good for you and it isn't good for Benji. Gage has no clue how to reassure you without seeming like he's pushing. You have to be loved, Rowan. Without it, you'll die slowly. Your heart will eventually fail as surely as Bennett's because you *need* to love. It's part of who you are."

"I'm so confused. So tired."

"Rowan, baby, come downstairs…come outside. Sit for a while and let's talk." Nina stood and James did, too, settling Benji more firmly on his shoulder. Holding out her hand, Rowan took it and allowed them to lead her to the first floor and out on the porch.

They settled on the chairs and talked for hours. When Rowan had to feed Benji, James stood and went to the edge of the porch, facing out to give her privacy. When Benji needed to be changed, Nina took him inside and brought him back several minutes later. Conversation was easy and Nina told Rowan about the girls, about wanting to keep them.

"You will be the most loving, kindest mother on the planet, Nina. Those girls will get a second chance at life because of you." Nina teared up but said nothing. "And with two such beautiful parents, how pretty they are won't even be questioned. You can fill the rest of their lives with happy memories and keep them safe."

They talked about their houses, the one James was remodeling, and the one Rowan was thinking about building. They talked about Rowan's charities which were garnering so much attention. For almost eight months, she'd been able to hide out here.

Other than Bennett's assistant and her own assistant at the organization, no one knew she was quietly passing her days in a sleepy Texas town. James had been worrying for a while now about her safety and Benji's but she hadn't wanted to discuss it.

"We need to hire you a driver, Rowan. A nanny and housekeeper. Another bodyguard I can work with as well as a full security team. I know these are not things you're used to anymore, but Benji is the heir to a massive fortune, Rowan."

James turned to her, "I've been stressing about one of you being abducted. I love this house, but it isn't safe for you to keep living here. Eventually, someone is going to track you down. I've been doing some research and I'd like to get started if that's alright."

Rowan was distracted and they followed her gaze across the road, where Gage was moving cattle a quarter of a mile away on horseback.

He sat easily in the saddle with a cowboy hat sitting low over his eyes, cutting and riding around the field to guide the cows through a gate. He had two men working with him.

She watched him in silence for over an hour. She grabbed the chair when he glanced in their direction then did a double take. Calling something to the other men, they nodded and he started trotting toward them. Her heart sped and breathing was harder.

Twenty yards from the border fence, he picked up speed and jumped it smoothly – Rowan gasped in fear – then crossed the road and entered the outer yard to Miss Jeffries's property.

Rowan took in his shaggy hair under the hat, his hazel eyes bright as he kept them on her, his body lean and hard in the saddle. Rowan had never seen a more beautiful sight in her life than Gage Chambers on the back of a horse.

# **Chapter Twelve**

He rode up along the porch and nodded to James and Nina. When his eyes lit on Rowan, he smiled softly. "Rowan. I've never taken you riding before." He held out his hand and she whispered she wasn't wearing shoes. "I'll bring you right back to this spot, you won't need them."

She stood carefully and Nina took Benji. Gage lifted her around the waist and settled her in front of him on the saddle. Tensing, having never actually ridden a horse before, Rowan held her breath as Gage slipped his forearm around her waist and snugged her back against his chest.

"Just relax, Rowan. I'll keep you safe." Clucking to the horse, he winked at the couple standing on the porch with Rowan's baby. "I'll have her back in a while."

"She's good on feedings for another three hours," Nina provided helpfully. "We've got Benji, no worries."

James grinned beside her. "Please, take your time."

Rowan started to speak but Gage rode out of the yard. He walked the horse slowly along the shoulder of the narrow road. "I've missed you, Rowan. I've been trying to figure out a way to talk to you alone…truly alone…for weeks now."

She said nothing but seemed to be holding her breath. "I've wanted to show you something. Mama asks about you all the time, said to tell you hello." Rowan nodded. "Well, all my brothers started businesses of their own long before we lost Dad. When he passed, Mama was the only one living in the main house…I was still out in the apartment over the barn."

The horse made a sudden step and Rowan clenched. "He was stepping over a hole, honey. I've got you." The day was beautiful and Rowan realized she hadn't been outside in a long time. Other than Benji's doctor's appointments, she hadn't even left the house.

"When Mama remarried, she moved in with Bobby. I moved into the main house. I'm the only one working the company anymore, except for a couple of cousins who work for me. Dad left it to me since the others didn't want it. Earlier this year, I bought the rest of the property from Mama; the house, the barn, and all the land that wasn't already used for working the cattle."

Gage came to the entry of the Chambers property and held Rowan tight as he went down in the ditch to take the smaller of the two gates. The large one had a cattle grate to keep the cows from wandering off.

It was still as pretty as she remembered it. The main house was a huge two-story plantation-style house with lots of windows and a porch that wrapped all the way around it. Glancing at the barn, she experienced a moment of tension and he felt her body stiffen.

Gage's arm tightened around her. "That was then, Rowan. That will never be now."

Riding up to the porch, he said, "Sit tight," and swung down from the saddle. He reached up and she put her arms on his shoulders to be lifted down. Thinking he'd set her on her feet, she was surprised when he held her instead. Her arms and legs wrapped around him naturally and he carried her up the porch steps. Holding her with one hand, he opened the screen door then the main door and went inside.

Rowan had never seen the inside of the Chambers house. When they'd done picnics, she'd been careful not to wander too far from Nina and Miss Jeffries. Her first impression was one of warm woods and bright sunlight.

He took off his hat, dropping it on the bench just inside the door, and ran his long fingers through his hair. "Time for a tour." Room by room, he carried her and pointed out things he thought she'd find interesting. The place was huge. A library, formal dining room, enormous kitchen, two living rooms, two small bedrooms, two bathrooms, and a large laundry area made up the first floor.

"When we were little, Mama had a housekeeper and a cook who lived in these two rooms downstairs. The man who took care of the grounds and drove us sometimes lived above the barn." He stepped through a set of French doors and the porch extended into a huge deck that led down to a fenced back yard.

On one side was a pool and on the other was a children's play area, complete with an enormous fort and tire swings. "My brothers and I used to play out here for hours. Mama would watch us from her office in the library."

Back inside, he carried her upstairs and showed her six bedrooms. "This suite was where our nanny slept. It has its own bathroom and that door connects it to the nursery. Each of us slept in the nursery until we were two, then we got our own rooms."

Continuing down the hall he said, "That door leads to the attic. Part of it is enclosed storage; the rest is a game room. It's pretty hot since I haven't aired it out or turned the AC on but I'll show you that later." At the end of the hall was a set of double doors.

Pushing them open, he told her, "This was my parent's bedroom all the years of their marriage. It covers one whole end of the house. A seating area, huge closets, an enormous bathroom I had remodeled, and another little office. The fireplaces all work. There's one here and three downstairs."

Walking to the seating area that looked out on the backyard and forest beyond, Gage settled on a couch with Rowan over his lap and asked her quietly, "Do you like it?"

"It's beautiful...a very beautiful house. You must have been very happy here growing up." Rowan's voice was barely a whisper.

He nodded, "I was. My parents raised us all very well in this house." Gage stroked his hand over her hair. "I've called about adding more security, Rowan. The technicians will be here in the morning to add everything I'll possibly need to keep you and Benji safe."

She sucked air in hard and he acted like he didn't notice, "There's plenty of room for the help I know you're going to have to hire. If James will still watch over you during the day, I'd feel better when I'm working. He can find someone to cover the nights and they can use the barn apartment. I'm sure there will be a lot more to do, and we'll figure it all out."

He pushed her hair back over her shoulders. "Rowan, I know it isn't what you had when you were with Bennett. I also know it was never about money for you. Not with me the first time, not with Bennett, not now with me again. I recognize you have more money now than my family would make in ten lifetimes and that you'll likely rarely touch it. You won't need it for you and Benji because I'll take care of anything you need."

Opening a small drawer beside the sofa, he took out a little box and held it out to her. "I'm tired of living without you, Rowan. I need you in my house every day while you work on your charity work and raise our children. I need you in my bed every night. You already own my heart. Marry me, let me love you...let me show you how happy you can be."

She opened the box and gazed in wonder at the ring inside. A platinum band held an intricate setting of diamonds and sapphires. It was stunningly beautiful. "Isn't that...your grandmother's ring?"

Nodding, he said, "How did you know that? It's been in my family for generations."

"She...she took me aside during a barbeque when I was sixteen. We talked for a long time that day. I liked her very, very much."

With a huge smile, he told her, "Nana Birdie was said to be something of a clairvoyant. I remember that barbeque. It was the first time I noticed how gorgeous you'd gotten. You sat with Nana for hours and I watched the way your hair moved in the breeze. You were wearing shorts and a t-shirt, running shoes." He groaned in memory.

"My mom stepped in my line of sight and said, '*She is too young for you right now and I will whoop your ass, Gage*'. I just growled at her or something and she patted my cheek; told me anything worth having is worth waiting for."

"I...I can't believe I'd *forgotten*..." Rowan tilted her head, looking at a spot on the wall, "Birdie…she told me to call her Birdie…she said I was very pretty and I would have pretty babies. She asked me a lot of questions about myself. I'd never had anyone, an adult, talk to me like a person before."

She swallowed hard, "Birdie said I…I'd have my heart broken twice. That…it would be worth it. That every woman should experience one broken heart so she appreciated good love."

Clearing her throat carefully, she continued, "She said she knew I was in love with you but you were still too much of a boy, that I had to give you time to grow up so you'd grab what you really needed with both hands." She stared at him, "Then she said I'd forgive you. I said you hadn't done anything; you didn't even know I existed. She chuckled and patted my hand. That's when I told her how pretty her ring was and she told me she was very glad to know I liked it."

Looking at Gage she added, "She died later that year. I was very sad because she'd been the first person who actually seemed to see me. Not as a lost child, a ward of the state, or a girl who lived at the home. She said I was named for a tree; that my name was strong and I would put down roots and go through many winters but when my spring came it would be beautiful."

Reaching in the drawer again, Gage pulled out a small linen envelope with old-fashioned handwriting on the front. "Months ago, after my mother went to see you, she came here, and I talked to her about you. She went to the safe and took out this box and this envelope." He handed it to her and she withdrew the heavy paper inside.

*"My precious Gage, if you're reading this it is because you grew up and are ready at last to grab what you need with both hands. Treat her well and know broken hearts sometimes take a long time to heal but love is <u>always</u> sure to do the trick. I found her magnificent, even so young. Her roots are very strong and she's going to love the spring. I'm glad you're going to be there for the blooming. I wish you all the love and happiness possible. I always adored you, darling, and I know you will be a fine husband and father. By the way, tell her B is going to be achingly relieved to know she's being well-loved and protected…that you'll be there for his boy. She's to keep her promise. Nana Birdie."*

The page drifted from her shaking hand and Rowan clapped a hand over her mouth. Tears flowed from her eyes and she tried to scramble from his lap but Gage caught her before she'd taken a step and pulled her back to straddle his lap.

"No more running, Rowan. You've run so far and I'm not letting you go again." He moved the ring and letter to the table and pulled her against his chest. "Enough guilt, *enough*. I'm not letting you do this to yourself another day, Rowan. Not one more day." She fought but he held her tight against him. She was screaming and crying and cursing him but still he held her.

After ten minutes, Rowan went limp, breathing hard. She lay against him, silent and still for so long he wondered if she'd fallen asleep.

He felt her wipe her face and take a deep breath. She sat up and stared at him for a long moment. Then she was kissing him and pulling at his clothes, her movements telegraphing her urgency.

Gage was off the couch and carrying her to the bed in a heartbeat, standing her beside the bed as they tore the clothing from one another. When they were naked, he picked her up and lowered her to the bed, following her down. Her legs wrapped around his waist and then he was inside her, driving into her deep and strong.

She kissed him, bit him, and clawed his back to bring him closer. Her feet pulled him hard into her and he increased the power of his thrusts, pushing her desperation higher. The first time she came it hit her suddenly, taking her by surprise as her upper body slammed into his and she screamed his name to the silent house.

Gage pushed Rowan hard through it, not giving her time to think, to let her mind take over and doubt what she needed, what she wanted. He held her in place as he lowered his mouth to a nipple and nibbled it gently. When a bead of breast milk appeared it hit his groin hard, knowing her body nourished her child affecting him on a level he'd never felt before. He licked it from her and marveled at the sweetness of it on his tongue.

Running both hands under her back, he gripped her shoulders from behind and drove into her without mercy as Rowan dug her nails into his ass. She felt the orgasm exploding outward from her womb and the heated tingle spread over her.

Leveraging one leg on the bed, she shoved and rolled them, her hands on Gage's chest as she rode him hard. His hands dropped to her hips and he locked down on every ounce of control he'd learned in his life to keep from coming at the sight of Rowan above him.

She put her palm flat on his chest over his heart and smiled when she felt the strong thump under the skin. Raising her eyes to him, he understood…knew this had been the position Bennett died in, needing her to be on top and keep him from some of the physical exertion. He smiled and placed one hand over hers, watching as she came; she dropped her head back on her shoulders and let it take her.

Riding him through it, she dropped forward with her hands on either side of his head. "Come for me, Gage," she whispered then she kissed him hard and stroked his face, leaving her hand on his cheek. He thrust up hard three times and came roaring her name, his hands rigid on her hips. It was like nothing he'd ever experienced and when he realized why, he almost panicked.

Then he remembered this was his Rowan. The woman who would be his wife. It was okay and if she ended up pregnant, that was alright, too. He kissed her hard and rolled her to her back again.

"I love you, Rowan. I'll love you hard every day for the rest of my life. You can trust me to love you, to love Benji…to take care of you both. All I want is to love you…for you to let me love you."

She nodded and kissed him deeply, her fingers in his hair. Stroking her hands over him, kneading his muscles, and lightly scraping her nails over his skin. She kissed him, licked him, lightly bit him. Again and again she brought him back to her mouth and held him to her.

"I'm sorry I ran, Gage. I was scared. I do love you…I've loved you for so long. It could have only been you. I shouldn't have doubted that, shouldn't have been afraid to love you." She kissed him and his arms tightened hard around her. "Can you lie on your back?" She smiled at his puzzled expression. "I hate to break this to you, but I've literally had sex three times. Once with someone too sick to allow me to touch him. Once when I was a weather balloon with no mobility.

I'd actually like to check you out, Gage."

"You couldn't…I mean…I'm sorry, Rowan…never mind." He pulled from her carefully and rolled to his back. Rowan went up on her knees and leaned over his face.

"The first time Bennett kissed me, very carefully, he had to take a nitrous pill. I could not risk too much physical affection, even hugging sometimes. Unless he was asleep, I undressed in another room. That…last day, he took a pill before and…during."

A deep breath controlled the tears that wanted to fall. "He was devastated he couldn't allow me to touch him…that he had to limit how much he could touch me. In his prime, he'd been a legend as a lady's man. He was thirty-six years older than me and so very sick when I met him…I never knew the man he was before."

She let her heart fill with the joy of Bennett's love, how good he'd been to her, "But he treated me gently and begged me to love him through it. When his heart stopped, so did I. I don't regret giving him that because he'd given me so much in return." She kissed Gage with all the love in her heart. "The night I went to the barn was the first time I'd seen a naked man. The day Benji was born was the third. Life is pretty funny sometimes."

"I…I didn't know you couldn't even touch, Rowan. I'm so sorry. I can't imagine his frustration. Two years with you as his wife, unable to kiss you, to hug you, to make love to you…to even enjoy the vision of you naked. It makes so much more sense why he felt the price was worth paying in the end." With a half-smile, he said, "He was stronger than I would have been."

Rowan laid her cheek on his chest and listened to the steady beat of his heart while he stroked her hair. "I'm very healthy, very strong, Rowan. I'll have a check-up every six months so you don't worry."

"*Three…*" she whispered and Gage nodded. Rowan straddled his body and started at his hair, running her fingers through it and raking it back from his forehead. She kissed over his face as her hands moved to his shoulders and down his arms. She lifted his hands in hers and kissed each finger before placing them on her face.

He watched as she closed her eyes and sighed his name. She kissed one palm then the other and placed them on her thighs. She leaned to kiss across his body from one shoulder, to the other, and over his collarbone. Kissing over his heart, she licked his nipple and his body tensed beneath her.

Smiling against his skin, she tugged it gently between her teeth, released it, and licked it again before moving to the other and repeating her attention. Gage's hands were fisted in her hair and he breathed shallowly, leashing his body's reactions to beautiful Rowan. Her hands never stopped moving on him as her mouth made its exploration.

Crawling further down his body, she kissed over each rib and the sculpted lines of his abs. When her tongue licked around his belly button, he sucked air hard through his teeth. Further down the length of him she moved, kissing the lines of his hip and across his pelvis.

Gage stared at the ceiling and tried reciting cattle statistics in his mind as Rowan wrapped her fist around his cock. She investigated every inch of him, running her nails through the light patch of hair around the base and cupping his balls in her palm, squeezing gently as if testing the weight.

Grinding her fingers into the muscles of his thighs, she took him in her mouth and his entire body locked down. She ignored his groans as she learned him, tasted him, and sucked him. Setting a rhythm, she moved over him until the top of Gage's head felt like it was going to blow off.

His heels dug into the bed, his fists clenched in the linens, his jaw was locked as he tried to hide the deep groans of need in his chest. Gage felt when his balls drew tight and he whispered, "Rowan, I can't...I can't hold back. You need to let me go, baby. Oh baby...please. Rowan, I can't stop it, I'm coming, baby."

The come left the head of his cock hard enough to leave him lightheaded as the tension left his body. "Oh, honey, thank you...yes, Rowan. That feels so good, so much better than I ever imagined. Thank you, baby."

Rowan felt when his body relaxed into the bed and she licked the head, planting a kiss there before curling up at his side. His arm came around her tugging her tight to his side. "You taste delicious, Gage. I figured I'd be so bad the first time you wouldn't be able to come. I feel better actually."

Rolling her to her back, he settled into the cradle of Rowan's body and kissed her breathless. Then he laid his cheek next to hers and hugged her tight. "Thank you, Rowan. For letting me love you. I *need* to love you, don't run from me anymore, baby." She shook her head and hugged him just as tight as he was hugging her. "And now…it's your turn, Rowan."

Gage worshiped Rowan's body from her hairline to her toes, until she was weak and begging for him to be inside her. Only when she said, "I love you so much, Gage. I'll die if you don't take me again…right now. *I will die*," did he crawl between her thighs and enter her in one smooth stroke.

Driving her over the edge the final time, Gage went up on his hands and came hard, every muscle in his body drawn tight and beautiful under his skin, his head thrown back. Rowan watched his face above her, a hard alpha male claiming her as his mate and felt her heart truly begin to heal.

She sent Bennett a silent goodbye in her mind. She would *always* love him. No part of her would *ever* forget him. She also knew – for her sanity – that she had to let him go.

As if reading her mind, when Gage's orgasm ran its course and he had nothing left, he bent to kiss her possessively. His hands were everywhere as he pulled from her carefully and climbed off the bed. Walking to the table by the couch, he picked up the little box and removed the ring. He came back to her with purpose, a predatory light in his eyes.

Sitting her up, he tugged her to the edge of the bed and went to his knee in front of her. Her hand in his, he said with quiet determination, "No one will ever love you as hard as I'm going to love you, Rowan. I'll spend every day left in my life proving it to you. Move into my house with Benji…let him be *our* son in all but name…and let's make this our home. Sleep in my bed every night and let me give you a life filled with laughter and children. Marry me, Rowan and let me love you."

Her hands reached down to cup his cheeks. "I'll spend the rest of my life loving you. Just please don't forget I love hard. I'll worry about you when you aren't with me. I'll need you to always remember how I reacted to Bennett's death, Gage. It will be so much worse if I were ever to lose you. Don't take chances, not ever, and come home to me safe every night."

With a smile, he nodded and slipped the heirloom ring on her finger before he tackled her to the bed. One hand moved to cup her breast and he realized it was more full than usual. As he thought it, a pearl of milk appeared on the nipple and she laughed.

"Benji is no doubt awake and ready to eat, Gage. I'm afraid I lost track of time and the darling boy is like clockwork." She watched as he licked the drop away and asked, "You don't think me being like one of the cows is weird?"

"Um, no, in fact…I'm thinking I may be abnormal because it's making me hard as a rock." He kissed her breast and bounded from the bed, pulling her with him.

She stood staring at him standing naked and uninhibited in front of her and when she licked her lips, his cock twitched. Pressing the heels of his palms over his eyes, he whispered, "God, please give me the strength to leave the bedroom with this woman."

Then he quickly pulled jeans over his lower body and dropped his shirt over her head. "Dear lord, that only makes it worse. I know you're not wearing panties." With a heavy sigh he found her panties and jeans and pulled them up her legs. Kissing her mound, he couldn't resist running his tongue over her, causing her body to spasm, before he pulled the fabric in place.

When he stood she glared at him. "That wasn't nice, Gage."

He gathered her in his arms. "We get you settled in this weekend. Not kidding. I need you here." She laughed and pulled his t-shirt over her head to put on her bra. "Wait." She was wearing nothing but jeans and her black curls fell beautifully around her. He crossed her hands over her chest, positioning them where her nipples couldn't be seen.

Pulling out his cell phone, he took a picture of her and saved it. "That's going to be my wallpaper. You are just fucking *stunning*, baby."

Laughing, she got dressed and they went downstairs together. His horse grazed in the shade and she realized Gage had tethered him near the bird fountain for fresh water. He lifted her in the saddle and bounded up behind her.

She leaned back and his arms went tight around her. "You feel so good, Gage."

"If you could only feel what I'm feeling right now…dear god." With that, he nudged his horse into a walk. When they were on the road, he whispered, "Trust me?" She nodded and he urged the chestnut into a gallop. By the time they entered Miss Jeffries's yard, she was laughing, her hair streaming out behind them.

The three adults stood watching them with huge grins, the twins holding Nina's hands and Benji in James's arms. Gage swung down and pulled her from the saddle, carrying her like a sack of potatoes to the porch. He put her on her feet but pulled her by her belt loops to kiss him.

"One second, Rowan." He moved past her and held his arms out to James who placed Benji in them without hesitation. "Hello there, little man. You are solid as a rock. I was a real surprise to my mama; all my brothers were old farts when I was born. I grew up with all my nieces and nephews. I like kids…you and I are going to get along great."

Rowan stood on the porch and watched as Gage walked with Benji to his horse and set his tiny hand on the huge soft neck. "You're going to be around a lot of horses in your life. And cows. This is Second Chance…I call him Chance. I bought him the day after I lost your mama when she was eighteen. He's the best horse I've ever owned and the first one your mama ever rode."

He added in a mock whisper, "He'll be the first one *you* ride as soon as we get one of those little baby backpacks and some sedatives for

Rowan." Kissing his soft head, Gage whispered something in Benji's ear and for the first time, Benji laughed a full little baby laugh. He reached out to touch Gage's face, "Yeah, we understand one another, don't we, Benji? Okay, I bet you're starving. We'll talk more later."

With that, he carried the baby to the porch and set him in Rowan's arms. "What…did you say?"

He winked, "I told him not to be too hard on me. I've never been a dad before." Her mouth opened and closed several times and he kissed her before turning to the twins. "Pretty girls, you need to come meet my horse. He told me he wants you to ride him…think you'd like that?"

Their shy faces turned to bright smiles and they nodded. He picked up one and James the other. They went to Chance who stood utterly still while a little girl was loaded from either side. "Okay, you're going to hold onto the saddle horn, that's this right here. When you get really good, you'll hold the reins. You'll be to that point before you know it. Now you, sweetie, you hold around your sister's waist. There you go. It might feel bumpy at first but we're going to walk on either side so you don't have to worry. Alright?"

They nodded happily. Looking over the horse at James, he smiled and added, "We need to get them little nameplates or something…they look exactly the same. I can't tell them apart to save my life."

That seemed to open a flood gate of conversation and they chattered adorably for twenty minutes. "I have a freckle on my ear…see? I'm Tia. If you look on Tara's foot, she has a freckle I don't have. I like pink and she likes purple." On and on they chattered as the men walked them all over the place.

Nina sat on one of the chairs watching the men and little girls, smiling over the fact that life had somehow come full circle. Glancing at Rowan who was splitting her attention between the group in the clearing and little Benji at her breast, the ring's sparkle caught her eye.

"Oh my god! *Rowan!*" The men turned back and she waved at them as she stood and started trying to hug Rowan with Benji in the middle of dinner. "I knew it would happen, I just *knew it*. Oh, honey, oh I'm so happy. I love you so much!"

Kissing her on both cheeks and dropping one on Benji's forehead, she took off down the porch steps and threw herself at Gage. His shock and discomfort were obvious and it made James chuckle. "I'm so damn glad you love her, she's going to be so happy. And now we get to keep her…she's back where she belongs. Thank you for being a good man and waiting for her."

She kissed his cheek loudly and jumped down, going around the horse to James. "We're staying…we're all staying and everything is going to be so much better." He caught her up as she barreled into him and her legs went around his waist. Looking up at the twins she said, "You two are going to have more love than you know what to do with. I think we should make ice cream…with strawberries…what do you think?" They were nodding and smiling.

Later they all piled into Miss Jeffries's house and spent the evening cooking and listening to music, talking about the past and the future. Making plans none of them ever thought – only maybe hoped a little in their heart of hearts – they'd be making.

And Benji never stopped laughing.

*Damaged*

# **Scars by Shayne McClendon**

## **Chapter One**

The scar was always the first thing people noticed. Some people never looked any further.

During one of Brinley Thornton's rare dates, she'd been told she shouldn't smile so much because the muscles in her cheek pulled at it and made it more obvious.

Her response had been an instantaneous, "Fuck you." She'd gotten a cab and left the asshole sitting there.

For more than a week, she had subconsciously smiled less. When she realized what she was doing, she almost hated herself. Staring at herself in the mirror, she examined the rough, quarter-inch line that trailed from her temple, along her cheek, and around her jaw to the center of her chin. It wasn't pretty.

She accepted that her scar might look worse when she smiled…but the rest of her looked better. Her eyes were still her prettiest feature; a pale gray she'd always liked. Her mouth was a little too wide but she had nicely shaped pink lips.

Her body was built for work, not fashion, and usually she felt like she resembled a twelve-year-old boy far more than a grown woman. It didn't matter in boots and jeans on the back of a horse.

Even before her accident she hadn't dated much. It seemed like she attracted two kinds of men. The ones who wanted to control her, tame her, make her more girly or the ones who were too weak for her to abide.

She used to dream about a man who knew his own strength…and hers.

"I can't believe I let that guy get inside my head."

Her older brother ruffled her pixie-cut blonde hair with a smirk. "You're human. Now snap the hell out of it."

Bobby was her best friend, the only person who always told it to her straight. When she was mauled by a bull in the family stockyards, it happened too fast for anyone to stop it. She knew her brother blamed himself.

It was one small slip – certainly not the first one in all the years she'd worked there – and the bull's head swung around, stepping on her booted foot at the same moment its horn crashed into her head. She didn't remember anything after the impact of her skull against the corral post.

Her mother and aunts had been beside themselves. Her little sister still had difficulty looking her fully in the face. All of them lied to her, played with her hair, and told her it wasn't that bad.

It definitely *was* that bad. The plastic surgeon had done what he could to minimize the scarring but her cheek had been crushed and the horn had torn through to the bone. He rebuilt her cheek and the scar was far better than it had been the first year.

She now wore metal in her face and the back of her skull.

When the last bandages came off, Bobby tweaked her nose and said, "You're not going to win any beauty contests but when did you ever want to compete anyway, Brinley?"

And when she looked at it that way, she agreed. She went back to work and she worried her mother would have a coronary the first time she took the bulls.

She wasn't going to let one accident take her away from the work she loved. The job she'd been doing since she was still in high school.

## Chapter Two

Auction day. Her dad met her in the parking lot as she jumped down from her truck. "Hey, honey. Can you take over the second group? Bobby's leadin' in the first one now."

"Sure, Dad. Are there a lot of people today?"

"Packed stands. Great idea keepin' the auctions to fewer times a year. Build the demand."

Brinley reached into backseat of her truck and pulled her gloves and hat from her gear bag. "I bet you sell every head today, Dad." He gave her a shoulder punch and she laughed. The men in her family were rough. "We helping with branding after?"

"We got a few companies need it but Chambers will brand their own. Rowan came with Gage and his boys, by the way."

Her eyes went wide. "Did they bring Benji?" Gage and Rowan Chambers lived about twenty miles away and owned a huge spread. They were fiercely protective of their oldest son.

Ten-year-old Benjamin Jefferson was the heir to his biological father's massive fortune. Bennett Jefferson had died before he was born. Her mother tried to tell her the story but all Brinley knew was he was the funniest kid she'd ever met.

"They did and he already asked about you."

Grinning broadly, she said, "Tell him I'll catch up before they leave." Her dad nodded and headed back inside. Brinley buckled her chaps and tugged her gloves on. She locked her truck and headed for the south side of the facility.

Charlie snuffed happily at her hand, taking the offered apple slices. Someone, likely Bobby, already had her saddled. She checked the tack anyway.

When she was mounted, she took a moment to look around.

Auction days were always hectic. They had to make sure the potential customers didn't wander into the corrals trying to get closer looks at the merchandise up for bid. Today, they had horses, two breeds of cows, and hogs. Almost every pen was occupied, the corrals were full, and the top doors on every stable were locked open to view the horses inside.

One of the younger hands opened the main gate and a huge cow simply bumped him aside and ambled through. Brinley yelled for him to secure the gate and went after the female.

Charlie cut neatly through the milling people and circled the cow close. She dropped a lead over the big head and led her back to the corral.

"Sorry, Brinley!"

"No worries. Be real careful using the gates to come in and out. Best to go over the top."

"Yes, ma'am."

She left him to it and a few minutes later saw the signal from her dad to bring the second group through. With a combination of whistles and nudges, she guided them along the shoot to the auction floor.

The main room of the facility was loud and busy. For the next several hours, Brinley circled the cattle, driving them forward and separating the next head up for bid. She'd been working the floor since she was sixteen and convinced her father she was old enough and smart enough not to get herself killed.

Animals weren't mean, they simply went where they thought they had to go. They weren't malicious but they didn't exactly stop on a dime either.

So when a little girl slipped under the containment fence in the thick of the second group holding pen, Brinley wasted no time charging around the enclosure in her direction. Jumping the two lower barricades, she dropped from Charlie's back, and whistled for Bobby. He wouldn't make it to them in time so she worked her way through the huddle of shoving, nervous cows.

One heifer closest to the fence jumped when the auctioneer's microphone clicked on, jostling another cow...and the chain reaction started. The little girl was turning in circles, suddenly realizing she wasn't safe. She got scared and began to cry.

Brinley skidded across the dirt, sliding under a large belly as the cows rolled forward in a wave and knocked the little girl to the ground. With no way to get her out before she was trampled, Brinley threw her body over the child's, wrapping her tightly beneath her, and protected her head as the cows stomped and pushed one another around them.

She curled her body in closer as the girl began to scream. With her mouth next to her ear, she said, "It's alright. Help is coming to move the cows." A hoof caught her in the back and another in her side but she stayed calm. "What's your name?"

"P-Penny," she cried.

"I'm Brin…" She gasped as another cow stomped her calf. Taking a deep breath, "Brinley. I work the auction. Are you okay?"

"I scratched my knee when I fell. I'm all dirty."

Brinley laughed softly. "As soon as they move the cows we'll get you all cleaned up."

As if she'd summoned him, Bobby reached down to scoop them up as space cleared in several directions. She couldn't stand up straight. The pain in her ribs was excruciating.

"Where do you hurt?"

"Ribs, shoulder, leg, back," she managed quickly.

"I got you. Little one, I'm going to have Lou walk you out, okay?"

"No, I wanna hold Brinley's hand!" All of them could see she was on the verge of a meltdown now that the danger was over.

Without a word, Brinley grabbed her hand and led her to the small gate that had been opened for them. She walked slowly, hunched over, but made out of the pen in time for a teenage girl with bright red hair to drop to her knees in front of Penny. Her face was drenched with tears.

"Penny, I just looked away for a second. Daddy is going to kill me."

She was smoothing her hair, hugging her repeatedly, and uncontrollably sobbing.

Knowing the little girl was with her family, Brinley whispered, "I can't...Bobby, help." Her brother lifted her and ran for his truck.

## Chapter Three

She knew she was in the emergency room when she opened her eyes. "Why am I here? I just needed to catch my breath."

Her father's face appeared over her. "Actually, honey, you got a broken rib and it punctured a lung. Hairline fracture in your leg and a dislocated shoulder. Some serious bruises on your back. We just got the x-rays back. How you feelin'?"

"Ha! Like I got stomped on by cows?"

There was some sort of commotion in the hall.

She closed her eyes and whispered, "I hate this place. I want to go home." She heard the curtain slide back hard but didn't look. If it was someone who hadn't met her before, they'd stare and she hated staring. "Dad, please get me out of here."

"Miss Thornton?"

She sighed and knew she had no choice but to interact. The view that met her stole her breath. A man was leaning over her bed. His shaggy black hair framed a face with angular lines and lips almost too sensual for a man. It was his eyes – such a bright green they didn't look real – that made it impossible for her to speak.

"Miss Thornton, my name is Wayne Savage. You saved my daughter Penny. I wanted to thank you personally. You risked your life."

She swallowed hard. "You're welcome."

"I saw her from the stage. She was trying to get to me. I never would have made it to her in time." He picked up a cup of water from the side table and held the flexible straw to her lips. "You look a little dehydrated. Drink."

Without thinking, she did and her throat thanked her.

"Are you alright, Miss Thornton?"

There was *no way* she was telling this man her injuries.

Her father felt no such hesitation. Wayne never took his eyes off hers as her dad outlined what the doctors had told him. "Penny called you Wonder Woman. I don't think she was far off. All she has is a scratch on her knee. A scratch, Miss Thornton. You took every blow to your own body and still thought to keep her terror to a minimum."

He leaned closer, his hand stretching across her body to the bar on the other side. "I can never repay you for what you've done. I insist on covering your medical expenses." One hand lifted and smoothed her hair away from her scar.

"This isn't the first time you've been hurt." She shook her head, stunned as his finger traced down her cheek and tilted her jaw. "This injury could have killed you."

No one touched her scar. Not even her family.

She wasn't sure why but she desperately wanted to cry. She never cried. Gulping, she fought the feeling, refusing to let them fall. His surreal eyes stayed on hers for a long time.

"I won't think less of you if you cry, Miss Thornton. In fact, I'll admit to my share after I realized my little girl was protected by your small body and you kept your cool despite the pain you must have been in."

Brinley cursed the tear that slid from the corner of her eye into her hair. Wayne wiped her skin and leaned lower to whisper at her ear. "I owe you. Remember that. I will." He kissed the skin just in front of her ear and she drew air in sharply. The shock slammed into her.

He'd kissed her scar.

"I'll let you get some rest." He lifted the hand of her uninjured arm and kissed the back. "Thank you again, Miss Thornton."

Unable to do more than nod, she watched as he gestured to her father and they left the room together. A few minutes later, the nurse added pain medication to her IV and she drifted to sleep.

The last thing she thought about was Wayne Savage.

*In keeping with the "Damaged" theme...here's an excerpt of "Obsession" – a novel about a young woman who experiences one of the worst things that can happen...and doesn't let it break her. You're going to love Ellie and Hyde.*

# Obsession by Shayne McClendon

**Prologue** (*May*)

Why am I in so much pain?

Where am I?

How did I get here?

What is the *last thing* I remember?

My name is Elliana Fields...right?

Yes. Elliana Monica Fields. My family calls me *Ellie*.

It smells musty here. It's dark as night but that doesn't seem right. Why doesn't it seem right?

*Come on, Ellie. How many episodes of* Criminal Minds *have you watched? Too many hours to be healthy. Think, damn it!*

The last thing...I was jogging.

Yes, I was jogging my usual trail around the municipal airfield and community park. I stopped at the halfway point to hydrate and stretch. Running again...I remember the sound of two small planes taking off. One was likely a crop duster from the sound. The other was a rich man's toy.

A small dog running full out for the main entrance as a little girl in pigtails tried to catch his leash. Her winded mom couldn't believe I caught the hellion of a Shih Tzu who would have surely become a fluffy greasy spot on the blacktop. The little girl going on and on about me saving little Biscuit's *life* like a *hero*.

Laughing and calling goodbye before running again. I passed Little League practice where boys were working on sliding home. They were the age Preston would be now. Maybe a bit older. Thinking of Preston always makes me smile even as my heart hurts.

Banishing my sad thoughts, I ran for the woods that surrounded the park on three sides and loomed ahead. Shade and cooler temperatures beckoned and I stayed on the path as it wound through the greenery.

I took out one of the ear buds to my MP3 when I noticed a shadow behind and to my left.

*Turning...*

A flash of pain then darkness.

I'm lying on dirt, I think. I can't see. I can't tell if it's dark or my eyes simply aren't working. I try to lift my arm but searing pain brings tears to my eyes. I think it may be broken.

Carefully, I try the other arm. Pain but not so bad I can't move it slowly towards my head. My face is wet and dirty, horribly swollen around my cheeks and eyes. A huge lump is seeping warm and sticky blood behind my ear.

"Hello?" There is no way anyone will have heard that. My throat is raw and there is a foul taste in my mouth. It is something completely alien to me but I recognize it anyway and suddenly I'm frozen. I know what has happened to my body though my mind does not remember the details.

The realization causes my focus to clear with a snap and I take in the world around me.

I can hear the faint sounds of metal bats hitting baseballs. Further away, the sound of a dog barking. I'm still in the municipal park.

In the wooded section of the park there are large steel sheds that contain sprinkler pumps, electrical boxes for the field lights, and one that contains the landscaping equipment used to maintain the popular spot for families, couples, and joggers. I'm in one of those buildings. Landscaping, I think. I smell fresh grass and wood mulch.

Running my hand over my torso, I confirm my nudity and a shudder of revulsion wracks my frame.

"Hyde?" I manage to whisper. There is no answer and dread fills me.

Swallowing, which is the reverse of what my body is *screaming* I do, I take as much air in my lungs as possible and shout, "Help!" Though it is still not as loud as I would like, the steel walls around me help to magnify my voice.

Resting only a few seconds, I gather my strength and try again. And again. And again.

From outside, I hear a young boy's voice ask, "Mom? Did you hear that?"

I shout again, desperate now. So tired and *hating* my weakness.

"Mom, someone's calling for help!"

"Ricky, are you *sure*? I didn't hear anything. I don't think you should be playing by these buildings, honey."

This time, I put everything I have left into a scream for help that translates to sheer agony throughout my entire body. I hear the mother of my savior trying to open the heavy door of the building I'm in. The scraping of the metal is both beautiful and horrific. I can see a lightening on the other side of my eyelids so I believe it is still daylight.

She is closer now and I hear her gasp, "Oh my sweet god, no." Two steps back to the door and she yells to her son, "Ricky, stay back, honey. Run and get Daddy *right now* and have him call 911. Go, baby. As fast as you can."

Then the woman is kneeling by my side. She takes the hand of the arm that isn't broken in hers and just holds it. "My name is Jamie Vasquez. We're going to get you help. I don't want to frighten you but I'm going to lay my jacket over your body. I can't move you, I'm sorry. But I'll stay with you until help comes." The woman has a slight Hispanic accent and seconds later I feel fabric settle over my breasts and upper thighs. "Can you tell me your name, honey?"

I hear the pounding of many feet on the hard-packed dirt path where I'd been jogging. I know they're coming closer. With effort, because I have no resources left to draw on, I tell her, "My family calls me Ellie. Don't let anyone disturb the scene."

"Okay, I'll do everything I can, I promise. Are you a police officer, Ellie?"

"*Criminal Minds*." Then blackness reaches out for me and I'm thankful, so fucking *thankful*, to slide into it. "Find…Hyde. He's hurt. He must be hurt so bad."

*Available on Amazon.*

# THE GREAT OUTDOORS

*Getting out there is half the battle.*

If you liked "Damaged" —you're going to love the four-novella series "The Great Outdoors"…survival erotica at its best featuring lead heroines and heroes who have jobs outside. Meet a few characters that overcome their pasts, tackle their dreams, and never let anything get in their way.

Available on Amazon.

# **YES TO EVERYTHING**

*Life at the top isn't all glitz and glamour.*

Brooke Kincaid's life takes a turn for the better when she's asked to join the country band Broken Bronco – founded by the gorgeous Bradshaw brothers. In a single moment, her struggle to care for her younger siblings after the death of their parents is a thing of the past.

She soon realizes fame and fortune have a price like anything else. Finding the love of her life in the last place she would have thought to look, Brooke embraces the realization of all her dreams only to have happiness ripped away in one act of brutal violence.

Starting again and healing her heart take courage she isn't sure she has but love always has a way of finding its way home.

# IN THE SERVICE OF WOMEN

*When you sell your body you lose little pieces of your soul...*

When Sarah is recruited as a high-end call girl servicing women, she embarks on a journey of passion and self-discovery that will alter her view of herself and her life.

Initiated into a world of passion and excess, she accommodates her clients' every carnal desire, until she learns they may need more from her than sexual release.

After two years spent in the world's oldest profession, she walks away from it with lessons that will change her forever and no regrets.

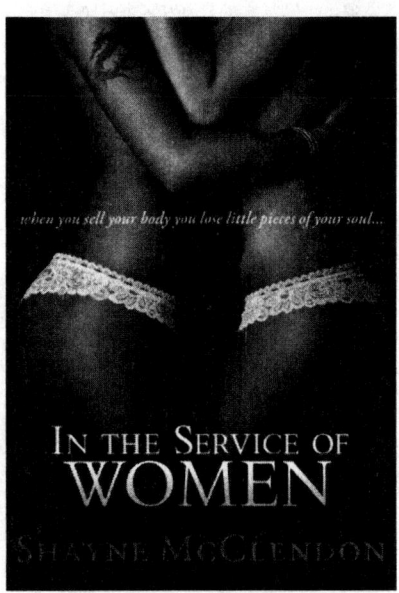

## **About Shayne McClendon**

*Shayne McClendon is an indie author who has received rave reviews for her premiere novel "The Barter System". Other stories recently released are "In the Service of Women", "Yes to Everything", "Obsession", "A Little Bit Country", "Being Delightful", "The Great Outdoors" collection, and "The Hermit" among others.*

*Shayne believes love crosses all boundaries, social castes, races, genders, and belief systems. If you are lucky enough to find soul-deep love, you should fight for it. She currently lives in Oklahoma wrangling teenagers, opening doors for her pets, and running her content-writing company.*

*She dreams of peace, quiet, travel, and always having plenty of coffee.*

*Shayne loves to hear from her readers…especially if you connect to her work. You can contact her by email at shaynemcclendon@gmail.com or stop by her Always the Good Girl Facebook page and join thousands of other survival erotica fans. Visit her web page www.alwaysthegoodgirl.com, where you'll find dozens of free short stories. If you subscribe, you get a free never-before-published novella!*

*All of Shayne McClendon's work is available in digital edition on Amazon.*

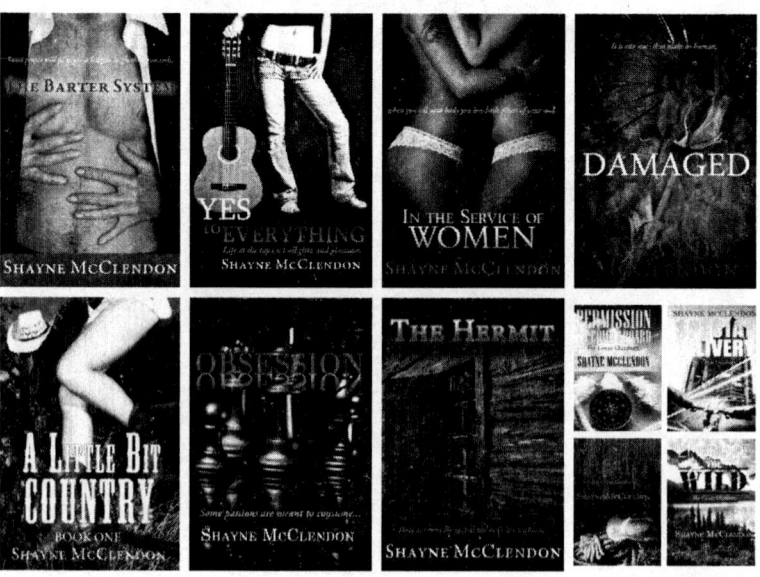